SOWING
POISON

SOWING POISON

A Thaddeus Lewis Mystery

Janet Kellough

DUNDURN
TORONTO

Editor: Allison Hirst
Design: Jesse Hooper
Printer: Webcom

Library and Archives Canada Cataloguing in Publication

Kellough, Janet
    Sowing poison : a Thaddeus Lewis mystery / Janet Kellough.

Issued also in electronic formats.
ISBN 978-1-4597-0054-3

    I. Title.

PS8621.E558S68 2012   C813'.6   C2011-906014-0

1   2   3   4   5   16   15   14   13 · 12

We acknowledge the support of the **Canada Council for the Arts** and the **Ontario Arts Council** for our publishing program. We also acknowledge the financial support of the **Government of Canada** through the **Canada Book Fund** and **Livres Canada Books**, and the Government of Ontario through the **Ontario Book Publishing Tax Credit** and the Ontario Media Development Corporation.

Care has been taken to trace the ownership of copyright material used in this book. The author and the publisher welcome any information enabling them to rectify any references or credits in subsequent editions.

J. Kirk Howard, President

Printed and bound in Canada.
www.dundurn.com

Dundurn
3 Church Street, Suite 500
Toronto, Ontario, Canada
M5E 1M2

Gazelle Book Services Limited
White Cross Mills
High Town, Lancaster, England
LA1 4XS

Dundurn
2250 Military Road
Tonawanda, NY
U.S.A. 14150

In memory of Zeke
(1951–2010)

Acknowledgements

Although Thaddeus Lewis, the hero of this work of fiction, is a documented historical figure, I have taken many liberties with the story of his life, and deviated greatly from the details in his autobiography of 1865. I have, however, attempted to portray him as the upright and honest man that he was. I tried to do the same with Archibald McFaul, who was for many years one of the leading citizens of Wellington, and whose house, Tara Hall, still stands majestically on that village's main street.

Many sources were consulted in an effort to provide authentic background details for this novel. With regard to what Wellington and Prince Edward County might have been like in the 1840s, a number of publications were invaluable: *The County — The First Hundred Years in Loyalist Prince Edward* by Richard and Janet Lunn (Prince Edward County Council, 1967); *The Settler's*

Dream: A Pictorial History of the Older Buildings of Prince Edward County by Tom Cruickshank, Peter John Stokes, and John de Visser (the Corporation of the County of Prince Edward); *Tremaine's Map of the County of Prince Edward Upper Canada, 1863* (Philip J. Ainsworth's transcription of 2006).

Special thanks to naturalist Terry Sprague for his description of the Sandbanks of the 1840s and his knowledge of the habits of muskrats.

Information on food, furniture, and decoration was found in *At Home in Upper Canada* by Jeanne Minhinnick (Clarke Irwin, 1970; Stoddart Publishing, 1994); and *Home Made* by Sandra Oddo (Galahad Books, 1972).

Details of Lake Ontario shipwrecks were taken from *Canvas & Steam on Quinte Waters* by Willis Metcalfe (South Marysburgh Marine Society, 1979).

A history of the introduction of the Orange Lodge into British North America was found in *The Sash Canada Wore: A Historical Geography of The Orange Order in Canada* by Cecil J. Houston and William J. Smith (Global Heritage Press, 1980, 2000).

A number of medical websites provided descriptions of some of the many syndromes associated with cleft palate.

"The Murders in the Rue Morgue," by Edgar Allan Poe, was first published in *Graham's Magazine* in 1841 and is often cited as "the first detective story."

And, as always, *Colony to Nation*, by Arthur R.M. Lower, Ph.D., F.R.S.C., Longmans, Green & Co. provided a succinct summary of the politics of the day.

Thank you to my editor at Dundurn, Allison Hirst, for her astute observations and for knocking the rough edges off my County accent. And again, many thanks to Rob for his patience and support.

Chapter One

Nathan Elliott had been missing for twenty-four hours and everyone had pretty well given up any hope of finding him, including Thaddeus Lewis, who knew that an injured man had little hope of surviving a second night in what had been a particularly frosty Canadian autumn.

When the call went out, Lewis had answered immediately. He joined the meeting at Murphy's Tavern, where the local constable was laying out his plan to organize the men into a search party. There were plenty of volunteers. The lakeside village of Wellington lost more men to the water than anywhere else, and search parties were often formed to comb the shores for the bodies of sailors or fishermen who had been reported lost from a vessel wrecked in a storm.

But a person who had gone missing on land was a novelty, and the tavern was full, with not only local

men, but a number who had arrived from the neigh-
bouring villages of Bloomfield and Raynor's Creek.

Constable Williams sorted them into pairs, and
then Reuben Elliott led them all out to where he said he
had left the wounded man — his brother Nathan. They
had been cutting firewood from the woodlot at the back
of their farm, he said, when he had attempted to fell a
widow-maker, one of those trees that falls the wrong
way and gets hung up in the surrounding branches.
They were tricky, these trees, for there was no way to
predict how they would come down. Reuben was an
experienced woodsman, however, and knew what he
was doing. But it had been a long time, he said, since
his brother had engaged in heavy farm labour.

"I told Nate to stand well back. But the top branches
wouldn't budge at first. I cut away the trunk, but it just
hung there. He ran forward to help just as it finally let
go. A big branch landed right on his head."

Nathan had been unconscious and bleeding, but
still breathing apparently, when Reuben ran to get help,
but when he returned with a neighbour they had been
unable to locate the body. They'd searched for hours,
but found nothing, and by the time the constable had
been contacted, it was growing dark. A further search
was delayed until morning.

Reuben led them straight to a clearing in a heavily-
wooded section at the back of his property.

"I'm sure this is the right place," he insisted in
response to a comment that they might be in the wrong
part of the woods. "Look, you can see the fresh cuts on
the stumps, and there's the pile of logs we were going

to haul out. Besides, do you think I don't know my own land? He was here, and now he's gone."

The searchers fanned out from the body-less clearing, two by two, calling Nathan's name as they went. Some of the men had brought their dogs, which barked and yapped crazily as they tore off through the underbrush, far more likely to run down a rabbit than anything else, Lewis figured. He hoped that if they did find Nathan Elliott, the dogs wouldn't tear him to pieces before their masters were able to call them off.

Lewis was teamed with Martin Carr, a young lad of fourteen or so, and was grateful for the boy's sharp eyes. His own eyesight had once been keen, but he knew that it was beginning to fail, and he found that he had to squint to see anything at a distance. Betsy had been urging him to get spectacles, but he resisted. He had to admit that there was a certain amount of vanity in this resistance; he didn't like the notion that he was growing old and felt disinclined to advertise his creeping infirmities to the world.

He and Martin set off in a northwesterly direction, sweeping back and forth in a zigzagging motion, checking under bushes and in thickets.

"Look over there." Martin pointed off to his right. "The grass has all been flattened down."

Lewis squinted, but could see nothing. He walked over to where Martin had pointed. The boy was right, there had been something there, but it was almost certainly the trampling of deer as they made their slow autumn move into deeper woods. They followed the trail that led from this, and at intervals they found coyote scat and mounds of rabbit pellets scattered amongst the fallen leaves. It was obviously a well-worn thoroughfare for animals, but there was nothing to indicate the recent passage of a man.

The trail led them into buckthorn and spindly poplar. In places there were gulleys and swampy areas, where they had to pick their way around, the footing too unsure to risk climbing through.

"If he came through here, he'd be pretty scratched up," Martin said. "There isn't much of a path."

Martin was in front, trying as much as he could to shoulder the hard work of breaking trail, but mostly managing to let go the branches at just the wrong moment so that they snapped back into Lewis's face. Lewis was certain that Nathan could not have come this way. Even if he had regained consciousness and wandered off in some sort of dazed delirium, he would scarcely have been in any condition to battle his way through these thorns and brambles. Lewis's hands were badly scratched after only a few minutes in the scrubby growth.

Finally, they reached a line of thick dogwood that stretched in both directions. Martin bulled his way through the dense bushes and Lewis followed his trampled path. Beyond the dogwood was a stream.

"If he did come through here, surely he would've followed the crick along," Martin said. "There's only a little water in it and it would be easier than walking through the bush. Which way do you figure we should go?"

It was not a wide stream, more, as Martin said, a creek, whose course dried in the heat of summer and at other times of the year flowed only strongly enough to prevent the dogwood from gaining hold. It could well peter out to nothing; if not, it would almost certainly flow into West Lake. If Nathan had followed it south, Lewis figured he would have soon reached the main road between Wellington and Bloomfield. He would have been able to find his way to a house easily enough from there.

If he had somehow crossed the road without being seen, he would then have been halted by the open water of the lake. It was true that at one end of this lake there was a vast reedy marsh, and if Nathan had wandered into this wild area and fallen, his body would probably never be found. But the marsh was well to the east. It was a possibility, but not very probable.

Lewis wasn't sure how far the creek ran in the opposite direction, but if they followed it north he knew they would reach the road that divided the lakeshore lots from the farms on the next concession. There were pockets of woods on all these lots, but none of them were large, not big enough to swallow up a man. The inland concession was more sparsely settled, the farmhouses farther apart; even so, someone would surely have noticed Nate Elliott if he had wandered through the trees and come out on the road.

Better to look in the thickest part of the woods, he decided, and so they headed south.

There were no signs along the creek. Occasionally, they would climb the bank and cast about in the surrounding bush for any sort of trail, broken branches, or trampled grass. They found nothing.

"This is getting us nowhere," Lewis said. They had followed the stream to where its course had been diverted to empty into a small pond behind the Elliott barn. "The sun will be setting soon. We'd better rejoin the others and see if they've had any better luck."

They hadn't. Most of the other searchers had returned to the clearing by that time, as well, but not even Lem Jackson, who was the best tracker in the district, had been able to pick up a trail.

"Looks like a horse came through here and headed off north," he said. "But we hit that ridge of hard rock that juts up and I couldn't make out where it went from there. There's no tellin' how long ago it was either."

"Well, we'd best leave it for today," Constable Williams said. "If we can't find a man in broad daylight, our chances will be next to nothing in the pitch black."

It was the right decision, but a difficult one. The risk of one of the searchers being injured by a misstep or losing his way in the dark was great and no one wanted to lose another man in pursuit of the first. But the cold north wind promised another heavy frost that night and they all knew that if Nate Elliott was still alive, he probably wouldn't be by morning. Lewis could sense the spirits of the crowd plummeting, and they muttered as they began to shuffle down the path that led home.

Lewis glanced at the brother of the missing man to see how he was taking the news. Reuben's features were crumpled into a mask of despair. "We can't leave him out here another night!" he cried.

"I'm sorry, Reuben, but we can't risk it," the constable told him solemnly.

"But what am I going to tell my father? Nate has only just come back again after all these years and now he's gone again. Pa's going to want to know why we're not out looking for him."

The others edged away, uncertain how to react. It was Lewis who hurried his pace to fall into step beside Reuben. His years as a minister had given him experience in offering comfort where hope was scarce.

"Perhaps he's found shelter somewhere," he suggested as they walked. "It's possible that he came to while you were gone and wandered off in a stupor. He may have stumbled upon an old cabin somewhere and decided to hole up until he felt strong enough to walk out. Or maybe he drifted into someone's farmyard and they're looking after him even as we speak. For all we know, we could hear he's been found when we get back to the village."

Reuben was unconvinced. "I know he's gone, I just know it," he kept saying, his voice hoarse from a day of shouting his brother's name. "Wolves got him, or a bear maybe."

It had been many years since the bigger beasts like wolves or bears ran thick in the settled Prince Edward District. Lewis couldn't take this suggestion very seriously, and dismissed it as hysteria on Reuben's part. He knew that it was important to keep the man talking, however, and so he asked, "How long has your brother been away?"

"He left nearly twenty years ago and hasn't been back since. I know my father is dying, and it was his one wish that he see his son again before he goes. I finally tracked Nate down in New York and persuaded him to come home. He's only been here a few days … and now this has happened."

"Don't worry, we'll look again tomorrow."

Reuben shook his head. "Tomorrow's going to be too late. He's already gone."

Upon their return, there was no news in Wellington that would prove him wrong. No one had reported seeing Nate, no one had welcomed a dazed stranger, and no one offered any clue as to what had happened to the missing man. The searchers promised to meet again the next morning before turning away to head home.

Chapter Two

The woman pulled her cloak a little closer around her neck, but no clothing seemed able to protect her from the insidious damp that seeped into everything, even the bench she sat on, which still felt clammy underneath her after so many hours. Her neck was stiff and sore and her legs hurt from bracing herself against the roll of the vessel. She hadn't expected the constant climbing and slamming as the steamer fought its way through the choppy water, nor the bitter cold that gripped the cabin in spite of the small stove that puffed away in the middle of the room. Even when she managed to ignore her discomfort long enough to doze a little, the steamer whistle would startle her awake whenever they approached another squalid little lake port, where she would straighten herself up in her seat as other passengers departed or boarded.

After the porter announced that Wellington was the next stop, she was ready for the shriek of the whistle and jumped only a little as it signalled the ship's approach. She had never been so glad to see the end of a journey.

For her son's sake, she had tried to make their travels seem like an adventure, and when they first set off he had been intrigued by the passing sights along the Hudson River and the wonder of watching the mules pulling the ship through the canal. This had soon palled, however, and he had become bored and whiney. They were both relieved when they finally disembarked and made their connection to Niagara Falls. Here their spirits had been revived by the sight of the great cascades of water rushing over the cliff to the whirlpool below, and she had taken off her hat and leaned as far as she dared over the railing so the spray could wash her face clean.

Her exhilaration had quickly worn off when she discovered that accommodation in the resort town was expensive, even for the tiniest of rooms. She and her husband had divided what was left of their money before they split up. There wasn't nearly as much as there should have been — they had both spent lavishly in the mistaken belief that the flow of income would never end. She knew it would be unwise to try to augment her purse here in this border town — it would draw far too much attention and there were many Americans at the hotel. Niagara Falls was a popular destination for New Yorkers looking for a change of scene, and any one of them could give her whereabouts away with a casual comment once they returned home. Better to bide her time until they were all together again. Then they would test the winds of circumstance and set a course for their next destination.

Day after day she waited, as the money drained away. After a week, she decided that she could wait no longer. She was told that there was a fairly reliable coach service that would take them on to Wellington, but that there would be several time-wasting stops along the way. She was also informed that if the road was muddy, the passengers were expected to get out and walk. She found this an unappealing prospect.

The steamer was more expensive, but if they went by coach she would have to pay for an inn wherever they stopped, with no prospect of finding any customers during the short overnight stays. Besides, she didn't think she could abide the jostling of a coach for so many miles.

Ultimately, she decided that it was faster and cheaper to go by water. She briefly considered neglecting to settle her hotel bill, but decided that this would draw too much attention to the fact that she had been in Niagara Falls. Reluctantly, she handed over what she owed. The few coins she had left were barely enough to cover the steamship fare, with nothing extra for private quarters. So she and the boy spent the entire journey sitting up on the benches provided in the public cabin. As a result, she was sore and exhausted and the boy had begun to whine again. She looked at her son anxiously; he was pale at the best of times, but now his face had an ashen tinge to it that matched the slate-coloured sky that stretched away to the horizon.

As soon as the captain had signalled their approach, she had risen and gone to the cabin window. She could see that Wellington was no bigger or better than any of the other towns they had called at along the way, and she felt a twinge of homesickness for the chaotic bustle of city streets. There were several men waiting with carts at the wharf, and as soon as the gangplank was lowered she directed the porter to load their luggage into one of these. It was little more than a hay wagon, with a board laid across to serve as a seat, but it was no worse than any of the others, and the carter looked friendly.

"Where to ma'am?" he asked as he helped her up onto the seat.

She hesitated. Should she go straight to the farm or find a quiet inn where she could stay until she found out what had happened? But the village was too small for that. She could scarcely pass as a stranger. Best to talk to Reuben first. Besides, her husband could well be waiting there, delayed by some unforeseen event and his message to that effect gone astray.

"Ma'am?" The carter sat, reins in hand, waiting for her instruction.

She made her decision. "Do you know the Reuben Elliott place? I'm told it's not far from here."

The carter nodded and set his team in motion with a flick of the reins. He seemed uncurious about who she was or what her business might be with the Elliotts. She blessed the man's stolidity as they rumbled down Wellington's main street.

An hour later they were rumbling back again. Reuben had seemed annoyed when he realized who it was at his door. He had admitted her only as far as the front hall while the carter waited with the wagon.

Reuben had imparted little information other than the bare facts that her husband had disappeared nearly a week previously, and that he had no idea what had happened to him after that. He had not offered accommodation, or any sort of assistance. Reluctantly, she had climbed back into the wagon and directed the carter to return her to Wellington.

Her mind was in a whirl. Something had gone wrong, that much seemed clear. *But what?* Until she knew what had happened, she decided, she would stay the course.

As they drove along the main street, she realized that the village was even smaller than it had appeared from the water.

The carter took her to a tavern. As he halted his team, the tavern door swung open and two men staggered outside. It was still only early afternoon, but it was apparent that they were already drunk.

"Is there anywhere else?" she asked her driver. "A respectable inn, if such a thing exists. Somewhere a lady might stay with her son without fear of interference?"

The carter wrinkled his brow and seemed to think deeply for a moment. Then his face brightened. "Well now, there's the new place. The Temperance House. It doesn't serve liquor. It seems very respectable, although I don't know of anyone who's stayed there. It's new, you see."

"Perfect. Please take me there." *No drunks to chase the women away*, she thought, for she would have to work while she waited. *Easy pickings. But I'll have to be careful.*

* * *

After days of searching, it was evident to all that
although Nate Elliott's body might yet be found,
there was little hope that it would still be breathing.
After the second day, the number of volunteers had
dwindled. Many had either been called away by their
own business or had become discouraged by the lack
of progress. Lewis was among the stubborn few who
continued to rendezvous at Murphy's Tavern each
morning, but as the constable could do little but direct
them to go over the ground that had already been covered, it seemed a futile exercise, and after the fifth day
the search was officially called off.

Lewis had found the long hours of tramping across
fields exhausting, and, relieved of this duty, he settled
in that afternoon to the pleasant pastime of looking
through the papers that were provided for the conve-
nience of the guests at the Temperance House Hotel.
The dining room was deserted by two in the afternoon,
as the hotel currently hosted only a single guest, who
by that time had long since finished his dinner and
departed. The morning chores were done, the evening
chores not yet pressing, and Lewis spread the pages
out on one of the tables and read while sipping his
cup of tea. With this indulgence, his aches and pains
began to subside. He felt only mildly guilty. In a way,
he felt that he had earned this luxurious diversion.
Prior to his recent exertions, he had spent four years
tracking a killer, and when the chase had finally ended,

he had continued to ride the circuits saving souls for the Methodist Episcopal Church. During it all, he had been aware of a profound sense of weariness. Part of it was physical; he had gone back to the travelling life too soon, he now knew, after a plunge into the icy waters between Kingston and Wolfe Island had nearly killed him. Every winter since, he had developed a hacking cough that plagued him until spring, and long hours on horseback through wind and rain and snow sapped his strength and made his bones ache.

He also knew that part of his fatigue was emotional. He had caught a murderer and watched him die, and although the crimes had been stopped, he was still trying to make sense of them. He had come to realize how much he treasured his family and how transient life could be, for five women, including his own daughter, had been killed, and his granddaughter had almost been taken too, all because of the twisted passions of the Simms family. He had been deeply shaken by the evil he had uncovered.

As a result, Lewis had been mulling over his options as he attended to the constant round of prayer meetings and sermons, study classes and Sunday schools. For a long time he had persisted in what he had always considered his true calling, but it had been a struggle. And then his wife, Betsy, precipitated a crisis that put an end to his travelling days.

Nearly a year ago, just before Christmas, she had taken an alarming turn that had rattled him to the core. She had been fighting mysterious fevers and agues for several years, but he had been sure that she was on the mend. Then one terrible day, he had arrived home to find she had fallen, insensible. She had stayed that way for five days. At the time he thought he would lose her, and he tried to steel himself for what appeared inevitable. But just as mysteriously as it had arrived, the pall of unconsciousness had lifted. An apoplexy, the doctor said — a small one, but a warning of what was to come.

As with the fevers, her recovery was erratic. Some days she could barely move from her bed, and when she did she walked with a pronounced limp and had difficulty speaking or using her left arm. On other days her infirmity seemed slight, and as long as she didn't overdo it, she could tidy up her own kitchen and direct both Thaddeus and their granddaughter Martha in the household tasks that they both performed clumsily. Lewis thought that eight-year-old Martha was actually more help than he was, but he tried to do Betsy's bidding without complaint, for he knew that the next day could find her once again unable to stir from her bed.

Even so, he wasn't sure how they could have managed without the help of their landlords, Seth and Minta Jessup, who lived in the other half of the house behind Seth's smithy in the town of Demorestville. Minta had helped to nurse Betsy through the initial stages of her illness, but Minta had a young family who quite rightly claimed a great deal of her attention. Seth had not pressed Lewis for the small amount of rent he charged them, but it was clear that they could not continue to rely on the Jessups' charity, as much as the couple appeared willing to help.

And then he had received a letter from his sister, Susannah. She wrote that she and her husband Daniel had leased a hotel in the village of Wellington, a small village some fifteen miles or so southwest of Demorestville. Although his father had left him a farm, Daniel was tired of farming and had fastened on the idea of entering the hotel business. Lewis wasn't sure that it was a wise move; Daniel had never done anything but plough fields and milk cows. But the pair seemed determined. Furthermore, Susannah had written that there was a small house — nothing more than a cabin, really — at the back of the property, which he and Betsy could have if Lewis was willing to lend a hand now and then when business was too brisk for the two of them to manage.

It seemed a sensible arrangement. They could take their meals at the hotel, Susannah said, relieving them of the daily struggle in the kitchen. There would be no rent to pay, and surely Lewis could find something to do that would provide enough money for any of their other needs, which at the best of times were modest. Perhaps there were enough Methodists in the village to support a located preacher; if not, he was sure that someone in the bustling town would need occasional help — clerking or bookkeeping or private tutoring. He was too old for anything very physical, but as an educated man and a former minister and teacher, he was sure his skills could be turned into some source of ready cash.

As far as he could see, the only problem with the suggestion was a promise he had made to Betsy.

He had been appointed to one different circuit after another over the years, and she had cheerfully moved from district to district with him. Two years ago, however, she had abruptly announced that her moving days were over and that she intended to stay put in the half-house in Demorestville. She would have to release him from his promise not to make her move again before he could accept his sister's offer.

He had underestimated his wife's practicality.

"It would be a relief to me," she said when he read the letter to her. "I've been worrying about how much we ask of Seth and Minta, though they've never said a word to me. Minta has enough to do, what with looking after Henry and little Rachel, and we've trespassed on Seth's generosity long enough. I'll be sorry to leave here, but I don't see how we can stay, do you?"

He didn't, and so he had written to his sister to accept their invitation.

The newly named Temperance House Hotel was a large, rambling three-storey building with a graceful double verandah fronting on Wellington's main street. It was perfectly situated to offer accommodation to travellers on the Danforth Road, the main route between Toronto and Kingston, or to farmers bringing their produce to the wharves at the nearby harbour. A hotel situated on such a well-travelled thoroughfare should have been a going concern, but Daniel had decided to offer only wines and ale at the hotel, and to forego the sale of hard liquor, and, furthermore, to advertise that fact in the hotel's name. Lewis approved of his brother-in-law's decision. There was too much drunkenness in Canada West, liquor too easily obtained, and at the hotels that also served as taverns the noise of rowdy patrons was a constant source of annoyance to those trying to sleep in the rooms above.

"People need a place to stay where they won't be accosted by drunks," Daniel had said. "Someplace that's respectable enough for a lady to stay. Clean beds, good food, quiet rooms. You'll see — it will be appreciated by the more *discerning* customer."

But temperance was not a particularly popular concept with the majority of people in the Province of Canada, and so far only one customer had proved discerning enough to appreciate the quiet rooms — a Mr. Gilmour, who had been with them now for more than a week. This gentleman neatly fit Daniel's notion of what a desirable guest should look like, for he wore a fine tweed chesterfield coat over a brown suit of superior cloth, topped with one of the tall hats that had lately come into fashion. He further accessorized his elegant costume with an orange silk cravat tied into a wide bow at his throat and a matching handkerchief tucked into his breast pocket. He carried a gold pocket watch, which he consulted frequently. He did not, however, state his business in Wellington, although Daniel had done his best to find out.

"I ask him every morning if he's going out and he always says yes," Daniel reported to Lewis. "I ask him every evening if he's had a satisfactory day, and the answer is the same, but he never elaborates any further. It's very puzzling."

"You shouldn't be so curious," Lewis told his brother-in-law. "People don't want their innkeeper poking around in their business."

"I'm not poking, I'm just being polite. You know, expressing an interest in my customers."

"Well, they won't thank you for it, you know. Just serve up their food and keep your questions to yourself. You don't want to drive him away."

Lewis thought that Daniel would be less curious about the mysterious Mr. Gilmour if he had a few more guests to look after. But until that happened, the slow traffic at the hotel promised ample opportunity for Lewis to indulge in tea and papers, and with the search for the missing Nate Elliott disbanded, he had only to wait until their solitary guest departed for the afternoon, before he made for the dining room with his steaming cup and a sigh of contentment.

As he spread the newspapers across the table, he noted that the front page of the new Toronto paper, *The Globe*, was full of the consequences of the recent election. Responsible government had seemed such a fine idea back in 1839 when Lord Durham had suggested that the two Canadian colonies be united into one province, but no one had given much thought to the actual mechanics of making it work. Over the intervening five years it had become apparent that neither Upper nor Lower Canada — or Canada West and Canada East, as they were now called — could dominate the provincial assembly. They needed to cooperate, and to a certain extent they did, but no one had defined their responsibilities nor delineated their powers. The assembly had limped along until the arrival the previous year of Sir Charles Metcalfe as governor general, a man who seemed to assume that being a governor meant that he should govern, and that allowing a recently rebellious population to make decisions for themselves was a ludicrous proposition. In spite of this, he had initially attempted compromise with his upstart assembly, going so far as to agree that the rebels of 1837 should be granted amnesty and allowed to return home; but he would make no further concessions to the notion of the province controlling its own affairs.

The entire assembly had resigned in protest over Governor Metcalfe's insistence on controlling government appointments. The Province of Canada had responsible government in name only, it seemed, as Metcalfe had simply carried on without these elected representatives until he was sure enough of his ground to call for a new vote. He had trotted out the old bogeyman of "British loyalty" as a campaign platform. Any further handing over of responsibilities to the assembly was, according to Metcalfe, tantamount to disloyalty to the Crown.

His strategy had worked, especially in Protestant Canada West, but Lewis had been surprised by some of the people who had supported it. Egerton Ryerson, self-appointed Methodist spokesman and editor of *The Christian Guardian*, had written in defence of the governor, to howls of outrage and general vilification by those who supported reform. Lewis read that Ryerson had now been appointed superintendant of education for Canada West, and wondered if that had been the price put on his support. Lewis had never liked Ryerson, and there were many Methodists, himself included, who often found themselves in disagreement with the man's opinions. Shaking his head over the chronic chaos of government affairs, he abandoned *The Globe* and turned instead to the inside pages of the *Cobourg Star*.

These were more entertaining by far. One article reported on the recent international cricket match between the United States and the Province of Canada, which took place at the St. George's Cricket Club in New York. Due to bad weather the match had been extended to three days of play. Lewis read with pleasure that "the British Empire's Canadian Province" had emerged victorious by a margin of twenty-three runs. Another item detailed some of the many wonders that had been unveiled at the Paris Industrial Exhibition, including a new musical instrument called the baritone saxophone. Its inventor, a Belgian man by the name of Adolphe Sax, intended the new apparatus "to fill the gap between the loud woodwinds and the more adaptable brass instruments" according to the article. Lewis hadn't realized that such a gap existed, never having heard an orchestra, only a few of the military bands that accompanied British troops in Canada.

He then became absorbed in an article about General Tom Thumb, a wonder of nature who was featured with Barnum's American Museum. A perfectly formed child, who at the age of five stood only twenty-five inches high and weighed only fifteen pounds, Tom could sing, dance, and impersonate Napoleon

Bonaparte, apparently. His act, along with the Feejee Mermaid, was drawing huge crowds as the exhibit travelled across the United States.

Wonder or freak, Lewis wasn't sure, but in any event his enjoyment of the article was interrupted and he never did get the chance to return to it. A horse and wagon had pulled up in front of the hotel and he watched through the window as a seemingly endless number of trunks and cases were pulled down from it. It appeared that Temperance House was about to acquire its second customer.

Lewis knew that Susannah was in the kitchen dicing vegetables for the evening's stew and he had seen Daniel disappear upstairs sometime earlier, so he supposed it was up to him to greet their new guest. Lewis sighed and took one last hasty sip of his tea, folded the newspapers into a neat pile, and walked out onto the verandah just as the carter handed down a striking woman who was dressed in a fashion that signalled her origins; her finely cut cloak spoke of the city and shops, of the latest fashion and of clothing made with the greatest attention to detail. She wore a hat that fit snugly to her head, with a small brim and ribbons that matched the satin loop on the muff she carried. It was quite unlike the flowered and feathered headwear that Canadian women generally wore when they dressed up. This woman wore no cap under her hat either; instead, her face was framed on each side by long curls that dangled down to her chin. She was quite unlike anything Lewis had ever seen.

"How do you do, ma'am," he said as she looked up at him. "Could I be of assistance?"

She smiled, an action that gave her heart-shaped face a distinctly cat-like appearance.

"How do you do. I wonder if I might take a room — a very private room, please." Her voice was high-pitched, almost shrill, with a telltale twang that spoke of somewhere in the south of the American republic. It grated on Lewis's ears and he found himself hoping that he wouldn't have to listen to it for long.

"Of course," he said. "Please come in and I'll fetch the innkeeper."

The bell on the front door jangled as he opened it for her. Daniel must have heard it and came running down the stairs, wiping his hands on the filthy apron he had tied around his waist after breakfast and had neglected to remove. However, when he saw the woman, he hastily tore it off.

"Welcome, welcome," he said, beaming at her. "Are you looking for a room, miss? We have a pleasant one on the ground floor. It has a view of the street and there are two beds in it."

"I should prefer a second- or third-floor room if that is possible," she said. "Horatio must be away from the awful dust that is thrown up from the street."

Lewis hadn't noticed the small, pale boy who had entered behind the woman. He must have been hidden amongst the trunks and hatboxes that the carter had stacked beside the wagon. Whatever dust had been in the streets of Wellington had long since dissolved into a muddy mess with the cold rains of autumn, but perhaps this woman from away was unfamiliar with the usual state of the streets in Canada in the fall.

"And I must insist that it be well-curtained," she went on. "Poor Horatio needs a great deal of rest and I must be able to draw the curtains against the light if he's sleeping, poor lamb. And is there a sitting room attached? If not, could I ask you to also furnish a good table and a few chairs?"

Lewis knew that he should go and help the poor carter, but he was mildly intrigued by the woman's requests, and so he remained standing in the hall to see how his brother-in-law would respond.

"That's no problem, ma'am," Daniel said with barely a moment's hesitation. "We can prepare rooms to your specification if you give us but half an hour. Perhaps you would like to take tea in the dining room while we make it ready?" He shot Lewis a glance, as if to tell him to get busy with the luggage, and then he almost bowed as he showed the woman the way to the dining room. "And of course we'll ensure that the rooms are adjoining, although I must inform you that there will be an extra charge for it."

"That would be lovely," she said with a wave of her hand. "Thank you."

Daniel reappeared gleefully a short time later, just as Lewis set the last of the luggage down in the hall.

"I was able to charge that woman more for two rooms than we normally get in a month for the whole lot," he said in a low voice. "She didn't bat an eye when I told her how much it would be."

"Who is she?" Lewis asked.

"She's Nathan Elliot's wife. She says her first name is Clementine. I don't recall ever meeting a Clementine before, but then she's American, and they do have strange ways, don't they?"

As a veteran of both the War of 1812 and the more recent Patriot Hunter invasions, Lewis had to agree. Still, he wondered why Nathan Elliott's wife and, presumably, his son, would choose to stay at a hotel instead of at the Elliott farm.

"I wonder why she didn't come with her husband in the first place," Lewis said as they carried a large trunk up the stairs.

"Hiram Elliott wasn't expected to last nearly this long," Daniel replied. "I expect Nate thought he could just skip up here, pay his last respects, collect his inheritance, and then skip back home again. Apparently, it's the first time he's been to visit his father in twenty years. I hear it was always Reuben who danced to the old man's tune."

"Well, everyone must be regretting the visit now," Lewis remarked. "Poor woman. It's a desperate reason for a visit."

Susannah was busy in the kitchen making the tea that had been promised and was unable to supervise the preparation of the rooms, so she had given Daniel strict instructions about what needed to be done.

"Apparently, we need to turn the bed," Daniel said as they stood in the large front room he had chosen for their guest.

"Why?" Lewis asked. "No one's slept in it for weeks." But he took one side of the floppy feather mattress and helped Daniel flip it over.

Fresh linens were necessary, as well, apparently, and after a struggle the two men managed to make the bed adequately, although the coverlet refused to hang straight.

"Should I find some extra blankets?" Daniel asked. "They won't be used to the cold nights."

"Do it later," Lewis said. "We've got to move the beds out of the other room and find a table and some chairs to move into it. And there are still bags and boxes that need to be brought up."

They went through the connecting door between the front bedroom and the smaller one beside it. The latter held two small beds. They moved one of them into the big room for the boy. The other they heaved out into the hall for the time being. They then brought up a small table and some chairs from the dining room. When they had finished, Daniel surveyed their handiwork.

"Well, I don't expect it's what she's used to, but it's the best we can do on short notice."

Lewis carried the rest of the luggage up the stairs while Daniel went to inform their new patron that her accommodation had been prepared. There were three heavy valises and a number of bandboxes, besides the trunk he and Daniel had already deposited in the bedroom. Rather a lot of luggage for what Lewis assumed would be a fairly short visit, but then what did he know of city ladies and their sartorial needs? She probably changed her dress every day. He could only hope that it wouldn't be he and Daniel who would be expected to do her laundry.

Clementine wafted into the room just as the two men had delivered the last bag. "Oh, this is lovely," she said, and again Lewis found himself slightly irritated by the timbre of her voice. She turned and smiled at Daniel. "Thank you so much for going to such trouble."

Daniel reddened, and stammered in return, "You're most welcome, ma'am. And now I'll leave you to get settled."

Obviously he found her high-pitched drawl of no concern. It was obvious, to Lewis at least, that he found Clementine Elliott quite charming.

Chapter Three

Over the next few days, Mrs. Elliott appeared to charm nearly everyone else in Wellington, too. As a widow, or at least a presumed widow, she was the subject of a great deal of sympathy.

"I expect we'll find her husband's body in the spring," was Susannah's opinion. Unlike her husband, Lewis's sister generally took no delight in idle gossip. She did seem, however, quite willing to report on Clementine Elliott, as the community's sympathy turned to curiosity and then, in certain circles anyway, admiration.

"The men fall over themselves to cross her path so they can tip their hats," Susannah said. "I don't see what the attraction is myself." At which point Lewis noticed that Daniel blushed. At least he had the good sense not to make any comment.

She went on. "The only topic of conversation amongst Wellington women is the cut of her dress and the amount of ribbon used to trim it. Meribeth Scully says they've been bought right out of satin."

The Scullys ran the local dry goods store, and although they carried a large selection of cloth and bobbins of thread, their supply of ribbon was limited to the plainer types required by local housewives and the two tailors in the village, mostly grosgrain in black or a dignified brown. This did not amount to a great deal of ribbon in a year, especially as there were so many Quakers in the area, and they, of course, used no ribbon at all.

Lewis knew from their sidelong glances that Daniel and Susannah were expecting him to launch into a diatribe about the folly of letting personal vanity occupy the attention that should rightly go to spiritual concerns — it was what was expected from a Methodist minister — yet he found that he could quite understand the interest in this display of exotic female finery.

In all the years of their marriage there were few ribbons that had ever come Betsy's way, yet there had been one time when he had been paid for a christening with a few yards of cloth. It had been a pretty calico print, with a blue background and a scattering of pink and yellow flowers. He should have taken the bolt to the nearest town and traded it with some storekeeper for flour or sugar or even a few coins, but something had held him back. Instead, he had taken it home and suggested to Betsy that it was time for a new summer dress. Her eyes had lit up when she saw the cloth and he chided himself for not thinking of her more often. Even then, she had said something about their daughter's wardrobe, but he had insisted that she use it for herself.

Women needed things like pretty clothes once in a while to offset the harshness of their lives in this hard place, to take the edge off their constant round of looking after houses and children and husbands. Betsy had looked lovely in her new dress and he had told her so. Let the Scullys sell as much ribbon as they could lay their hands on, and if Clementine Elliott had raised the bar of Wellington fashion, then so be it. What real harm could it do if it was but a transitory thing and made women happier creatures?

Of more concern was his brother-in-law. He knew that Daniel had a bit of an eye. After all, it had been what attracted him to Susannah in the first place. She had been an extraordinarily pretty girl and was still a fine-looking woman, but Lewis knew that she had begun to fret about the fine lines that had etched themselves into the skin around her eyes and mouth, and once he had surprised her at the mirror in the front hall. She had been pulling at the slightly sagging pouch of flesh under her chin. She'd blushed a little when she saw him, and he had not commented. He had no real reason to think that any part of Daniel would rove except for his eye, but he was anxious that his sister's feelings not be wounded by even this small transgression. If necessary, he would have a word with him, but he hoped it wouldn't come to that.

Mrs. Elliott had dutifully attended her father-in-law the day after her arrival, but what the old man made of her was unknown, for by now he was apparently so far gone that it was unlikely that he even realized she was there. She must have concluded the same thing, for she made no move to return to the Elliott farm. Instead, she wandered the town, her small, pale son in tow, and handed her cards to everyone she met. Daniel had a supply of these cards, for she had asked him to leave a pile on the table in the entrance hall. He showed one to Lewis. *Psychic Guide*, it said in an ornamented script, and underneath, in plainer letters, *Mesmerism, Transportation and Spirit Communication, Dr. & Mrs. Nathan Elliott. Rates upon inquiry.*

"What nonsense is this?" Lewis said. "Spirit communication? What's that supposed to be about?"

"I asked the same thing," Daniel said. "Apparently, Mrs. Elliott has the ability to contact the dead, and helps their relatives speak with them, make sure they're all right, that sort of thing. It all seems very odd, doesn't it?"

Lewis was quite prepared to overlook the obsession with dress that Clementine Elliott had ignited, but this was something he could not countenance.

"This is wrong," he said flatly, "a desecration. Not only that, I suspect it's impossible anyway. This can't be anything but a parlour trick."

Daniel shrugged. "It's got everybody talking."

"I expect it has," Lewis said. "That doesn't mean it's right. Has any fool actually taken her up on it?"

Daniel appeared unconcerned. "Not yet, but I suspect it's only a matter of time. There are plenty enough people who are desperate over the loss of a loved one. And there will be plenty of people who are curious enough to come at least once, just to see what it's all about."

"You'll have to tell her she can't do that sort of thing here."

Daniel bristled. "Now, why on earth should I do that? It's none of my business ... and she's a paying customer."

"But it's fraud," Lewis protested. "You'd be a party to it."

"I don't see how you can come to that conclusion. All I do is rent the rooms. Besides, how do you know it's a fraud? Maybe she *can* do what she claims."

"You know that can't be true, Daniel."

"No, I don't know for sure," he said. "Maybe she can. Whether she can or not, all she's really doing is bringing a little comfort to folks. What's wrong with that?"

"But it's a lie."

"Oh, leave it alone, Thaddeus. She's not hurting anybody. Not everybody has your conviction, you know."

In spite of his certainty that contacting the dead was both impious and impossible, Lewis had to concede that there was a certain element of truth in this argument, for he, too, had once been guilty of a longing to communicate with his lost daughters. He wondered if he would have availed himself of a similar service had it been available at the time of his most intense grief. In spite of his moral objections, he rather suspected that he might have considered it.

Chapter Four

Clementine stood at her upstairs window and watched as two women struggled down the street toward the hotel. She recognized one of them; the woman had been at the fusty little dry goods store the day before when she had called, and had seemed quite interested when she had been handed a card. The woman's eyes had been red-rimmed. *A recent loss, and a heavy one from the look of it,* she had thought at the time. She would have spoken with the woman at greater length, but she had barely been able to get a word past the prattling of the little dressmaker who worked at a table in the corner. Fortunately, the gossipy woman had happily filled Clementine in on the details she needed to know after the woman had left.

"That's Mrs. Sprung. Poor lady lost her little girl in an accident just a month ago. She's only just managed to pull herself together and go out once in a while."

"How dreadful," Clementine had murmured. "Whatever happened?"

She was treated to a blow-by-blow account of a runaway horse, a small child slipping in the street in front of it, broken, shattered bones, and the wails of the mother when it was discovered that the life had been battered out of her child. She had filed each detail away in her memory. The dressmaker had a very loose tongue, and Clementine made a mental note to frequent the store as often as possible.

Clementine had known that it was only a matter of time until the grieving woman came to her, but she was surprised she had come so soon. It was nearly always a woman who made the first approach, and most often they brought someone with them the first time, for comfort and support. The second woman in the street beside her could be safely ignored.

"Is the room ready?" she asked the boy, over her shoulder.

"Yes, Mama."

"Bring me my shawl."

"Yes, Mama." His tone was flat. The boy always did what she asked, and with his father gone he had proved to be an enormous help to her; but she realized that she was never quite sure what this pale son of hers was thinking. There was no time to worry about it now, though, for the two women had arrived at the front door.

* * *

Clara Sprung hesitated as she and her companion reached the hotel. If her husband, Ezra, knew what she was doing, he would be furious. She had wondered at it herself all the way down the street, but the prospect of once again talking to, maybe even seeing little Amelia, was a possibility that she couldn't ignore. One part of her mind argued that the whole enterprise was a waste of money, and that Ezra would be sure to notice the missing coins. Another insisted that this woman could indeed hold the key to finding out what had really happened to her darling Amelia, in spite of the assurances of the preachers that the little girl had without doubt gone to heaven and was even now basking in the glow of God's blessing. She needed to know firsthand. But just in case her judgment had deserted her entirely, she had decided to bring her sister Harriet with her.

She was a little taken aback when she stepped inside and saw Mr. Lewis in the hallway. Everyone knew about him, of course. He had tracked down a notorious killer and brought him to justice. The whole village had been atwitter when he and his ailing wife had moved into the community. But she had been so flustered at the thought of speaking with her sweet little girl again that she had forgotten that Lewis was now helping to run the hotel. She had attended Methodist meetings on occasion, before she had settled into the habit of going along to the Church of England, and she was fairly certain what this preacher's view of trying to contact the afterlife would be. Would he remonstrate with her, right here in the front hall of the hotel? Send her away; tell her she was nothing but a foolish woman?

But he merely nodded and showed her up the stairs to Mrs. Elliott's sitting room. She and Harriet were invited to take a seat at the table and the door was firmly shut in the preacher's face.

Lewis didn't know either of the two women who disappeared into the sitting room, but Daniel passed them in the hall and was quick to fill him in.

"One of them is Ezra Sprung's wife," he informed him. "They lost their little girl a while back. I expect that's why she's here, to see if Mrs. Elliott can help. The other is Mrs. Sprung's sister. Sad, isn't it?"

With the arrival of a paying customer, Lewis's dilemma regarding Clementine Elliott's activities had suddenly moved from the theoretical to the actual. He tried again to persuade Daniel to put a stop to it. "Do you really think we should be subscribing to this?" he insisted. "It can't be anything more than party tricks, and she's using *your* premises to perform them in."

Daniel was having none of it. "I don't see that it's any of our concern what she does in her rooms as long as it's not illegal or outright immoral. If she wants to carry on her business while she's here, who are we to stop her?"

Lewis felt that this statement was on extremely shaky ethical ground. "But if it's fraudulent in any way, that would be neither legal nor moral. And you could be held culpable in the consequences."

"I don't see how," Daniel scoffed. "Besides, who's to say that she doesn't have a genuine ability to communicate with the afterlife? God has wrought greater miracles. Think of Daniel in the lion's den, or Shadrach, Meshach, and Abednego in the fiery furnace."

Lewis was at a loss as to how he should counter this argument. God had indeed wrought many miracles in the Bible, but the preacher had a great deal of difficulty believing that the same agency was at work in a hotel room in Canada West. But as Daniel pointed out, it was a difficult argument to uphold. How could you convince people of the miracle of God's grace if you denied them what they perceived as evidence of that grace, especially when it was impossible to prove it otherwise?

It was obvious that Daniel was not to be persuaded. For now, all Lewis could do was keep his eyes and ears open. When he had collected enough information to make his case, and he was certain that he would, he would once again ask Daniel to put a stop to the nonsense.

Lewis made sure to be standing near the landing when the two women descended the staircase two hours later. Tears were running down Mrs. Sprung's face and she dabbed at her eyes with a handkerchief. Whatever had happened upstairs must have been upsetting, indeed, he thought, but then he realized that her sister wore a puzzled expression that was tinged with more than a little awe.

"There, there, Clara," she said, patting the woman on the back. "It's what you wanted, after all."

"I know, I know, it was wondrous to see her again. It's just that it's given me such a turn."

Lewis stepped back into the dining room before the women spotted him. He was puzzled. Whatever had happened in the upstairs room had affected Mrs. Sprung profoundly. Her sister less so, perhaps, but she had obviously been impressed. *How had Mrs. Elliott convinced them that a dead girl was communicating from beyond?*

Chapter Five

Clara Sprung might well have remained Clementine's
only client if it hadn't been for the early winter storm
that blew in the next evening.

Lewis had known it was coming. One of the
enduring effects of his wife's prolonged struggle with
ill health was her ability to foretell the weather. All
would appear to be fine until, in the middle of cooking
dinner or sweeping the floor, she would suddenly stand
stock-still with a preoccupied expression on her face.
The next moment she would be clutching the table, her
legs barely able to support her weight, and it would be
a struggle for her to make it even as far as the kitchen
bed, where she would collapse in agony. This pain was
merely a herald. After an hour or so of lying immobile
she could often get up again and resume her chores,
but she would know that the respite was temporary,
for as soon as the wind started to blow in from the east
she would have to return to her bed.

He found her there when he carried in the supper Susannah had made for them. Martha, like the good girl she was, had fed the fire to boil up some tea, but was struggling to lift the heavy kettle off the stove without spilling it on herself.

"Storm coming?" he asked, and Betsy's groaned reply was all the answer he needed.

By the time they finished eating, the wind was pounding in great gusts against the house, making the pottery rattle and setting up a multitude of draughts that whistled through the windows and sought out even the coziest corners of the room. Lewis chased Martha off to bed and got an extra quilt to cover Betsy. He would spend the night in the chair by the stove, both to keep an eye on his ailing wife and to feed the fire. It was no hardship for someone who had spent many years on horseback in all weathers, with many a night passed huddled under just a cloak in a barn somewhere or in an indifferent bed provided to him by some well-meaning but indigent Methodist supporter.

He dozed off for a while, but was awakened by the sound of ice pellets pattering on the roof. This was a nasty one, he reflected, and he sent up a prayer for anyone caught in the open country, or on a ship out on the lake. He slipped another log into the stove and glanced out the window. He couldn't see a thing. The small pane of glass was completely glazed over with a layer of ice. He felt Betsy's hand under the covers. She seemed warm enough, so he returned to his chair and had soon dozed off again.

He slept heavily until morning, when he woke

to the sound of Martha filling the kettle from the water bucket. Betsy seemed better now that the storm appeared to have blown itself out.

"Could you run up to the hotel and ask Susannah for a couple of biscuits?" he asked the little girl. Betsy's recovery would be faster if he could get her to eat a little biscuit softened in her tea.

Martha ran to the door and pulled at the latch, but nothing happened. She pulled harder, but still it remained stubbornly closed.

She turned back to Lewis. "Can you help me, Grandpa? I can't get the door open."

"What? Have you gone all feeble all of a sudden?" he teased, but when he pulled at it he could get it to budge no more than she could.

He doubled his efforts, but the door remained stubbornly fast.

"Well now, there's a conundrum," he said, as Martha's eyes grew wide.

"Are we stuck here forever?"

"Oh, no, don't worry. I think it's just frozen shut. The ice will melt in the spring and then we'll be able to go outside."

For a moment her eyes betrayed the fact that she considered this a real possibility, but since her grandpa had teased her in this way often, her brow quickly wrinkled as she dismissed his assertion and considered other possibilities.

"Oh! I wonder if the shed door will open," she said.

There was a woodshed off the kitchen, with a door leading to the outside. It had been in the lee of the

storm and was not nearly as iced up. With a smart
tug, Lewis was able to jerk it open. He was astonished
at what he saw. Thick layers of ice coated every surface, and the weight of it had bent the trees over nearly
to the ground. Many of the hardwoods had broken
under the strain and there were downed trees and great
branches littering the side street that ran past the hotel.
The Donovan house, directly across the street from
Lewis's, had been damaged by one of these; a thick
piece of oak had fallen or been blown onto the roof,
and he could see a gaping hole where it had landed.
Lewis stepped out into the yard — he would go and
see if the Donovans needed help — but as soon as his
foot hit the ground, it skidded out from underneath
him and he had to brace himself against the side of the
shed to keep from falling.

"Are you all right?" Betsy called. Martha ran
back into the kitchen to report that the ground was
too slippery to walk on.

"There's been a lot of damage," he told her as he
went back in to collect his coat. "There's one roof gone
just from what I can see from the back door. I'd better
go and see if I can help anywhere."

She nodded. "Yes, go. I'm much better. Just get me
a cup of tea first, will you? And don't fall and break
anything, all right?"

Lewis's years on the road had been spent on horseback, not on foot, and he possessed no walking stick.
He rummaged in the shed until he found a stout branch
that had not yet been cut for kindling. It was about the
right height, and he pounded three long nails at an angle

through one end, so that the points protruded. This would give him a little extra purchase on the icy surface.

As he stepped out the back door, he saw Mr. Donovan creeping gingerly to the front of his own house. He, too, had to come through his woodshed, but had the presence of mind to bring a heavy mallet with him.

"The roof's fallen on my boy," he said in response to Lewis's hail. "I'm just going for the doctor now. I don't think there's anything more to be done inside until the doctor comes, but would you see if you can get the front door open?" Lewis nodded and, with the aid of his homemade ice pick, slithered across the road and took the hammer from the man.

"Here, take this," he said and he handed Donovan the stick in exchange. "You'll go faster."

It took ten minutes of beating at the Donovan's door to loosen it, for the ice came away in bits and pieces instead of falling to the ground in a sheet. When he had finally cleared it enough to open it, he poked his head inside and called. Mrs. Donovan appeared at the top of the stairs.

"Is there anything else I can do for you?" Lewis asked.

"No, we just need the doctor. The boy has come to now, but he got an awful blow to the head. He was insensible for a terrible long time. I tell you, I thought he was dead when I first found him. I just hope he's not addled as a result."

"I hope so, too," Lewis replied. "I'm just going to free my own door now, and then I'll be at the hotel if you need anything before your husband returns. Just yell across the street. I'll tell my granddaughter to listen for you."

He set to work to open his own door with the borrowed mallet, and by the time he finished, Mr. Donovan had returned with the doctor. Lewis returned the mallet and retrieved his makeshift ice pick.

The yard between his house and the back of the hotel was littered with icy branches and he judged that it was safer to make his way along the side of the street to the front door. Even so, the walking was treacherous, and the distance he had to travel was twice as long as it should have been. He had to pick his way around several large branches that partially blocked the road, and at the same time he was careful to stay well away from the eaves of the hotel. Every few minutes a long icicle would let go its tenuous hold and come crashing down, smashing on the ground with a shattering explosion.

Daniel had just finished freeing the hotel's doors when he arrived.

"Have you ever seen anything like it," he said in greeting.

"No, and I pity anyone who was out in it. It's too early for any kind of news, I suppose."

"Yes, people are only just getting out and about. We'll just have to pray that no one's been killed in this. I'm fine, for now. You go on and see what you can do."

Lewis made his way up one side of the street and down the other, but it appeared that the rest of Wellington had suffered only minor damage from the ice. Beyond a few torn roofs and smashed windows, all its buildings stood, and the only casualty reported so far was the Donovan boy. It would take many days, however, to clear away the mess.

By the time Lewis returned to the hotel, the ice was softening underfoot, for in the wake of the storm the temperature had risen. The sun would wear a lot of it away by the end of the day, but in the meantime the water collecting on the ice surface promised to make the footing even more slippery.

Lewis busied himself with the morning chores and was just sweeping out the kitchen when he heard the bell at the front door. Surprised at anyone venturing out on such a day, he went to see who it was. It was Mrs. Sprung, this time without her sister. He waved her up the stairs and shook his head at the notion of anyone venturing out on such an unnecessary errand when good sense dictated staying safely at home.

"We used the last of the bread for breakfast, didn't we?" Susannah said to him as he returned to the kitchen.

"I wish I'd known sooner," Lewis said. "I could have stopped at the bakery when I was out. I'll go now, if you like." He was a little annoyed at the prospect of having to make a second trip down the slippery street, but he supposed it was more interesting than sweeping.

Susannah must have the heard the annoyance in his voice. "No, no, I'll go now that the dishes are done," she said. "There's plenty of time before I have to start dinner."

Lewis finished tidying up the kitchen and swept both the stairs and the second-floor hall, and when he realized that Susannah had not come back yet, he returned to the kitchen and started to peel the potatoes for the noontime meal. There was still no sign of his sister by the time he'd started them boiling. Come to think of it, he had no idea where Daniel had got to either. He was beginning to notice that his brother-in-law seemed able to disappear for long stretches of time, but where he went and what he did were a mystery. It was nearly eleven o'clock, and soon the Elliotts and Mr. Gilmour would be descending the stairs in expectation of their dinner. Lewis needed to return home to check on Betsy, but he didn't want to leave his sister to cook and serve at the same time.

At last, the bell at the front door sounded and Lewis assumed it was the tardy Susannah. After a few moments, when she had not appeared in the kitchen, he went into the hall to discover that his sister had, indeed, returned, but not in a state he expected. She was being carried on a door by the baker and Mr. Scully, and her left leg was tied firmly down to it with a couple of belts.

"Someone's gone for the doctor," Scully reported. "We thought it best to get her in out of the cold."

"I'm so sorry, Thaddeus." Susannah smiled weakly. "One of those icicles came crashing down from a roof and I jumped to avoid it. Unfortunately, I jumped right onto a stretch of half-melted ice, and I went down hard."

It was obvious from the strange angle of her boot that the leg was broken, and that the doctor would need to set it, for it was unlikely to be a simple fracture.

Her lips were set in a taut line against the pain and her face had lost all colour.

"Susannah!" Daniel had finally returned from wherever he had been and was standing in the kitchen doorway, aghast at the sight of his injured wife. "Bring her through here," he said, directing the door carriers to the downstairs room at the back of the hotel.

They set the door down on top of the bed and left Susannah strapped to it. If they tried to move her, they could well do more damage to the injured leg. Besides, there was no point in putting her to bed just yet, for who knew what the doctor would need to do — a wooden door was easier to wash if it proved to be a bloody affair. In the meantime, Lewis could hear footsteps on the stairs and he knew that Mrs. Elliott's morning session was at an end. She and the boy would be heading for the dining room shortly.

Daniel turned to Lewis. "Do you think you could finish dinner?" he asked.

"Probably not. It's only half-ready," Lewis said. He had no confidence in his abilities as a cook.

"Could you stay with Susannah, then?"

"Yes, but then you have no one to serve. Maybe we should ask everyone to go down to the tavern this one time."

"Maybe, although by rights we should offer to pay for it." This was a prospect Daniel found less than appealing, in spite of his concern for his injured wife.

Lewis nodded, but as he headed to the bottom of the staircase to intercept the guests, he noticed that Mrs. Sprung was still in the hall.

"Has there been some trouble?" she asked. Her handkerchief was still in her hand and she dabbed at her eyes as she inquired.

"Yes, the proprietor's wife has broken her leg." A sudden thought had just occurred to him. This woman apparently had no need to be anywhere at any specific time, judging from her return visit to the hotel. Perhaps she had some time to spare. It might even do her good to have someone else to think of for a few minutes.

"I wonder if you might sit with her while we serve dinner?" he asked. "We're waiting for the doctor. You don't have to do anything," he assured her when she hesitated, "If she needs anything, you have only to come and fetch me."

"If it would be a help, then of course," she said.

He showed her to the room and ran back to the kitchen.

He quickly refried some of the bacon that had been left over from breakfast while Daniel dished up the potatoes that had by now boiled to a watery pulp. They then carried the bowls through to the dining room where Mr. Gilmour and the Elliotts were waiting. There was no bread to go with the dinner; no one had thought to bring the loaves that Susannah had dropped when she fell. The Elliott boy made a mewling noise when the food was set down in front of him.

"Now, Horatio," his mother admonished. "Be thankful for what there is."

"I'm sorry there are no other dishes," Lewis explained. "I'll fetch a bowl of pickle to round this out and we'll do better tonight, all right? We've had a bit of an upset this morning. My sister has fallen and broken her leg rather badly, I'm afraid."

"I'm sorry to put you to so much trouble," Clementine said. "It's just that Horatio is so delicate, his digestion is easily upset. I do hope that your sister isn't in too much pain." She smiled, and just for a moment Lewis could understand why the men scrambled so to tip their hats. Then the smile left her face and he was left wondering if his eyes had deceived him, for in repose her face was hard.

When he returned with a bowlful of pickled cabbage, he noted that Horatio appeared to have finished eating, having consumed nothing but a few spoonfuls of the potatoes. He removed the boy's plate without comment, even though the waste of good food aggravated him. Ah, well, they pay for it anyway, don't they, he thought, and the pigs will eat it up well enough.

Lewis had finished scrubbing the pots by the time Dr. Keough arrived to confirm what they already knew — Susannah's leg was broken in two places.

"I need you to hold her down while I set it," he told Lewis and Daniel. "And you, ma'am." He nodded to Mrs. Sprung. "Perhaps you could grasp her foot, just so."

"I … well … all right," she said tentatively. "I guess I could." She looked most alarmed at the prospect.

Keough knew his business well and it was only a short time before he announced that he was satisfied with the alignment. He fixed two wooden splints to the leg and wound it around with heavy bandaging to hold them in place.

"Fortunately, the bone didn't puncture the skin," he said. "It should heal without difficulty, although she may have a bit of a limp for the rest of her life." He sighed. "What a morning."

"Would you have tea?" Lewis asked, and the doctor gratefully accepted his offer. Mrs. Sprung declined. "I must go," she said. "I've been gone too long now."

So she did have somewhere she needed to be, Lewis thought. "Well, thank you for all your help."

"I don't believe we've been introduced," she said. "I'm Mrs. Sprung. I do know that you're Mr. Lewis, though. You're the man who caught the murderer."

"Yes, that was me," he said. It wasn't a reputation that he welcomed, but it was one that seemed to follow him around. "Again, thank you for your help, Mrs. Sprung." She smiled and made her own way to the front door, and he was relieved that she didn't, like so many people, pry into the details of his pursuit of Isaac Simms.

The doctor was full of news as he drank his tea. The Donovan boy would recover from his head wound, although, as he pointed out, "You can never tell with these things. He may be a little odd as the result of it."

There had been numerous sprained ankles — less dire outcomes of spills on the ice than Susannah's. Mr.

Harry, the headstone carver, had sliced open his hand when he attempted to free his front door with one of his own chisels; and Sarah Bowerman had taken a bad fall, an incident that caused some alarm as she was in the family way again. Thankfully, it appeared that no harm had been done.

"Minor stuff, fortunately," the doctor said. "Most of the damage appears to have occurred elsewhere. There were several ships damaged, I hear, and the *Anthea* hasn't been heard from. She was due in at Picton last night. We can only hope she found safe anchorage somewhere, or better yet, didn't set out at all. I would hate to have been out on the lake in all that."

"Were there any local men on the ship?"

"Oh, yes. Peter Spencer's brother is the captain, and his sister is the cook. I'm not sure where all the crew was from, but they may have picked them up in Oswego for a last run."

A great number of the shipwrecks that occurred on the Great Lakes happened in November. Fall was a time when sudden storms swept seemingly out of nowhere, like the one of the previous night. Deciding when to end the shipping season was a perilous gamble for the shipowners and captains, and there were always a few who were willing to bet that they could get "one last run" in before laying the ships up for the winter. All too often, the last run of the season ended up being the last run *forever*.

The Spencer family was Methodist, Lewis knew, as he remembered having seen them at several meetings. Not that that should make any difference, really, but normally he would have gone to the family to offer whatever comfort he could. But as a result of Susannah's mishap, he would now have too much to do at the hotel, and he set about doing it as soon as the doctor had finished his tea and gone on his way.

Betsy received the news of her sister-in-law's accident with dismay. "How are we ever going to manage?" she asked. "Surely, you and Daniel can't do it all."

"I know. I'll try to help as much as I can, and we can certainly keep things going for a few days, but I don't know what will happen after that. Daniel's not much help at the best of times, and neither of us knows our way around a kitchen."

"Is there anything I can do? This latest bout seems to have passed, and I'm feeling much better."

Lewis looked at her face, still pale, and with traces of the pinched look it got when she was unwell.

"No, I don't think you should try to do too much. You'll just get sick again. I wonder, though, if it might be a help if you could spend part of the day sitting with Susannah. It might save Daniel some steps if he doesn't have to run back and forth, and she's sure to be happier with a woman there to see to her needs."

"Of course."

"And Martha can lend a hand. She's old enough to run errands and do a little sweeping."

He had to laugh a little at the look on Betsy's face. The little girl was quite willing to turn her hand to whatever she was asked to do, and he knew that she was a real help to Betsy when he wasn't there, but when he was at home he often stopped her in mid-task and sent her out to play instead. "They grow up too fast as it is," was his reply when Betsy protested. "Let her be a little girl."

He knew this was spoiling her, but he couldn't help himself. Her mother had been his favourite child, and her premature death at the hands of a murderer had nearly destroyed him. That he himself had brought the murderer to justice had allowed him to close the door on his mourning, but the fact that the killer had nearly taken Martha as well was almost more than he could bear to think about, and it coloured his dealings with his granddaughter.

Betsy and Martha walked across the yard to the hotel with him. The warmer temperatures and the bright sunlight had softened much of the ice. The patches of roadway that had seen the heaviest morning traffic had cleared entirely. By picking their way carefully, they could find secure footing. Even so, Lewis kept a firm grip on Betsy's arm and Betsy on Martha's.

Daniel looked relieved when they arrived, as did Susannah when she realized that Betsy would be there to keep her company. "Yes, yes, much the best solution," she said.

Martha was sent to the bakery to fetch some bread for the evening meal. Supper was always a much simpler affair than dinner, with the leftovers from the noon meal serving as the main course, rounded out with a good soup and a pudding; except that today there were no leftovers from the poor meal they had served up at noon. There were, however, two apple pies that Susannah had prepared that morning, which only needed to go into the oven. That would do for dessert, and they could put some cheese with each slice, as well.

Surely, Lewis thought, he and Daniel could manage to fry some chops and potatoes and boil up some carrots or turnip. With a generous serving of bakery bread and a selection of the pickled vegetables that Susannah had done down that fall, it would be an adequate menu for a supper. *It's better than what I gave them for dinner, anyway*, Lewis thought. He resigned himself to the fact that in the next few weeks he would undoubtedly be forced to learn far more about what went on in a kitchen than he had ever wanted to know.

Chapter Six

The following day was a Sunday and Betsy helped them spit a nice piece of beef for dinner. Then she and Lewis and Martha walked to the Methodist meeting, leaving Daniel with strict instructions regarding the importance of frequent basting.

The Elliotts had retired to their rooms after breakfast and had not re-emerged since, which surprised Lewis a little. Clementine had gone to great pains to acquaint herself with the inhabitants of the village, and Lewis had assumed that she would consolidate this beachhead by making an appearance at one of the Sunday services. Perhaps there was no church of her persuasion here, although there were plenty enough to choose from — his own Methodists, the Presbyterians, the Anglicans, and even the Roman Catholics, who presided over not only a church but a boarding school that housed nearly a hundred students.

This school existed largely due to the efforts of one Archibald McFaul. McFaul had arrived from Ireland as a penniless boy and through intelligence and industry, had risen to become one of the most successful businessmen in Wellington and a leader in the community. His success had been shouted to the world when he built a large brick house on a knoll overlooking the lake. It was an extraordinary building, grandly constructed with stone lintels, four large chimneys, and elegant French doors that graced the façade. McFaul had dubbed it "Tara Hall" in honour of his Irish origins.

It was McFaul who was in a large part responsible for the lively Catholic presence in Wellington. As soon as he had been able to afford it, he had fetched a priest from Ireland to establish a church and a school. And then, a few short years later, he turned his graceful house over to the priests. There were differing motives ascribed to this astounding gift — some said it was McFaul's sense of piety that was responsible. Others claimed that his extensive enterprises, in particular his far-flung shipping business, had suffered heavy losses and that he could no longer afford to maintain the massive home. Whatever the reason, the gesture had only elevated McFaul's status within the community. The church elected to use Tara Hall as a boarding school, and soon Catholic families across the province were sending their offspring, boys and girls alike, to be educated in Wellington. On Sundays, these pupils traipsed along to the wooden church that had been built behind the school.

If Lewis had been forced to guess, he might have expected Mrs. Elliott to attend this church. For some reason he had a vague notion that there were many Catholics in the southern states. But there were many other denominations, as well, and he supposed it wouldn't be surprising if Mrs. Elliott belonged to one that was peculiar to that part of the country, and therefore declined to attend services here.

It was not really any of his business what the hotel guests did, he reminded himself. The Elliotts could honour the day in any way they thought fitting.

When Lewis and his family arrived at the Methodist meeting house there was a knot of people on the sidewalk passing the time of day before they went in. All of the conversation was about the ice storm and the damage that had been done. Of particular interest was the fate of the missing *Anthea*.

"We can only hope they read the weather signs before they left Oswego," said Alonzo Jones, who had fished the waters of Lake Ontario nearly all his life. "If they were out in the lake, they'd have been in trouble with all that ice on their sails. Their only chance would be to steer for Main Duck."

Main Duck was one of the islands that stretched across the eastern end of Lake Ontario. Situated almost exactly halfway across, just outside American waters, it often served as a haven for ships in trouble. The island was used as a fishermen's base in the summer, but the owner grazed livestock, as well, and there would be a man or two left there all winter to see to the cattle. In a violent storm, a ship's captain might well make for

Main Duck, sure of a safe anchorage for his vessel and food and shelter for his crew.

"Peter Spencer is beside himself," Jones said, "with his brother and his sister both on board. He's always claimed there's no storm on the face of the earth that Matt Spencer can't sail through, but I don't know — with the ice coming down so fast the way it did, I don't know how any ship would survive. In spite of what he says, Peter's worried all right. You can tell just by looking at him."

"Well, we'll just have to pray that the *Anthea* never left port," Lewis said. And with the rest of the faithful Methodists, he entered the meeting house and did exactly that.

When they returned to Temperance House after the service, the roast was a little burnt on the outside, and Daniel had forgotten about making any gravy, but in a few minutes Betsy had set everything right and they served up an excellent Sunday dinner.

At mid-morning the next day Clementine Elliott steeled herself to enter the dry goods store. When she had first started making the rounds of the village shops, she had always made a point of making a small purchase or two, often lingering over her choices for an hour or more. She had soon zeroed in on Scully's store as one of the hubs of conversation in Wellington, especially for the women.

Nearly everyone who came into the store would pass a pleasant word with Mr. Scully, who would inquire as to the health of his customer and his customer's family, but it was his daughter Meribeth, the dressmaker, who always took the inquiry farther, following up with questions regarding neighbours, acquaintances, and far-flung relations. She had a prodigious memory for the details of family connections and, in particular, the history of disputes and disagreements between them.

Having a dressmaker right in the store was a good business practice for Mr. Scully. Meribeth often commented on which qualities of cotton or bombazine would be appropriate for which style, and which colour would most suit the customer — although black and brown remained the most respectable colours for married women. She made suggestions regarding how each item should be trimmed, whether with ribbon or lace, and which styles were currently in fashion in London or New York. Many customers felt uncomfortable with taking the cloth away to sew themselves, or to another dressmaker when Meribeth had been so helpful in its selection, and so they would contract with her to cut and assemble the article, as well, doubling the profits for Scully, for every penny made was put into the store account, and few coins found their way back to Meribeth.

This was only fair as far as Scully was concerned, for he knew that he would be responsible for his daughter's keep as long as he lived. There was no point in setting aside a dowry for Meribeth. No man was ever likely to come courting her, for she had been born with a twisted spine, a malformation that had killed her mother in the birthing. The fact that the child had survived at all was a shock to everyone, and for a time Scully had hoped that the deformity would correct itself as she grew older. Instead, it grew worse, and her corkscrew back bent her over at the waist, so that she had to tip her head up and sideways in order to meet anyone's eye.

Her father had decided to put her to work, teaching her the intricacies of cutting cloth and of making fine, even stitches. She had shown a surprising aptitude for tailoring, and an ironic interest in the latest fashion. Her willingness to share her expertise made her popular with Scully's female customers, particularly the young girls. They listened to Meribeth's advice, for they knew that there was no element of competition in her suggestions. She would not ever lure away the young men they had their eyes set on.

Meribeth whiled away the tedious hours she spent with a needle in her hand by tracking her neighbours' business. She heard every item of news and piece of gossip that passed through Wellington's lively and extensive grapevine, and mentally fit it into the giant jigsaw puzzle of events and personalities that comprised the village's social life. She shared her knowledge with whoever came into the store, for the passing on of one item would often prompt the offer of another.

She had been aware of the arrival of the exotic Mrs. Elliott almost immediately. Bella MacDonald had been passing Temperance House as Clementine alit from the wagon, and after taking careful note of her cloak and hat, had scurried to Scully's to report their cut and colour to Meribeth, in the hopes that she might be able to copy it. Bella was to be married the following year, and was busy assembling her trousseau.

Meribeth was intrigued, and hoped that Mrs. Elliott would soon grace the shop. She had the latest available patterns, of course, and kept herself as up-to-date as possible with new trends in dresses and hats, but styles took a long time to work their way across the ocean from London and Paris, and often she had only written descriptions or drawings to guide her. Actually being able to examine a stylish outfit firsthand would help her immeasurably — she would be able to see how the cloth was cut and inspect the details of how it was assembled.

When Clementine first entered the store, she had very graciously removed her cloak and hat and allowed Meribeth to look them over carefully while she made a show of inspecting the bolts of cloth and spools of lace on offer. As far as Clementine was concerned, these were of poor quality. Eventually she had purchased a small packet of pins, just for the sake of buying something, but by then she had listened to a full half-hour of the dressmaker's prattle.

She had been able to formulate a very clear picture of the village just by listening. She knew not only who was angry with whom, which village men were drunks, and which had an eye for the girls, but also who had suffered a loss, who was grieving, who was expecting a child. The next day she returned with a magazine, a newer one than Meribeth had seen, that had a number of drawings of the necklines currently fashionable for evening wear in New York. From then on, it seemed natural and easy to drop in every day.

Clementine knew that she had caused a sensation in Wellington and that the women remarked on her fashionable clothes, while the men remarked on her. It was not difficult to impress these villagers, she thought, stuck as they were in such a backwater place. She also knew that her regular appearances at the dry goods store had elevated Meribeth's status by the mere fact of association, and some of the village women who had previously not frequented the store, now began dropping by in the afternoon just on the off-chance that they might get a peek at Mrs. Elliott's clothes. Mr. Scully was delighted; for it meant that each of these women could be counted on to purchase at least some small item. And each time, in the course of conversation, they would impart a bit of news that Meribeth would happily repeat to anyone who would listen.

Until now, Clementine had simply let the little dressmaker chatter away, taking the information as it came, tedious though that had been. Now she judged that it was time to start directing the conversation into specific areas of interest. She took a deep breath, mounted the steps, and opened the door.

Mr. Scully beamed when he saw her. "Mrs. Elliott! How grand to see you. And how are we today?"

"Good day, Mr. Scully, I hope things are well with you."

"Never better, never better," he replied, bowing slightly as he did so. "And what could we do for you this afternoon?"

She had no chance to answer as Meribeth bustled over from her corner.

"Mrs. Elliott, how wonderful to see you," she said. "My goodness me, I've just started the rosettes on Bella MacDonald's bodice. You're not in such a hurry that you couldn't take a look at them for me, are you?"

"Well." Clementine made a show of hesitation, then began peeling off her gloves. "Perhaps I could take a quick look."

Meribeth was full of the usual inconsequential details of village life. Sarah Bowerman was still resting, apparently, after her fall on the ice, but it looked as though it had done her unborn child no harm. The Presbyterians had still not collected enough money to begin building a church, in spite of a concerted subscription drive. The Carrs were still struggling after the death of Mr. Carr, although Martin was working at the sawmill and taking his entire pay home to his mother.

"I hear there is great concern about the missing ship," Clementine said when the dressmaker stopped to draw a breath.

"Oh, my goodness, that's a terrible thing! We can only hope they'll turn up safe and sound. It's happened before, you know, a ship caught in a storm and presumed lost, and then some time later you find out that everything is fine. It's worrisome, though."

"How long will it be before we know for certain?"

"Sometimes you never find out," Meribeth said. "It's a peculiar thing. Sometimes the lake never returns the wreckage, especially if the ship went down where the lake is deep. Other times, weeks might go by and then a body might be discovered on a shore far distant from where anyone would expect. Then again, it might be thrown up in front of the victim's own home. There's no accounting for what could happen, and all anybody can do is pray and wait."

"That's assuming that the ship was wrecked in the first place," Clementine pointed out.

"Oh, my yes, the best news possible would be that they stayed snug in port somewhere. Even then, it might take some time before they felt it safe to set out again. You just never know about these things."

"They tell me the captain is a local man."

"Matt Spencer, yes, and his sister is the cook." And at that Meribeth settled in to relate everything she knew about the Spencer family.

Lewis was at a loss to explain why Mrs. Sprung kept returning to the hotel, but each morning since her first visit she had walked through the front door just before nine o'clock. Now that she knew where the Elliott rooms were, he simply nodded a good morning to her and waved her up the stairs. During the course of the morning he would hear various rappings and thumpings from upstairs, and then Mrs. Sprung would depart again a couple of hours later, clutching a handkerchief and dabbing at her eyes.

That morning he had just finished scrubbing the last of the breakfast dishes when the front door opened. He assumed it was Mrs. Sprung again, and it wasn't until he heard someone clearing his throat that he realized it wasn't. It was a ruddy-faced man who looked vaguely familiar to Lewis, but he couldn't quite come up with the name.

"I'm looking for Mrs. Nate Elliott," he said, and his face reddened even more.

Lewis directed him up the stairs, and it was only later that he realized the man was Peter Spencer. This was an unwelcome realization. There could be only one reason that he would be visiting Clementine Elliott; he was hoping she could help him discover the fate of the missing *Anthea*.

Lewis went fuming back into the kitchen, wishing he could think of some way to get his brother-in-law to put his foot down in this matter.

Daniel had taken a cup of tea in to Susannah, relieving Betsy of her invalid-sitting duties for a few moments. Lewis had arrived back in the kitchen only just in time to stop his wife from peeling the mound of potatoes that were set out for the noonday meal.

"I'll do those later if Daniel doesn't get to them," he said, although he sincerely hoped that this wouldn't be necessary. "Come and sit down for a minute. There's something I want to discuss with you."

She looked puzzled, but obligingly settled herself down at the kitchen table.

"It's not your hotel," she pointed out, when he outlined his concerns about the activities taking place in the upstairs room. "It's Daniel's place to stop it if he thinks it's wrong, but he has no qualms about it at all."

"That's because Mrs. Elliott has bewitched him," Lewis grumbled.

"No, it's because Mrs. Elliott is a paying customer. Enough people turn away because there's no drink here. If Daniel starts questioning everyone's business, he won't have any customers at all. It's bad enough the way he keeps pestering poor Mr. Gilmour."

"You don't think it's some sort of witchcraft or something?"

"Of course it isn't. We can't communicate with the dead. You know that as well as I do, Thaddeus. There's no doubt in my mind that there's some sort of jiggery-pokery going on, but I honestly don't see what you can do about it. If she was asked to leave, she would no doubt simply move down the street to the other inn, or operate from the Elliott farm, and in the meantime you would have deprived Daniel and Susannah of most of their current income. I know it seems wrong, but I don't think it's wrong enough to make a fuss over."

As usual, Betsy's opinion was one of good sense, but he kept an eye on the hall after that. Within an hour, Peter Spencer came down the stairs with a satisfied look on his face.

"I knew it," he said to Lewis. "I knew there was no chance that Matt could ever drown. He was born with a caul, you know."

There was a persistent opinion that babies born with a caul were impervious to death by drowning, that somehow the birth membrane protected them from a watery death. Lewis subscribed to no such notion, but he was reluctant to snatch away whatever hope this man held.

"You'll see," Spencer said. "They'll turn up. Mrs. Elliott said they were happy where they were, and she thought they might be near an island. They were on their way from Oswego, you see, so an island makes sense. They probably put in at Main Duck and can't get away again."

If that were the case, if the crew was indeed comfortably housed in one of the cottages on the island, they might well take a few days to ensure that the weather was fair enough to continue. In the meantime, it would be impossible for them to notify their relatives of what had happened. Similarly, if they had never left Oswego at all, they could bring news of their own fates as quickly as anyone else. If Spencer and Mrs. Elliott were right, it was not surprising that no news had reached their ears. Lewis could only hope Peter Spencer's optimism was not ill-conceived.

"We can only pray that this is the case," Lewis said, and Spencer appeared satisfied enough with this half-hearted response.

Chapter Seven

Since his arrival, Martha had been intrigued by the pale boy who was staying at the hotel. The only time she saw him was when he appeared for meals with his mother. He would sit at the table across from her and pick half-heartedly at the food that was placed in front of him, occasionally wrinkling his nose in disgust at a particularly fatty piece of meat or an underdone crust. His mother would chide him gently, but this admonishment was never enough to make him eat more than a few mouthfuls.

He didn't go to school. Martha had started classes in the fall and her excitement at going off to the schoolhouse down the street from where they lived had soon faded at exposure to the constant repetition of the alphabet and counting to one hundred every day. She could already read — her grandma had taught her — and in spite of the thrill of spending her days with the other children, she was too easily bored by the routine. She was mildly envious of the boy, Horatio, who had all of his days free to do as he pleased; he just didn't ever seem pleased to do much of anything, she thought, and she made it her mission to befriend him.

Martha was used to making friends wherever she went, but when they lived in Demorestville her customary playmate had been Henry Jessup, Minta and Seth's little boy, who lived in the half-house next to them. Henry was quite a bit younger, and although he had tried to keep up with whatever game Martha chose to invent, he was timid and clumsy and sometimes she became very impatient with him. After Grandpa moved them all to Uncle Daniel's hotel, Martha had missed Henry dreadfully. Although Horatio was older than Henry, and would probably not be as eager to do her bidding, Martha was determined to give him a try. So when school was done each day, she returned to Temperance House and offered to help with whatever she could manage, just so she might catch a glimpse of him. But he appeared not to notice her at all.

She wasn't sure how she should go about getting his attention, until fortune smiled on her endeavour. As Martha was walking home from school, her eye was caught by something shiny lying on the ground in front of the meeting house. It was a penny, probably destined for the collection plate when someone dropped it without noticing. She debated whether or not she should attempt to find its owner, but quickly rejected this notion; after all, the first person she asked was apt to say, "Yes, of course, that's mine," whether it was or not, and then she would have to give it up.

She knew what her Grandpa would say. He would say that the penny had been meant for the church, and that was where it should go, but if she put it in the collection on Sunday her opportunity to win a new friend would be lost. Besides, what if it hadn't been meant for their own church, but for one of the others — perhaps the Presbyterians or the Catholics? Surely Grandpa wouldn't expect her to donate so willingly to his rivals. And with this rationalization, she felt that her conscience was in the clear.

So off she went to Henderson's store, where she figured Mrs. Henderson could be counted on to give her the best value for her money. After all, the Hendersons were Methodist, and Grandpa was a preacher, or at least he had been. Surely that should be worth an extra couple of candies in the bag.

She agonized over the selection, limited as it was. Eventually, she decided on lemon rocks and molasses candy. There were a few pieces of marchpane on the counter, which sorely tempted her for a time, but she could get a greater quantity if she chose the more common offerings. And sure enough, Mrs. Henderson added a few extra pieces to the pile on the counter before she bundled the candy up in a twist of paper so Martha wouldn't lose any on the way home.

"My goodness me," she said as she packed the candy. "Aren't you a lucky girl to have a penny to spend."

"Yes, ma'am," Martha replied, but wisely decided to comment no further. She hoped Mrs. Henderson wouldn't mention the purchase to anyone. If either of her grandparents came to hear of it, she would have to explain, and she wasn't at all convinced that the conclusion she had reached over the ethical ownership of the penny would be endorsed by either of them.

She allowed herself only one of the lemon drops as she walked back to the hotel. When it had melted away in her mouth she was tempted to gobble the whole mess down at once. She didn't often get real *boughten* candy. She resisted the temptation, however, and after consideration of the best hiding places the hotel had to offer, she snuck down the stairs to the root cellar and put the twist of paper in the corner behind the apples, which were spread out on the wide shelves for winter storage.

Then she went to her Uncle Daniel to persuade him that she could help wait on tables.

"My goodness me, really?" Daniel said when she suggested it. "Well, aren't you just the best girl to help like that." He gave her a hug and said they could see how it went.

Initially the boy continued to ignore her, although she sometimes caught him casting sidelong glances at her while she placed a plate or a glass of water in front of him. She began to talk to him whenever she was near, something that was quite a natural thing for her to do. Grandpa claimed that she chattered every moment she was awake, but he always smiled when he said it, so she didn't think it could be a bad thing. Eventually she appeared to wear the boy down with the sheer volume of words thrown in his direction.

"What's the matter? Didn't you like it?" she asked that evening as she cleared away his plate. There was a mound of food on it, and his knife looked as though it hadn't been used.

He shook his head.

"Want something nicer?"

"Like what?"

"Come out to the front stoop in a little while and I'll show you." She was bursting with excitement at having finally coaxed a couple of words out of him, but she nevertheless sauntered out of the dining room as if she were unconcerned. She was quite proud of herself for this show of nonchalance.

She took the plate she was carrying to the scullery. Uncle Daniel was still busy in the kitchen, her grandfather was clearing the rest of the dishes from the dining room, and her grandmother was nowhere to be seen, although Martha was fairly sure she was sitting with Aunt Susannah. She was confident she had at least a half-hour or so before she would be called to her own supper, which would be eaten at the big pine table in the kitchen, so she scampered down the steps to the cellar to retrieve her loot, then slipped on her coat and went out the back door.

Horatio was waiting for her on the verandah.

Wordlessly, she held the candy out to him.

His eyes widened. "Where did you get this?"

"I bought it. You want some?"

"Yeah." He took three pieces of molasses candy and crammed them into his mouth. "Wash or nay?" he asked.

"Pardon?" His mouth was so full she couldn't understand what he was saying. "What's a nay?"

He shoved the wad to one side of his mouth. "It's something a horse says."

She was puzzled for a moment, until she understood the pun. She began to giggle. He began to laugh with her. At that point, Martha figured the friendship was established, so she reached for a lemon drop.

"I'm Martha. And you're Horatio, right?"

He made a face. "Yeah, Horatio. But you can call me Joe if you like."

"Horatio Joe, that rhymes. How come you don't go to school?" Lemony saliva dripped down her chin as she spoke.

"Because I have to help Mama."

That made sense to Martha. She often had to help her grandmother, especially on the days when she wasn't feeling well. She would have been happy to stay home and help her all the time. It was her grandfather who was insistent about her attending school every day.

"How much do you have to help?"

"Mostly in the mornings. She goes out in the afternoon."

"Wanna go play tomorrow afternoon? When I'm done school."

"Play what? I'm not going to play girl stuff."

"Nah. I don't want to play girl stuff either. We could go down to the docks."

Horatio appeared to consider this proposition. Martha hoped he didn't think she was too bossy. She didn't realize that he was so bored in the afternoons that he would have agreed to play anything, even if it did involve dolls. "All right," he said finally. He helped himself to three of the lemon drops from the twist and Martha took a molasses candy.

"Martha! Supper!"

The call came from inside. No one had noticed that she'd gone out, but there was little chance that she would be able to slip back in without being seen. She wasn't worried about being outside with the boy; it was the candy that would be hard to explain. She looked longingly at the three candies left, but then she remembered that the whole point of the enterprise had been to win over Horatio.

"I've got to go," she said. "See you tomorrow?"

He nodded.

"Here." She thrust the paper twist into his hands and ran back inside.

Chapter Eight

Lewis was on his way to the bakery the next morning when he saw a knot of people in front of McFaul's store, the wheelwright Ed Fisher holding court at the centre of the crowd.

"They've been found!" he shouted as Lewis joined the group. "The ship foundered, but the crew made it to Main Duck! The captain of the *Cinderella Davy* saw the signal from the island and brought them in to Picton safe and sound. "

This was news indeed, and in spite of the fact that myriad chores awaited him at the hotel, Lewis was prepared to take a few minutes to hear the details of the miraculous survival of the crew of the *Anthea*.

As had been feared, the ship had been caught on the open lake when the storm hit. Every surface of the vessel had soon been covered with a layer of ice. The cook, Jemima Spencer, had taken the wheel, as was the customary drill, while the crew took oars and beat at the sails in an attempt to free them from the stiffening shroud of ice. This effort had been enough to give them at least a little steerage way, but with so much ice on their canvas, Captain Spencer didn't dare try to ride out the storm in open water. It would only be a matter of time before a mast snapped and the ship was rendered helpless. Jemima steered for Main Duck, hoping to tuck the vessel into the lee of the island. After an exhausting struggle, she successfully piloted the vessel into Schoolhouse Bay. The captain hoped he could throw out his anchor and at least try to get his crew ashore.

The wind had continued to howl and heavy seas washed over the *Anthea* while the ice continued to rain down on them. The lifeboat was washed away by a huge wave as they attempted to launch it, and then an eddy wind parted the anchor chain. The ship struck hard against the rocks that lay near the shore, staving a great hole in the stern of the vessel. She began to take on water.

The crew's only hope was that someone on shore would see them and attempt a rescue. But night was falling fast, and Spencer knew that at this time of year there would be only a couple of men on the island and that their chores would have been completed long since. It was unlikely that they would venture out of doors again in such a storm, and even if they did, how would they ever see the ship? Against all odds, the first mate managed to keep a lantern burning, but the fuel soon ran low and the crew's spirits plummeted as it winked out.

Now in total darkness, they huddled at the bow of the ship as water continued to pour into her stern. Though they were only a hundred feet from shore, the heavy surf and blinding sleet made any attempt to reach it suicidal. They would have to wait until dawn.

As the first light brightened the eastern sky, Captain Spencer made his decision. He removed a hatch cover, tied a rope to it and threw it overboard. They would have to jump in after it one by one and hope to reach it before being swamped. The added buoyancy of the hatch might give them a chance to kick their way to shore. What would happen after that he had little idea, for he knew that his crew was cold, wet, and exhausted, and in all likelihood they would be unable to climb the high bank or walk far enough to reach a dwelling. The alternative was to stay where they were and hope that the ship held together against the buffeting of the waves and wind. His guess was that it would soon start to break up, and that they would be thrown into the water regardless, with no chance of survival.

Jemima jumped first. If she failed to reach the hatch, the captain would jump next and try to pull her to safety. She timed her jump well, however, and bobbed up to the surface a foot from the cover. The first mate followed, and he, too, jumped well. The sailor who leapt next was not so lucky. As his head came to the surface he was caught by a huge wave, which swept him away from his target.

At this point a miracle occurred. One of the caretakers of the island appeared on the shore in search of a steer that had wandered off. This man, taking the situation in at a glance, grabbed one of the large branches that had fallen in the storm and waded out into the frigid water. It was a close thing, but the very tip of it reached the struggling sailor. He was able to grasp it and was pulled to shore.

The branch was used to good effect for the others, as well, and with the boost in confidence that the promise of assistance gave them, the rest jumped to the cover, from where they could grab hold of the branch and be pulled in.

"The hardest part," the captain was reported to have said, "was getting to the nearest house. We were so cold we could barely make our legs work."

There they had stayed for the next three days, warm and fed, until a passing ship could be hailed to take them to the mainland.

After he had gathered all the pertinent details, Lewis continued on his way, relaying the welcome news to the baker and whatever customers were in his shop. They in turn passed the details on to whoever they met. It was all anyone could talk about, and Lewis heard the news discussed and dissected countless times over the course of the day. He was not at all surprised when Peter Spencer appeared at the hotel the following morning.

"I told you Matt could never drown," he said with a grin, "and Jemima can steer a ship better than most men. I have to tell you, though, I despaired for a while there, but it was Mrs. Elliott who gave me heart when things looked so bleak. I've just come round to thank her for that."

Clementine and Horatio were just finishing breakfast, but Clementine rose and came out to where they were standing.

"I can't thank you enough, ma'am," Spencer said when he saw her. "You were right all along, although I don't know how you do it. Is there anything I can do for you in return?"

She smiled her cat-face at him. "We have only to listen to the spirits to learn the truth," she said. "Their voices can help us to deal with the tribulations of this mortal life."

"Still …" Spencer shuffled awkwardly, "it seems to me that the information you gave was worth a lot more than I paid you for it. It sits kind of uneasy, you know, and I'd like to put it right."

"There is no need," she said, still smiling. "I would freely share the wisdom of the afterlife with all who cared to hear, if only I were able. Alas, I am forced to ask for a small remuneration only to keep myself and my poor boy. Beyond that, I ask for nothing. Except, perhaps…" she paused and looked at Spencer squarely, "perhaps you could offer your friends and acquaintances some verification of my abilities."

"Of course. Of course I will," he said. "I'll tell everyone. And thank you again, ma'am. Thank you so much."

Lewis happened to glance into the dining room as Spencer spoke. Horatio was sitting at the table with his chin in his hands, his elbows on the table, something his mother was constantly chiding him about. As Clementine asked for Spencer's aid in advertising her talents, her son rolled his eyes. Mr. Gilmour was listening, as well, and his eyes narrowed as Clementine made her pitch.

Chapter Nine

By the middle of November snow had begun to fall, not in a blizzard, but gently and intermittently over the course of several days, blanketing the roads and fields with an obliterating white. The mud froze into ruts on the road, and horses were harnessed to sleighs instead of to wagons. Instead of hurrying to the constant round of toil that claimed them in good weather, farmers indulged in second cups of breakfast tea and dreamed of next year's crops. The hectic pace of summer business slowed in the towns, as well, and there was time for meetings and lectures, dances and dalliance. The gentle inward-looking respite gave everyone a chance to catch their breaths and prepare for the quickening that would come with the spring.

Lewis became aware that Martha had somehow won over the Elliott boy and that for some inexplicable reason she called him "Horatio Joe."

"Because it rhymes," she had said when he asked her about it, and she seemed to have no better answer than this.

Lewis had been convinced that she would never get the boy away from his mother. Clementine liked to keep him close, and usually he was in their rooms with her whenever she had visitors. The boy functioned as a sort of chaperone for her, he figured. Horatio was so small and pasty-faced that Lewis wasn't sure how well he would tolerate Martha's boisterous activities anyway. He seemed to be a boy more suited to drawing rooms and the company of his elders. Lewis found him sitting at the bottom of the stairs one afternoon, however, and when Martha arrived after school, she hastily deposited her slate in the kitchen and the two scurried outside.

Martha hesitated on the front step. The snow presented opportunity for an abundance of activities, but daylight disappeared so rapidly in the late afternoons at this time of year that there would be little time to do much before darkness descended and they would have to go back inside.

"Do you want to toboggan?" she asked him.

Mr. Henderson at the general store had given her an old piece of board that had been worn smooth on one side, and showed her how to drip some wax over its surface to decrease the friction.

Horatio scowled. "What's a coboggan?"

"You know, going down a hill on a board."

"Oh, sledding," he said. "I've done that!" Then he reddened. "At least, I've heard about it. We don't have much snow in Carolina, you know."

She was puzzled. "What do you do in the winter then?" Horatio only shrugged.

Martha was in a lather to try her new plaything, but was uncertain where to do it. There had not yet been enough snow to heap up into the huge mounds by the side of the roads that would serve well enough for a slide later in the winter. There were some gentle slopes here and there in the village, but there would be older children playing there, including some of the bullies from her school who would be sure to wrest her toboggan away from her and use it roughly. She had no confidence in Horatio Joe's ability to protect her from these boys; in fact, his presence would certainly only intensify their unwanted attentions.

"Let's go down to the lake," she finally suggested. "We can walk to the dunes and go down the banks and onto the ice."

Wellington's situation was peculiar in that it stretched along the shores of two nearly separate bodies of water, with only a narrow channel to connect the two. One part of the village fronted on the vast expanse of Lake Ontario. This was where the bigger ships docked and where wharves and piers had been built to accommodate the lake traffic. From this harbour everything from grain and peas to flour and huge quantities of fish were shipped across the lake to New York State or down the St. Lawrence River to

Montreal. The eastern part of Wellington was built along West Lake, virtually an inland body of water, although it had probably once been a bay. The far end of this small lake was covered in acres of reedy marsh, but the water deepened near the village and was usable to small craft. A long bar of sandy hills formed the boundary between the two, it's width so narrow in places that it was a wonder that the pounding waves from Lake Ontario did not some stormy night break through it and merge the waters again into one. Quite the opposite appeared to be happening, however. If anything, the sand piled up higher every year. This thin thread of sand was but an outcropping of the massive dunes that lay farther south. Unsuitable for farming, these sand hills were covered with a vast, undisturbed forest of cedars. The trees thinned as the dunes marched toward Wellington, however, and the sandbar that Martha proposed to play on sported only scrubby poplars and a blanket of marram grass.

These small hills formed a steep slope with a short run, not ideal for tobogganing purposes, but Martha figured they could at least test their makeshift sled. They poked along the bar, looking for the best place. They finally found one that was relatively free of trees, but it was on the Lake Ontario side. Martha tested the skim of ice that had formed in the shallow water along the shore, and it appeared to be solid enough to hold them just in case.

"Do you want me to go down first, just to show you?" She was concerned about Horatio's apparent lack of experience.

He shrugged, so she leapt on the homemade toboggan and pushed herself off. There were still patches of ice under the snow that sped her downward to where the slope levelled out, at which point she hit a frozen rut and spun crazily around, until finally the board slowed and stopped. Laughing, she hauled it back up the hill.

It was Horatio's turn next. He opted to fly down the bank on his stomach, which distributed his weight a little more evenly so that he had a far smoother ride, and was carried farther, out to the edge of the lake. In spite of what he said, Martha was certain that he had done this before.

When he arrived back at the top of the bank, he suggested that they go down together.

"There will be more weight on the board and we'll go farther," he said.

"Is there room for both of us?" Martha asked doubtfully. "It's not that big."

"Well, let's try it. If one of us falls off, we'll only land in the snow anyway."

So Horatio scrunched himself up at the front while Martha knelt at the back. She was unable to find any piece of the sled to hold on to, so her only option was to grab the back of Horatio's coat. That meant that if one of them toppled off, the other would probably follow.

With two of them on board, the sled was slower going down the bank, but halfway down it again rammed against a lump of frozen snow that sent them off in a crazy direction, and they went skidding onto the lake ice, and directly toward the open water. Martha responded to this peril in the only sensible way she could think of — she threw herself off the board. The sudden lightening of the load seemed to make the sled, with Horatio still aboard, go faster, and she watched it skew around and come to a stop just short of where the water lapped against the thin shelf of ice. As Horatio attempted to rise, the edge of the ice broke away and he plunged into the water.

"Horatio Joe! Are you all right?" Martha yelled. She hoped he wasn't about to drown — that would require an awful lot of explaining. But as she watched, he hauled himself upright, and she realized that he had landed in only a couple of feet of water. He was soaking wet from the waist down, though, and she judged that tobogganing was over for the day. They needed to go home right away and get him some dry clothes; otherwise his trousers would freeze to his legs, chilling him to the bone.

They had wandered quite far from the harbour, however, and she realized that it would take some time before they could even reach the wharves where someone might let them stand inside a building for a few minutes to get warm.

"I'm okay," Horatio said. "Let's go down again."

But Martha had been warned too often of the perils of getting wet and cold and was determined that she wasn't going to lose her new friend to pneumonia after only their first adventure.

"No, we have to go *now*. You'll be sorry later if you don't."

He protested some more, claiming that a little cold water couldn't hurt him. Nevertheless, he followed her as she marched determinedly back along the sandbar.

If they hadn't been arguing, they might have noticed the strange apparition far sooner. As they wound their way through the line of poplars that crested a dune, Martha suddenly stopped and screamed. At first she was unsure whether it was a man that stood in front of her. His coat was made of animal skins of every description; she could see muskrat, fox, raccoon, and rabbit pelts, greasy and matted, many of them with the tails and feet still attached. She could tell that they must have been bush-cured, for a gamy, rotting smell emanated from this eccentric cloak. For some reason, the toes of the man's boots had been sliced open and she could see his bare feet poking through them. It was this fact that helped her decide it was, indeed, a man.

His attire was by no means the most remarkable thing about him, however; those were only the things she noticed once she was able to tear her gaze away from the hideous sight that was his face. The creature's upper lip was split in two, the cleft running jaggedly upward to slice into his right nostril. A runny puss dripped from this, down onto the blackened stumps of teeth that she could see in what she thought must be his mouth, for his lower jaw sloped away to meet his neck, the two nearly indistinguishable. The rest of his face was flat under drooping lower eyelids rimmed with red.

Martha screamed again as the figure moved a step closer, gesturing with one hand. Through the tattered

bit of fur that served as his mitten, she could see that
some of his fingers appeared to be webbed.

She jumped when she felt a hand on her arm, but it
was only Horatio trying to pull her away.

"*Ah-oo-oo?*"

The voice that came from the man was high-
pitched and nasal.

"What?" Martha knew that the thing was attempting to communicate with her, but she was at a loss to
make out his words.

"*Huh-oo-oo-ee?*" He screwed his eyes up as he
said this, as if it were painful to speak.

"He's asking if we're all right, I think." Horatio
had stopped pulling at her, although one hand still
firmly grasped the sleeve of her coat.

"I don't think so," Martha said. "Who are you?"
she finally asked.

"*Huh-oo-oo-ee?*" he repeated.

With the repetition, the sounds began to make
a little sense to Martha. "You want to know what
we're doing?"

The man nodded.

"We're sliding down the bank." She pointed to their
piece of board.

"*Oh … ack.*" The man waved toward Wellington,
then turned and trudged off down the sandbar with a
peculiar shuffling gait.

They waited until he had disappeared into the
distance before they dared to turn their backs and
walk in the other direction.

"What was *that*?" Horatio asked as they walked.

"I don't know. I've never seen him before."

"Was it a man?"

"I think so," Martha said. "It must have been. Either that or it was a goblin."

"That's not what goblins look like."

"How do you know?"

Horatio ignored this. "He was nothing but holes. He had holes in his boots and holes in his face. Holes everywhere you looked."

"Maybe he was a wildebeest." She had read that word somewhere and it seemed to describe perfectly the thing they had just seen.

"I think a wildebeest is some sort of deer or something," Horatio said. "That was no deer. It was just a man with a lot of holes in him."

After that, whenever they spoke of the strange figure they had seen, they referred to him simply as the Holey Man.

Chapter Ten

To Martha's enormous relief, Horatio suffered no ill effects from his frigid dip. Although his teeth were chattering by the time they returned to Temperance House, he was able to slip upstairs and change into dry clothes without anyone noticing, and Martha merely entered by the back door and wordlessly started setting the tables for dinner.

In the wake of the miraculous salvation of the crew of the *Anthea*, however, Horatio's presence soon became required in the upstairs sitting room far more frequently than before. Peter Spencer had done what he promised and spread the news of Clementine's prediction far and wide. He needn't have bothered telling more than a person or two; after the details of the dramatic shipwreck had been fully digested, the whole village and most of the surrounding countryside could barely talk about anything but Mrs.

Elliott's miraculous talents. Several days after the news of the *Anthea* became general knowledge, two more women came to the hotel asking for her; the next day there were four. Clementine held sessions each morning for the next several days, and added two afternoon sittings, as well.

Horatio still managed to slip out in the late afternoon to play with Martha, though. They crossed the channel to the dunes looking for the Holey Man, and glimpsed him twice in the distance, but he never seemed to come close to where they were playing.

The increased traffic at the hotel resulted in more work for Daniel and Lewis, without contributing much to their fortunes. Occasionally, one of Clementine's customers might linger for a cup of tea and a biscuit in the hotel's dining room after they had visited upstairs, but not often. Most of them were distraught and shaken when they emerged from a session and anxious to ponder their experiences in private.

They left hurriedly, almost surreptitiously, unable to look Lewis in the eye or return his polite greeting. This was, he knew, because he was a preacher and they were afraid, quite rightly, that he disapproved of the whole enterprise. They tracked in an enormous amount of dirty snow, which melted in puddles in the hall, and left muddy footprints on the stairs and in the upstairs hall. He and Daniel had barely been able to keep up with the work prior to this influx of visitors; now they were falling farther and farther behind. Betsy helped whenever she could, but Lewis kept a close eye on her, and whenever it appeared that she was tiring, he sent her to lie down or to sip yet another cup of tea with Susannah.

So Lewis wrestled with this dilemma while traffic to the upstairs rooms continued to increase, but then, a couple of days later, there seemed to be a change in the clientele. An older couple, well-dressed and prosperous-looking, arrived asking for rooms — a welcome inquiry, for even though it would mean yet more work, it also meant more money. Lewis gave them the largest of the third-floor rooms, well away from the mysterious rappings and thumpings that frequently echoed along the second-floor hall. The rapping, however, appeared to be what they had come for.

"We're from Cobourg," the man said. "We heard about Mrs. Elliott from an aunt who has attended her with most excellent results. We're anxious to consult her."

Lewis expected that they would stay but one night. After all, they had only to see Clementine, be given the answer they were looking for, and depart for home again. To his surprise, they made no move to leave the next day. That afternoon a man from Belleville arrived, and on his heels a well-dressed woman who declined to announce where she hailed from, although Lewis checked the register after she had signed it and it said *Napanee*.

"We'll have to move you into the kitchen if this keeps up," Lewis joked with Susannah.

"Aye, this is grand, isn't it?"

It would be a great deal grander if there weren't so much mud on the stairs, Lewis thought sourly, and then he chided himself for being so uncharitable. It wasn't Susannah's fault that she had broken her leg, or that Daniel seemed to be so good at disappearing just when he was wanted most.

Even so, they should have been able to manage the rush of customers themselves, but the tasks were so unfamiliar to Lewis that they took him far longer than they should have to complete. He worked long into the evening, washing up the supper dishes and bringing in firewood, while Betsy and Daniel prepared as much as they could for the following day's meals.

Lewis kept a worried eye on Betsy, and when her limp became more and more pronounced as the day wore on, he took Daniel aside.

"We can't go on like this, you know. I'm quite willing to do whatever work needs to be done, but I'm useless in the kitchen and you're not much better."

Daniel wrinkled his brow. "I hadn't counted on having to hire help. I thought we could do it ourselves."

"We could if we hadn't lost Susannah, but if we keep on at this pace we'll lose Betsy, too, and then it'll just be you and me trying to cope. I think you should hire someone before that happens."

He knew that Daniel was worried about what it would cost, but he truly could not see an alternative.

"Look, the people who came here over the last couple of days came because of Mrs. Elliott. There's apt to be even more tomorrow. That's more business than you've seen in the last six months. Take a little of the money and hire some help."

"I guess you're right," Daniel grumbled. "I just don't know if we can find anyone suitable. There's not many will come to a hotel to work."

The problem, Lewis knew, was that too many of the families in Wellington were Quakers. No Quaker girl would wait on tables, and this severely limited the pool of available help. The Society of Friends were a sober and industrious lot, but they made peculiar distinctions when it came to working for others. An honest exchange of labour for wages was acceptable; anything that implied that they were subservient in any way was firmly declined. It was something the better class of English immigrants had complained of bitterly in the past, for this Quaker attitude had spread to others who, had they been in England, would have been little more than scullery maids and happy enough to tug their forelocks to their self-proclaimed betters. Here, the attitude of hirelings was summed up in the one word: *help*. It was no disgrace to move in with a family and "help," but the help expected to be spoken to civilly and to sit at the same dinner table as her employers. And no girl of good family, Quaker or not, would ever be allowed to work at an inn that had a tavern; but surely an inn that boasted temperance in its name might be more acceptable?

Susannah, who was well aware of just exactly how much work was entailed in looking after so many guests, readily agreed that some help was required. "I don't know of anyone offhand," she said, "but I do know who might. Go talk to the Scully girl. She seems to know everything about everybody, including half the things they don't know themselves. Surely she'll be able to think of somebody who would be willing to work for us."

Lewis knew that if he left it to Daniel the conversation would never take place, so the next morning he set off for Scully's store.

"You're Mr. Lewis, are you not?" Scully asked as he entered the shop. "You're over at the Temperance with your sister, isn't that right?" Lewis nodded his agreement. "What could we do for you today, sir? I can only hope that you're so busy over at the hotel that you've worn out the linen already and are looking for more."

"It's not the linen that's worn out, it's me," Lewis said. "I expect you know that my sister broke her leg. What you may not know is that my wife is not well either. That leaves me and my brother-in-law to manage things ... and we're not doing a very good job of it, I'm afraid."

"Oh, dear, that does sound dire," Scully said, "but how can *we* help you?"

"I was wondering if I might speak with your daughter. I've been told that she tends to have a finger on the pulse of the village, and that she might be able to point me in the direction of some industrious person who could take up some of the slack."

He had rehearsed his very diplomatic statement, not wanting to imply that Meribeth Scully was a busybody, although as far as he could ascertain, that was exactly what she was.

"Mr. Lewis! How *is* your sister? Recovering, I hope." The voice came from the corner of the store.

Lewis hadn't seen the girl behind the huge oak table. She was so short she nearly disappeared when she sat behind it.

"She's as well as can be expected, I suppose. Thank you for asking."

"You must have your hands full over there. I hear the inn is nearly booked up now that Mrs. Elliott is so famous. I don't know what to think of her, to be perfectly honest. It all seems so odd, but it certainly is good for business."

Lewis knew that she was fishing for more information about the mysterious sessions that Clementine held in her rooms, but he knew little more than she did, and even if he had, he wouldn't have said a word. She had, however, given him an opportunity to jump directly to the matter at hand.

"It's busy, that's the truth. And that's why I thought I'd consult you."

"Oh, if there's anything I can do, just say, Mr. Lewis."

"I'm wondering if you would know of anybody in the neighbourhood who might like to earn a little money. We can't keep up with the work over there."

She screwed up her face in thought. "Well, there might be one or two. It would depend on what you were asking them to do."

"The cooking, mostly," he replied. "Maybe a little cleaning. It's too much for us. My brother-in-law and I can manage to get the food to the table all right, but it's the business in the kitchen that we're having the most difficulty with."

She laughed at this. "I don't think there's a man alive that truly knows his way around a cookstove," she said. "Well, you might ask Sophie Carr, that's Fred Carr's daughter. You know, her brother Martin went with you when everyone was looking for Nate Elliott."

After Lewis recovered from his astonishment that Meribeth knew, much less remembered this small detail of such a wide search, he considered her suggestion. Martin had seemed like an intelligent boy, and if his sister was in any way similar, she could be a good choice.

"She's free at the moment, do you think?"

"I expect so," Meribeth said. "She spent the last year nursing her father, but he died three months ago. The family could probably use the money. They've been living on what Martin makes at the sawmill."

"Excellent. I'll go along and ask Martin about it right now."

"It's a funny thing, though, isn't it? About Mrs. Elliott, I mean."

"I don't understand." She was still fishing, but she'd get nothing from him. "If she is so good at communicating with the spirit world, you'd think she could tell us whether or not her husband is dead."

As he walked along the street to the mill, he had to reflect that, although Meribeth was a dreadful gossip, she was by no means a stupid girl, for he had been wondering about that very same point. Surely if Nate

Elliott was dead, and at this point it was almost certain that he was, Clementine would be in constant communication with his spirit. After all, she seemed to be able to summon up everyone else's dear and departed practically on demand.

Her activities at the inn had nettled him from the start. "Treating with the devil" would be the church's objection, and one that would easily explain his unease to anyone who asked, although no one else seemed to make any connection between the tenets of their faith and table-rapping or spirit-calling, or whatever it was she did. In all honesty, his objections were far more practical; he was convinced that she was a fraud.

He considered what Spencer had told him. "Near an island," she had said to him. Well, that wasn't difficult, was it? The *Anthea* had been in a part of the lake that had a number of islands, large and small, and an even greater number of shoals and bars. It wouldn't require clairvoyance to provide the insight that they might be near an island. He worried over "happy and safe," for that was the part of her prediction that had seemed so miraculous. He wondered what she would have done if the bodies had washed up on some shore, or if no news had ever been received as to their fate. And then he realized that the prediction had been so vague that almost anything could have been read into it by someone anxious for explanation. If they had simply disappeared, never to be heard of again, the claim could be made that they were happy and safe somewhere and just hadn't informed anyone else of the fact. Even in the worst of scenarios, if the actual bodies were found, Mrs. Elliott could play to the expectation of an afterlife and claim that their souls had gone to heaven, a place that, after all, promised well-being and happiness. The outcome didn't matter, he realized; she would be seen as prescient no matter what occurred.

That still didn't explain what had happened to Nate Elliott though. Lewis resolved to study the question more closely when he had time, but he would never have time if he couldn't persuade Martin Carr's sister to come to work at the inn.

So he continued down to the planing mill, past the piers and the huge reels that were used to wind up the fishing nets so that they could dry. They gave the harbour an eerie skeletal look, accentuated by the hulls of ships that had been stripped of their masts and booms and hauled up onto cradles for the winter. The mill appeared equally deserted at first, for there was little call for finished lumber in the wintertime.

Lewis entered the first door he came to and called out. He heard footsteps clattering on a set of stairs and Martin appeared.

"Mr. Lewis, good day. What can I do for you, sir?"

"I'm here to ask if your sister would be able to come and work at the hotel," Lewis said, getting right to the point of his visit. "We need some help, mostly in the kitchen. Can she cook?"

Martin grinned. "She does all our cooking and it makes my mouth water just to think of it. She's better at it than my mother is."

"Do you think she might be interested in a job? We've more work than we can handle by ourselves."

"That would be grand," Martin said. "I'm on short hours here because it's so slow right now, and even when it isn't, I don't make nearly enough for us all. I don't mind telling you it's been a tough go with Pa gone, but Ma's been reluctant to let Sophie go just anywhere. If it's you and your brother-in-law, and the Temperance Hotel at that, I'm sure she'll say yes, for she'll know that Sophie will be treated well, and there's no chance of her running into the rough bunch that go to the taverns."

"When could she start?"

"I'll ask tonight when I go home, but I expect it could be as soon as tomorrow if that suits you."

Lewis nodded his thanks and walked away a relieved man.

Sophie arrived early the next morning.

Daniel was in the sink room filling jugs with hot water to take upstairs to the guestrooms and Lewis was in the kitchen struggling with the beginnings of breakfast when a tap was heard at the back door. When Lewis opened the door, Sophie stepped in and introduced herself. His first impression was that Meribeth certainly seemed to have steered him in the right direction; the girl was neatly and demurely dressed, her hair tucked carefully under her cap. She was quite attractive — she looked a lot like her brother, but with the features softened into a pleasant femininity. He didn't care, really, what she looked like as long as she did the work, but it was nice that she was so presentable.

Sophie bustled into the kitchen and grabbed an apron. "Oh, good, I see you've got the porridge on. I'll start the biscuits. How many are there for breakfast? And are the tables set?"

Lewis had done this the evening before. He found that mornings were such a scramble that it was worthwhile to take a half-hour to brush off the cloths and lay the cutlery before he dragged his weary bones off to bed.

He did a quick mental headcount, relayed the information to Sophie, then showed her the pantry in the cold room just off the back hall.

By the time they returned, the kettle was boiling. He would start the coffee first, then re-boil the kettle for tea. It was a nuisance having to make both, but their American guests seemed to expect coffee at all hours. The Canadians, on the other hand, wanted their tea in the morning.

Sophie seemed quite at home in the kitchen, so when Betsy came in he left them to it. Daniel had already wrestled most of the jugs up to the rooms, so Lewis decided he would help him carry up the rest.

By the time the first guests straggled into the dining room, breakfast was ready, but Lewis noted that the menu seemed to have changed dramatically from the fare that he and Daniel had planned to provide. There were potatoes and bacon as usual, but Sophie's bacon had been fried to a crispy brown and looked far more appetizing than the burnt strips they had managed. She had also chopped some onion into the potatoes, and, in the short time since she had arrived, she had managed to produce a mound of light, fluffy-looking biscuits, an addition that made even Horatio's usually dour face light up. The porridge was free of the sodden lumps that appeared whenever he or Daniel cooked it and there were a handful of chopped apples on top. All in all, it appeared that Sophie would be a fine addition to the inn's staff.

Lewis left Martha to clear dishes away from the tables as the guests finished and went upstairs to help empty the slops and air the bedclothes. Normally he left these rather odious tasks to Daniel, while he washed the dishes and began the preparations for the noontime dinner, but Sophie had chased him out of the kitchen.

"I'm fine here," she told him. "I've already got the water boiled up for the dishes, so it's just a matter of doing them." She had smiled when she said this, revealing two astonishing dimples. "I'm sure there's plenty else you could be doing. I'll need a little more firewood in an hour or so, but nothing until then."

"Yes, ma'am," he replied. "I know when I'm not wanted." At this, she had smiled again, the working relationship between the two sorted out in the matter of a few sentences.

He found himself whistling a little as he climbed the stairs. Complete chaos had seemed suddenly averted, and for the first time since Susannah had broken her leg he was not operating on the edge of panic. Unlike most men, Thaddeus was aware of the amount of work women did, and tried not to take it for granted. But this business of looking after umpteen hotel guests every day was far harder than anything he had ever encountered in all his years as a circuit rider. Or maybe he was just getting old. After all, many families consisted of thirteen, fourteen, fifteen children or more, and someone cooked and cleaned for them all, didn't they? Of course, the older ones looked after the younger ones and pitched in with everything else. The problem, he decided, was that you couldn't expect guests to pitch in.

With relief he turned to the Elliotts' rooms. Mrs. Elliott appeared to be a very tidy soul, and extra clothing was hung on the pegs or had presumably been folded away, probably in the trunk that had arrived with her. He stripped the coverlets and sheets off the beds. He had extra time this morning, so he would turn the topmost mattresses over and smooth out the inevitable lumps and bumps that appeared as the goose feathers clumped together. Betsy had told him he should do this from time to time. (It certainly wouldn't have occurred to him otherwise.)

As he heaved the mattress off the smaller bed and onto the floor, a piece of paper slid out with the inevitable feathers that had escaped the confines of the ticking. It was a sheet of newsprint that had been shoved in between the many layers of bedding. It had been opened and folded to reveal the inside page and, as he retrieved it from the floor, an item in the top right hand corner caught his eye. It was the newspaper he had been reading when the Elliotts first arrived at Temperance House, or at least a newspaper with the same articles, for there was a description of Tom

Thumb and the Feejee Mermaid. Horatio must have been as intrigued by these articles as he had been and taken the newspaper upstairs to read.

But then his eyes slid farther down the page to rest on an article he hadn't noticed at the time. "Information Sought by Prominent Businessman," read the caption. The short item went on to state that a Mr. Augustus Van Sylen, a man of some means and prominent in New York financial circles, was offering a reward for information leading to the whereabouts of a certain Monsieur and Madame LeClair, who had been operating in the city as mesmerists and spirit guides. Mr. Van Sylen had contacted the couple to discover the whereabouts of his youngest son, who had run away two years previously and had not been heard from since. The LeClairs regretfully informed Van Sylen that his son had headed west and had perished in an Indian attack on the travelling party. They claimed to have made contact with the son's spirit in the next world and over a period of the next few months Van Sylen attended their sessions on a regular basis. He reportedly paid a great deal of money for this communication.

The scheme had fallen apart when Van Sylen's son was discovered in New Jersey, living under an assumed name with another man's wife. But by the time Van Sylen returned to demand his money back, the LeClairs had disappeared.

The newspaper itself was local, but a note at the bottom of the article indicated that it had been reprinted from the *New York Tribune*. Perhaps it was just coincidence that Horatio had happened to pick it up from the bundle of papers that were piled on the table in the parlour, but even so, why then would he have hidden it under his mattress? Mrs. Elliott had stated that she was from South Carolina, not New York, and her accent, with its honeyed twang, bore that out. But the description of the LeClairs' activities bore a startling resemblance to the services being offered on the second floor of the Temperance Hotel. What if one of their other guests read the article? Would they come to the conclusion that Mrs. Elliott, too, was a sham? It seemed reason enough to spirit the paper out of the parlour and away from curious eyes, but Lewis had to wonder if there was more to it than that.

He made a mental note of the date of publication and, once he had wrestled the featherbed back onto the frame, he carefully tucked the paper back where he had found it.

When he was reasonably satisfied with the way he had reassembled the linens, he quickly made up the larger bed and turned to the door of the adjacent sitting room. It was locked, and the key was nowhere in sight. He tried the door that led to the room from the hall, but this, too, was firmly locked. A guest was well within his or her rights to lock their hotel room, but in Lewis's experience few ever availed themselves of the courtesy, leaving their doors open so that the room could be cleaned and aired. Apparently, Mrs. Elliott preferred to keep the contents of her sitting room private. That being the case, he decided, she could clean it herself. He shrugged and headed downstairs to see what Sophie was planning for dinner.

Chapter Eleven

The fitful snow of late November had been but a harbinger of what was to come. As the year marched into December the wind switched around and blew in from the northeast, bringing a heavy storm with it. Even if Lewis had not noticed the signs — the sudden change in the wind, the great piling up of cloud on the horizon, the realization that a dull cold was creeping into his bones — he would have known that a storm was coming by the worsening of Betsy's lameness, her blinding headache, and the spike of fever that once again sent her to huddle under a blanket.

The blizzard began in the early evening and continued for two days. Snow piled into the fences and sides of buildings, drifted into sculpted dunes in unexpected ways, obliterated familiar landmarks, and transformed the landscape into an unrelenting uniform whiteness. Many of the guests commented on their luck in being inside with the guarantee of a bed, and not out on the road where they would be forced to find whatever shelter was closest at hand.

"We're warm and cozy enough here," said the man from Cobourg, for he and his wife continued to consult Clementine every morning. "We weren't too sure about the fare for a time, but that's nice enough now."

It was more than nice enough as far as Lewis was concerned. Within a day, Sophie had commandeered the kitchen as her exclusive domain. She sent Daniel to replenish their sorry larder from both McFaul's and Henderson's stores and augmented the usual pieces of beef and pork with mutton, haunches of venison, and local smoked fish. Succulent puddings and light-as-a-feather cakes began to appear as if by magic, and when the supply of eggs ran low, Sophie turned her talents to shortcake served up with jars of preserves.

Nor did she confine her efforts to pleasing the guests; she boiled beef tea for the invalids, and made up a posset that she said was called "stewed Quaker." This was gratefully received by both Susannah and Betsy, who appeared brighter and stronger as a result of her attentions.

By the afternoon of the third day it appeared that the storm had finally blown itself out and Lewis could hear the sounds of shovels and the good-natured banter that seemed to unify Canadians when confronted with an assault from the elements. As soon as Martha finished her dinner, she ran to claim Horatio for a few hours, for there was no school on stormy days and Clementine had cancelled her after-noon session in light of the inclement weather.

The children wound great woolen scarves around their heads and over their mouths and rushed out the door to investigate the wonderland that lay outside. Horatio had never seen such snow, he said, and he was delighted. Martha showed him how to make snow angels, lying on her back and flapping her arms and legs until a heavenly outline appeared. Then they turned their attentions to a snowman, begging an old carrot from Sophie for his nose. One by one the other children who lived nearby appeared and joined in happily. Clementine must have been watching her son from the upstairs window, because just as he was positioning the sticks that formed the snowman's arms, she appeared at the door to offer a scarf and a feather from one of her hats as the finishing touches. The feather gave the snowman a peculiar and rather rakish look, but the children seemed delighted with the contribution.

The next time Lewis looked out the window, there was quite a gang of children, and it was inev-itable that they would dig into the banks to make forts, and that snowballs would start to fly. He was intrigued and amused by the battle that was shap-ing up below, and checked on its progress at every opportunity.

He watched as Martha patiently attempted to teach little Rosie Carpenter from across the street how to aim her throws, rather than just wildly heav-ing them in every direction. The little girl had likely been sent out to play with her older brothers, but in the way of all older brothers, they had decided to ignore her. So Martha had taken her in hand. Rosie's inclusion on her team put them at a disadvantage, however. All of the other children were older and had mastered the art of the sidearm throw, harder and more effective, more often finding their targets. Rosie bravely attempted to copy them, but in an attempt to get it right she often stood up for too long, taking the brunt of the other team's attack. Lewis winced as a snowball struck her on the side of the head, the force of it knocking her down; but she bobbed up again a few moments later, refusing to acknowledge the discomfort of the hit.

The game disintegrated into disarray when Ed Fisher, oblivious to the war unfolding around him, wandered between the two forts just as Rosie let fly with a determined return salvo.

"Look out!" Martha yelled. Fisher turned his head in her direction at the sound, and for a moment Lewis thought that he would receive the full force of an icy snowball square on the forehead. All of the children dropped their hands and watched in dismay.

But Rosie's throw, though hard, had been crooked, and it curved in a wide arc around the pedestrian to land with a satisfying plump against the chest of the biggest boy opposite her. Her team cheered, drowning out Fisher's indignant protests.

"Rosie, you did it!" Martha crowed, and the little girl started to laugh with the excellence of it all. Martha laughed with her, and Lewis chuckled, as well, though he was quick to walk out onto the verandah, just in case Ed Fisher was prepared to make trouble.

"Are you all right, Mr. Fisher?" he asked.

"Darn kids. They never watch what they're doing. Why aren't these children in school?"

Lewis ignored this. Fisher should know that there would be no school until the village dug itself out from under its blanket of snow.

"Well, no harm done, is there? After all, you weren't hit."

Fisher stomped off down the street still muttering complaints about the manners of the young folk these days. As he left, one of the bigger boys threw a snowball after him, to the delight of the others.

Lewis was just closing the door when he saw another man approach Martha. The figure looked familiar, but he couldn't think why. It was only when he heard the man speak that his identity became clear.

"You must be Martha?" the man asked. "You look very much like your mother."

All the children stood in the yard and stared, their laughter forgotten. Finally Martha answered. "Yes, I am, but who are you, sir? I don't think I've ever seen you here before. Were you looking for a bed for the night? Shall I fetch the innkeeper for you?"

In the midst of his astonishment, Lewis noted that Martha had spoken well, politely, and in a way that would make a traveller feel welcome. He made a mental note to compliment her later. But the little girl didn't seem to realize that this stranger wasn't just a traveller looking for a room, but her father — Francis Renwell.

"No, actually," Renwell replied. "I was looking for you. And your grandmother, if she's nearby."

"Grandma's sick in bed, but Grandpa's here. Would he do?"

Lewis was through the front door and into the yard before Renwell had a chance to say whether he would do or not. He rather suspected that he wouldn't, for the man looked a little uncomfortable at this intelligence. He hadn't expected to find his father-in-law at home, and why would he? All too often Lewis had been off riding the circuits whenever someone wanted him.

"Francis. You've been granted an amnesty then?"

The rebels of 1837 who had escaped hanging and transportation and melted away into the United States had recently been invited back, all sins forgiven. All, that is, but those of their leader, Mackenzie, who would never be welcome again as far as Lewis could tell. The men who had followed the little rebel had crept back home again, some of them defiantly, some of them sheepishly, but all of them grateful that they could safely rejoin their families and resume their lives.

"Yes, I'm apparently no longer a mortal threat to Upper Canadian society," Renwell said. "Although I guess it's called Canada West now, isn't it? In fact, I've been in no danger of arrest for quite some time, but it took many months to find the money to come home. They say the United States is the land of opportunity, but fortune has eluded me somehow."

He spoke ruefully, and Lewis noted that although he was far better dressed than the last time they had met, the quality of the cloth was poor and his boots were worn.

"Come in, come in. Mrs. Lewis has been unwell, but she's better today and will be so pleased to see you."

"And you, sir?"

Lewis smiled. "I owe you a great debt, Francis. You will always be welcome in my house."

He turned to his granddaughter. "Martha, dear, why don't you come inside with us so we can all get warm."

Lewis led Renwell into the now-deserted dining room, beckoning to Martha to follow them. The little girl sat down, not at a table with her father, but at one next to it. She had known that she had a father who had gone off somewhere — her grandparents had made no secret of his existence — but neither had they belaboured the story. After all, they had expected never to see him again, and he had warned them as much himself. Lewis could see that Martha did not realize the identity of this man who had been invited in from the cold. He left the two eyeing each other uncertainly while he went to fetch Betsy.

He discovered her, not sick in bed, but up, dressed, and getting in Sophie's way in the kitchen. The weather had eased up enough to ease her pain, as well.

"We need some tea in the dining room," he told her. "We have a visitor."

"Who?"

"Just go on in. I'll set the kettle to boil."

"I'll do it," Sophie said. "You go on, too."

Lewis knew that Betsy would be expecting to see some neighbour, or a member of some former congregation, so her surprise was almost comical when she saw who it was.

"My word! Francis!" And she held her arms out to him in unconditional welcome.

She held her questions, although she was bursting with them, until Sophie appeared with the tea and a plate of leftover breakfast biscuits. As always, she began with the polite inquiries.

"Are you well, Francis? Where have you been living? What have you been doing?"

"I ended up in New York City, working on the docks." He folded his cold hands around the warm cup and Lewis knew that he would ignore the biscuits until he was invited to take one. When he did, he would devour them, for he had that pinched look of someone who has been on the edge of hunger for a long time. "It's dreadful hard labour and the pay is poor. There are so many immigrants in the city right now looking for work that the bosses can get plenty of men for a song. You can be hired on at a certain rate one day and find your pay cut the next. And you daren't protest, because there are fifty men waiting to take your place. And yet every one of them remains convinced that it's only a matter of time until he'll be living in a mansion and driving a fine carriage. It's far worse than any of the nonsense we ever put up with here."

"Have a biscuit, Francis," Lewis urged. "There's nothing like tea and biscuits to warm you up on such a cold day."

Let the man have a little dignity, he thought. He appeared to have so little left.

As Renwell gulped down four of the biscuits in very short order, his eyes kept sliding to Martha. Lewis decided to put him out of his misery before Betsy could distract him with any more questions.

"There's time yet to hear about what you've been doing," he said. "But first, I think there's an introduction to be made. Martha, come here, dear."

The little girl stood up and approached hesitantly.

"Martha, do you remember the stories about your father? About how he was a brave man and how he rescued me from the ice?"

Martha nodded. Renwell shot him a grateful glance. He hadn't known what Martha had been told, or if she had been told anything.

"Well, dear, this is your father, Francis Renwell, come to make sure you're all right. He couldn't come before, though he wanted to."

Martha nodded again, her eyes wide. She turned to look at the man who was her father. "How do you do," she said, relying on the good manners that Betsy had taught her. And then her brow furrowed. "What should I call you, sir?"

"Well," Renwell said, "why don't we start with Francis and we'll decide on something nicer after we get to know each other a little better. Would that be all right?" Lewis could see that he wanted to take her in his arms, pull her up on his lap, and cuddle her, but had wisely decided against it. It would be too much, too soon. He was still in her mind a stranger, a figure in a story. It would take some time to make him more.

"Why don't you go take Rosie back home?" Lewis said. "Then you can come and have some more tea with us."

It was a good suggestion. It would give Martha a little time to absorb the fact that her long-lost father had just walked in the door. They waited until she had left before they resumed their conversation.

"Are you just here for a visit, Francis, or do you intend to stay?" Lewis asked.

"It depends," he said. "I have no sense of how things are, whether or not there's a place here where a man can start over."

"Things are picking up. They're better than they were, at any rate. In the meantime, we have plenty of room for you — we have a little house of our own out back — and to tell you the truth we could use an extra hand just now at the hotel. In the meantime, you can look around and see what else there is." The inn promised to run far more smoothly with Sophie in the kitchen, but with so many guests, the addition of another able-bodied adult would be more than welcome, especially if Daniel didn't have to pay him anything but room and board.

It was odd that it was he and not Betsy who had made this offer, but then he realized what she had been preoccupied with. She was fretting about Martha. Obviously one of the reasons Renwell had returned was to see his daughter again. Would he want to take her away to live with him now that there was no price on his head and he could take his place once again as a respectable, if not yet respected, member of the community? Lewis felt a pang at the thought of losing his granddaughter. He knew that she had been Betsy's comfort and delight for some time now. What if Renwell decided, once he was on his feet, to head west, or to try his luck in the city? He and Betsy would no longer be an everyday part of the little girl's life. At the most they would be occasional visitors, grey-haired ghosts who loomed out of a hazy past she could barely remember. No wonder Betsy was preoccupied.

"That sounds like a perfect arrangement to me," Betsy said, endorsing Lewis's offer of hospitality. "You're welcome to stay until you find your way, Francis. It will give you the opportunity to get to know Martha, as well."

"I would appreciate that," Renwell said, "as long as you and your good husband are in agreement."

"Well, of course we are," Lewis said. "You're welcome here as long as you need to stay."

"No lingering doubts about me?"

"None."

Lewis had once thought that the man who sat across from him was a murderer; that he had, in fact, murdered his own wife and others besides. No, not thought it, *believed* it, and had pursued him with a vengeance that had blinded him to the identity of the real murderer. It was only when his own life had been in jeopardy that he had come to see how mistaken he had been.

"I thought you were dead when I left you that night." Renwell's thoughts had followed Lewis's own. "I was sure that the cold would kill you, if not right away, then sometime in the next few days. I didn't see how you could survive."

Lewis had been chasing Renwell across the river from Kingston to Wolfe Island when he had fallen through, clinging to the ice while the current pulled at him. He had not been sure that this man would come to his aid — it had certainly not been to his advantage to do so — but Renwell had turned back and dragged Lewis out of the icy waters and across the lake to a house on the shore. He had not been a murderer after all, but simply a pawn in Mackenzie's rebellion, fleeing a sentence of transportation, afraid of the government's revenge on all those who had taken part.

"He very nearly didn't live," Betsy said softly. "He was many weeks in bed, but he was just too stubborn to die. He's like that, you know."

Renwell chuckled. "He was certainly too stubborn to stop walking that night. I don't know how we ever reached the shore."

"That wasn't me," Lewis said. "That was you, pulling me along."

"You kept babbling about murder. I thought you were delirious."

"Unfortunately, I wasn't. I discovered afterward that I was right, there had been many murders, and all committed by a single hand. Not yours, as it turns out, but eventually the culprit paid for his crimes."

"And Sarah was one of the victims?"

"Yes."

Renwell's face furrowed as he digested this information. "This starting over is a funny business," he said with a sigh. "You think you can just walk away and return later with a clean slate, but there are so many things you carry with you, things you wonder about, questions you're not even sure you want to know the answers to. Why Sarah? I didn't think she had an enemy in the world."

"She didn't. She was merely in the wrong place at the wrong time."

"I still miss her sorely. I got quite a start when I walked up and saw Martha. She looks so much like her mother."

"Yes, she does," Lewis agreed. "It took me a long while to get accustomed to that, as well. But she's not Sarah. She's Martha. She's a delightful Martha, and very much her own person."

"I didn't expect to see her quite so suddenly. It was a shock." Francis seemed far in the past, sunk in a reverie about his lost wife, his lost life. Lewis and Betsy remained silent, too, until Francis straightened up and said, "What's this about helping out? I was told that Daniel and Susannah were the innkeepers here."

Francis had been unsure where exactly to find his in-laws when he had returned to Canada. "I went to Wolfe Island first," he said, "to the house where I dumped you on the doorstep that night. The woman there sent me off to Bath, where they told me you had gone to Demorestville. The shopkeeper in Demorestville sent me here. The shopkeeper's wife told me that Mrs. Lewis had been unwell and had gone to stay with relatives, but I was certain you'd still be riding a trail somewhere, Thaddeus."

"No," he said. "I gave the circuit up when Betsy got so ill. Daniel's the innkeeper here, but unfortunately

Susannah's laid up for the time being with a broken leg. We're trying to help out but have been making a pretty poor job of it so far. Fortunately, we've just found an excellent girl for the kitchen, but there's still more work to do around here than Daniel and I can manage. Martha helps a great deal, but we could certainly use your help, if you're willing."

"Of course. Anything you need."

Just then Martha returned from her errand. She approached the table slowly. Lewis could see that she looked wary, concerned. She must be wondering what would happen to her now.

Francis was magnificent with her. "Hello, Martha," he said. "Did Rosie get home safely?" When she nodded, he went on. "I see she was on your side in the snowball fight. It's a good thing that man wasn't too upset when the snowball nearly hit him, isn't it?"

She began to giggle at the memory of it. "I didn't think Rosie could throw that hard."

"It looked pretty hard to me. It just kind of went *splat* when it hit, didn't it?"

He reached into his pocket. "I've brought you something. I hope you like it."

Martha carefully unwrapped the paper package he handed her to reveal a salmon-coloured string of coral beads. "Oh, it's beautiful. Thank you!"

"Shall I help you put it on?"

She turned, and he fastened the clasp for her. "There."

Martha ran to the hall where there was a long mirror, and stood admiring herself.

Lewis felt a pang. The necklace was nothing special, just a cheap string of beads that might be found anywhere, but it was the sort of small extravagance that almost never made its way into his household. They kept Martha fed and adequately clothed, but her possessions were of the homemade variety, and they could offer little more. She had turned to her father, not to her grandmother, to help her with the clasp, but then he had been the source of this unexpected luxury, hadn't he? Lewis realized that he was being uncharitable; it was only natural that her father would want to please her in some way, to help make up for the long years of absence. He just hoped that Martha would be sensible enough not to bestow her affections solely on the basis of material gain. *No, of course she wouldn't,* he thought. She had been raised by Betsy, after all.

Martha bounced back into the room. "Thank you, Francis. It's very pretty."

Again Lewis was aware that Renwell expected physical contact, a hug or a kiss on the cheek, or at the very least a handshake, but Martha maintained her distance. *Good for you, little one.*

It was nearly time for supper and the tables had yet to be set, but as soon as Lewis moved to do this, Renwell leapt to his feet and offered to help.

"You'll have to tell me what to do for the first while," he said. "I'm afraid I have no experience with this." With four of them working, the task was accomplished in very short order, and for the next hour they were kept busy with the serving and removing of an excellent fillet of fish. Sophie was a marvel.

Chapter Twelve

The staffing arrangements at Temperance House had been resolved just in time, as it turned out, for after supper the Grand Master of the Orange Lodge arrived at the hotel to make inquiries regarding the use of the meeting room on the second floor the following evening. The Lodge had always met at MacDonald's Tavern, the Orangemen having shown a great fondness for drink at their gatherings. But now, thanks to the Lodge's efforts in the recent election, their numbers had grown beyond what could be accommodated at MacDonald's. None of the other taverns had tap rooms that were any larger either, and the only other place big enough, the ballroom at the Wilman Hotel, had been booked for a lecture by the Agricultural Society.

The Temperance's meeting room was by no means as large as the ballroom, but it was bigger than any tavern, and after a close inspection, the Master agreed that it could accommodate the number of Orangemen expected at the meeting. He grumbled a little when he was informed that wine and ale were the only refreshments that would be available and that no exception would be made to this rule, but as he had no other option, he supposed that Temperance House would have to do.

"I don't know what the boys are going to say when they find out they can't get whiskey," he said, shaking his head. "Ah, well, I suppose it won't hurt them for one evening."

"What on earth do you suppose he thought the *temperance* in Temperance House meant?" Lewis said after the man left.

"I have no idea," Daniel replied. "You would have thought it was clear enough, wouldn't you? Never mind, the rent is welcome. We'll need to move chairs from the dining room right after supper, though. There's but one or two up there now." He sighed. "And then we'll have to move them back again after the meeting. We'll need them all for breakfast in the morning."

"It sounds like a good job for Francis," Lewis said, and Daniel's face brightened a little at the thought that someone else would be doing the heavy work. Daniel and Susannah had readily agreed to the arrangement that had been offered to Renwell, and rather than have him stay with Lewis, had even insisted that he be given a tiny bedroom off the back hall, little more than a closet really, that he said would likely never be rented to a guest.

"You've little enough room where you are," Daniel had said, "and having him there is going to disturb Betsy on her bad days. If he stays here, maybe I could get him to tend the fires first thing in the morning."

Daniel was always slow to get moving in the morning, so the offer was not entirely altruistic on his part; but what he said was true, and Francis seemed happy enough with the arrangement.

Lewis started moving chairs the next evening directly after supper, and Francis jumped up quickly to help him, later cheerfully sweeping the meeting room floor.

Their regular dinner service had been lighter than usual due to the absence of the Elliotts. That morning, Clementine had informed Daniel that she and Horatio would be present for neither dinner nor supper. They would be spending the day at the Elliott farm, she explained, and wouldn't return until quite late in the evening. She had left by the time they realized that, even if they used all the dining room chairs, they might not have enough to accommodate the Orangemen.

"There are chairs in the Elliotts' sitting room." Daniel offered. "I wonder if we could borrow them just for tonight." But when Lewis checked, the doors to both rooms were firmly locked, and Clementine had apparently taken the keys with her.

"I wonder if the Donovans would loan us a few," Lewis suggested. "They seem very affable neighbours." Daniel looked doubtful, and when Lewis went to inquire, he discovered why. He hadn't been aware that their closest neighbours were among the small group of Catholics who lived in Wellington.

"I'm sorry, if it were anyone but the Orange Lodge, I'd say yes in a minute," Mr. Donovan said. "But I won't help them in any way, shape, or form. I hope you don't think badly of me for it, but you have to understand my position."

Lewis understood all too well, and apologized for asking in the first place. The popularity of the Lodge made him profoundly uneasy as well. It was an organization that had been imported into Canada by the great numbers of Protestant Irish who had immigrated here, and who had brought their homeland quarrels with them. At first they had seemed like a joke. After all, the fate of the united province depended on the ability of the mostly Protestant Canada West to get along with the mostly Catholic Canada East, a fact that had been amply demonstrated in the first united legislatures. It had become clear that no one could govern without the support of the members from Quebec, and Robert Baldwin of the western province and Louis LaFontaine of the eastern had forged an alliance that allowed the government to get on with business. Now, however, the new governor seemed prepared to dispense with this notion of compromise. As far as he was concerned, any attempt to further entrench the elected, and largely co-operative legislature as the rightful governors of Canada was an affront to the Queen and a usurpation of her authority.

This sentiment appealed to the voters of Canada West. They were a diverse lot — Loyalists who had fled the American Revolution, Scots crofters looking for a better life, Ulster Irish, and immigrants from England herself — but the two things they shared were a distrust of American republicanism and an unease at the necessity of sharing a country with French-speaking Catholics.

The Orange Lodge had smelled opportunity and played upon their disquiet. To the Lodge, loyalty to the Crown meant loyalty to its language and protestant beliefs; Quebec Catholics were, therefore, by definition, disloyal.

It was a philosophy that left a bad taste in Lewis's mouth. He had heard the same kinds of arguments trotted out against the Methodists not so long ago, when the Family Compact had reigned supreme in Upper Canada. They had branded Methodist circuit riders like himself as "American" and not to be trusted, and had used this accusation as an excuse to further entrench themselves in power. This old Anglican elitism had been rendered obsolete with the establishment of the new Province — the tracts of land that had been reserved for the benefit of the Church of England were now being broken up, and the jewel in their crown, the Anglican university, was slated to be secularized. But now the term "Anglican" had, in the upper colony, been replaced by the term "Protestant" in the public mind, and this broader definition of an officially sanctioned religion had far more appeal. But to Lewis it looked like the same old hag dressed up in a new bonnet.

Robert Baldwin, the influential Reformer, without whom no united government could ever have worked, had recognized this threat and had introduced legislation that would outlaw secret societies and their provocative public marches. It was an act that was directly aimed at curtailing the growing power of the Orange Lodge in Canada West, but in spite of the fact that the legislation had been passed, the governor insisted on reference to London for final approval. Baldwin's act had halted the marches on Guy Fawkes Day and the anniversary of the Battle of the Boyne in July — that much, at least, could be decided on without Britain's approval — but, Lewis thought, it was unlikely that the rest of the legislation would ever be heard of again. In the meantime, the Lodge was broadening its membership and its political influence was growing.

The Orangemen had done everything they could to influence the election in favour of the governor's position. They had harassed, threatened, and in some cases physically attacked anyone who declared for a Reform candidate. As a rule, the Prince Edward District had a basic distrust of rabble-rousers, but even here the Lodge had brought its influence to bear.

The vote had taken place during the week that Lewis was tidying up loose ends in Demorestville and preparing to move to Wellington. Some details regarding the expiry of his church appointment had taken him to Picton, and he had been drawn to the open-air poll by the shouts of the crowd gathered around it.

As each man stood on the hustings and declared his support, a group of men who seemed to have nothing more to do with their time than stand around all day would cheer or hiss according to the voter's choice. Elections were rowdy affairs at the best of times, and fistfights often broke out among the various candidates' supporters, but the continued presence of this group of toughs was intimidating in the extreme. Occasionally, when a particularly prominent citizen declared for Reform, one from the group of men would detach himself from his cronies and follow the voter down the street, shouting imprecations as he went.

Lewis could not vote. He did not meet the property qualifications — he had no house, owned no land. But had he been able to, he rather thought he would have spoken for Reform, just to annoy the toughs.

He was about to turn to leave the poll and carry on with his business when a small, thin man stepped forward to declare. There was a growl from the gang as the man called out his choice in a quavering voice: "John Roblin."

"Traitor!" one of the men shouted, for Roblin was the local Reform candidate. The group spread out to encircle the platform.

When the voter tried to shoulder his way through them, they gave way a little as he strode through the line near Lewis. Then, just as he was passing, one of the gang reached out and shoved him. He stumbled, but Lewis in turn reached out and caught him by the arm before he could fall.

"Hey, you, what do you think you're doing? Traitor helping traitor, eh?" The man who had pushed the voter had a thick brogue that spoke of the treeless hills of Scotland.

Lewis fixed him with an icy stare. "Pardon me, sir," he said. "I was born in this land; I fought for this land in the War of 1812. I bandaged more wounded than I could count at the Battle of the Windmill, and I buried the dead at the end of it. Where were you when I was defending British Canada? This man is free to vote as he pleases, and you'll have nothing more to say about it."

"Hear, hear!" said a voice at his side. "And you'll be letting these gentlemen go on their way now, won't you?"

A well-dressed man had joined Lewis's side. The Scottish thug wilted under his glare and took a step backward. The gang of men around them grumbled, but they too moved away, unwilling, for the moment anyway, to escalate the conflict. The gentleman ambled along behind them for a few steps, just to make sure, then turned back to Lewis, who by then was standing alone, for the skinny little voter had taken the opportunity to slip away unnoticed.

"Well spoken, sir, and thank you for saving that man a tumble in the dust. He's a neighbour of mine and I wouldn't like to see anything happen to him."

"It was nothing," Lewis replied. "Anyone would have done the same."

"Not with that gang of Orangemen, they wouldn't," the man said. He stuck out his hand. "Archibald McFaul."

"Pleased to meet you. Thaddeus Lewis. Now, I think we'd best be getting on with our business before this crowd gets rowdy again."

The man nodded briskly and strode away. His name meant nothing to Lewis at the time. It was only after they moved to Temperance House that he realized he had met one of Wellington's leading citizens.

And to Lewis's surprise, John Roblin carried the day and was returned to the legislature, in spite of the best efforts of the local Orange Lodge.

The dilemma of the extra chairs was answered quite neatly by Francis, who offered to knock together a couple of benches from some old planking he had discovered in the woodshed.

"It will only take a few minutes," he said. "They'll be crude — I'm no cabinetmaker — but they'll serve well enough for an Orangeman's arse."

Lewis should have chided him for the vulgarity, but he just chuckled.

The Orange Master, when he arrived prior to the start of the meeting, requested that refreshments "of the liquid variety" be served to the members at nine o'clock.

"I'll signal you when we want 'em," he said to Daniel, "but I'd appreciate it if you stayed out of the room until then."

Lewis and Francis hurriedly washed the goblets and glasses that had been used for supper and carried them on trays to the top of the stairs. They would bring the wine and beer up in decanters and jugs when the time came. As they passed the meeting room door, they could hear the murmur of voices inside the room, and snatches of song, although it was hard to make any of it out.

"...on the Twelfth I love to wear the sash my father wore" was the only bit they could understand, because it was shouted out at the end of each verse with great enthusiasm.

At a quarter to nine, Lewis climbed the stairs. He stationed himself just outside the door in anticipation of "the signal," at which point he would call to Francis and Daniel to start bringing up the jugs.

Just as he reached the landing, he thought he heard footsteps and a faint bang as a door was pulled shut. One of the other guests, he thought at first, but there were only three rooms on the other side of the hall from the meeting room — the Elliotts' chamber and sitting room, and the bedroom assigned to the enigmatic Mr. Gilmour.

Lewis walked down the hall and noticed that the door to the Elliott bedchamber was slightly ajar. This must have been the door he heard closing, but it hadn't latched and had swung open slightly. He was sure that it had been quite securely locked; after all, they had attempted to get inside to borrow chairs only that afternoon. Puzzled, he pushed the door open and went in.

At first it appeared that nothing had been touched. The room was neat and orderly, as it was every morning when the linen was aired and the room swept out, but then he realized that the coverlet had been rucked up on one side of the small bed, the side where Lewis had previously discovered the newspaper. When he turned, he noticed that the trunk that was normally firmly locked had been opened. A small piece of white gauzy material protruded from the lid, as if whoever had been looking at the contents had shut it hastily. He noticed nothing else amiss.

Should he straighten the coverlet, return the white material to the trunk? He decided against it. It appeared that someone besides himself was very curious about Clementine Elliott's activities. Maybe if she knew that, it would be enough to scare her away.

He left the room as it was and went to wait for the Orangemen to stop singing.

Chapter Thirteen

Whenever Clementine was not occupied with whatever it was she was doing in the upstairs rooms, she would go out. She and Horatio would breakfast early, and they were almost always the first to come down. Then they would retire to their rooms again to await the procession of visitors that continued to solicit her services.

On afternoons when she held no sessions, she would don her cloak and one of her stylish hats and go out for the afternoon. Had Lewis thought about it at all, he would have assumed that she had gone to the Elliott farm, perhaps to sit with the old man while Reuben attended to the business of the household. He couldn't imagine her doing much more than that. No one as elegant as Clementine could be pictured bathing a frail old body or changing soiled linen, administering whatever medicine was needed, or spooning broth into an insensible mouth. No, she would read to the old man perhaps, or sit quietly, ready at a moment's notice to call someone else should he require something.

Sometimes she took Horatio with her when she went out, but not often, confirming the statement she had made when she first arrived, that she disliked the notion of exposing him to a sickroom. Although the boy was certainly small for his age, which he said was nine, and white as a January snow, Lewis could see no signs of this reputed delicacy. He certainly had no difficulty keeping up with Martha — no mean achievement in itself — and now that Sophie was queen of the kitchen and the edibility of the fare had improved to such an extent, he consumed rather a lot of food for such a small boy.

After the discovery that someone had been in her rooms, Lewis took more note of Clementine's comings and goings. He quickly realized that the mysterious Mr. Gilmour's schedule coincided with hers to a surprising degree. Both would leave the inn at more or less the same time every morning, Gilmour always just a few minutes behind.

He had not previously been sure when either of them returned; he was not curious about the guests in the same way Daniel was, and had no basic interest in who they were, or where they were from, and seldom ventured any personal inquiries. He had hoped for an opportunity to prove that Clementine's self-proclaimed talent was nothing more than deceitful illusion, but this intention had sprung from ethical and moral objections, not from curiosity about the woman herself. But now he was convinced that Gilmour was spying on her, and he doubted that it had anything to do with moral conviction.

One late afternoon a few days after the Orange Lodge meeting, when Sophie had chased him from the kitchen and Francis was taking care of other chores, Lewis suddenly discovered that he had nothing to do. He decided once again to indulge himself with newspapers, with the justification that he was "keeping an eye on the front door." This sounded, he knew, like a feeble excuse, however true he knew it to be himself, but in any event, he suspected that staying out of everyone's way was perhaps the most useful thing he could do at the moment. So he settled himself happily on one of the stuffed chairs in the sitting room, which for once was free of guests.

He noted in a front page article that politicians in London were continuing to agitate for repeal of Britain's Corn Laws. He, like every other Upper Canadian, hoped they would fail. The Corn Laws gave Canadian wheat preferential treatment, and a move to free trade would be devastating to the new province's fledgling economy.

In the United States, the agitation over the boundary of the Oregon Territory continued to attract high-flown rhetoric and some alarming sabre-rattling. America insisted that it had the moral right to expand its territory all the way to the Pacific Ocean and as far north as they could get away with. Lewis had no expectation that Britain would make much effort to protect its claims on the west coast of the continent and would probably agree to continue the border along the 49th parallel to the sea.

He read these articles as a matter of principle, but soon turned to the stories of new wonders, which seemed to be popping up everywhere. Samuel Morse's system for sending messages over a wire was being adopted widely, he noted. He had no idea how this astounding invention worked, but it was a marvel to all.

The Life and Adventures of Martin Chuzzlewit, a serial by the English author Dickens, was provoking howls of outrage from American readers who felt that he had cast them in a very unflattering light. Lewis had not read any of Dickens's works — he had not ever had the time to delve into fanciful tales — but he found the descriptions of the book intriguing and wondered if he might be able to find it somewhere.

He was deeply absorbed in an article about a new process that promised to make rubber more useful, when he heard the front door open. He glanced through to the hall and realized that it was Mrs. Elliott and that there was no need for him to rise. To his surprise, instead of continuing up the stairs, she came into the sitting room and took a chair close by the stove, removing her gloves and holding her hands to the warmth.

"Good afternoon," he said, prepared to leave it at that and continue reading.

"I can't get used to this climate," she said ruefully. "Cold as a miser's heart one day, nothing but mud and damp the next. Is it always like this?"

She seemed to want conversation, so Lewis put his paper aside. "Well, at this time of year, yes," he said. "In the summer it's sometimes so hot you can hardly bear it, and it's damp then, too. The only time it ever seems dry is in the winter, but then of course it's *too* cold and *too* dry. It's a place of extremes, that's a fact."

"I grew up in Charleston, South Carolina. It's nearly always hot there, so that's something I'm used to."

So he had been right. She was from the southern regions of America. It wasn't an accent one heard often in Canada. Southern Americans were scared away by the climate. He wanted to ask her where she had met Nate Elliott, but he realized that the inquiry would be insensitive under the circumstances.

Then, as if she had read his thoughts, she said, "It's a funny old world, isn't it? Who would ever have imagined that someone who was born in South Carolina would fall in love with a man from the Canadian wilderness? The chances of us ever meeting must have been remote. Of course, Papa moved us all to Philadelphia when I was sixteen, so I reckon the chances improved then, but still ...." She sighed. "It must have been fate that brought us together and now fate has wrenched us apart."

"God willing, you'll be together again," he said. He didn't like this mention of fate, as if lives were pre-ordained. That was more along the lines of the way Calvinists thought, and he had always believed that actions counted for something. After all, why bother otherwise? He knew that in all conscience he couldn't offer this woman any hope that her husband might still be alive, but perhaps this was an opportunity to talk to her about the true meaning of eternal life. He doubted that he could persuade her to give up her table-rapping with argument alone, but felt obliged to at least try.

"Oh, that's right," she said, "You're a preacher, aren't you? I must say you have more forbearance than others of that profession I've met. Most of them would have had me thrown me out of the hotel by now."

"I must admit, if it had been my inn, you'd have been gone long ago. But it's not, it's my brother-in-law's, and there's little I can do about you while he has the say of it."

To his astonishment she began to laugh, and the timbre of her voice, which had been so high and irritating to him, changed with her amusement. It became deep and throaty and altogether not what he expected.

"I admire forthrightness in a man, even when it's one who is so disapproving," she said. "However, I will conjecture that you and I are not so different — we're both concerned with the state of the soul, aren't we? The difference is that you talk to God, while I talk with those who are with Him."

"It's not the same thing at all," he said sourly.

"But wouldn't you like to know for sure that all of those you have loved are truly in Heaven as you expect? Would that not be a confirmation of your faith, to know that they are well and happy and in God's grace?"

This was sophistry, and worse, near to heresy. "My faith needs no confirmation," he said, but even he could hear the slight hesitation in his voice. His belief had been fed all these years by his wish to see his daughters again, to know that they were in a better place and all suffering had been extinguished. It was something he had clung to, this trust in the mercy of

God. It was why he had given up farming and taken up the call.

He shook his head to clear his thoughts. No, this was nonsense, what she claimed to do. Even had he not been a man of God, he would have known in his bones that there was something not quite right, something spurious about her claim, and it seemed to him that this must be the Devil's tongue at work. He was sure that this woman was a charlatan. He was certain that the parade of visitors who came calling every day were receiving false hope in exchange for their money. He just had no means to prove it.

Just then he caught the sound of the front door opening again, but there was no accompanying ring of the bell. Clementine's eyes slid toward the doorway. She had heard it, too. Whoever had entered had taken care to do it quietly.

"Well," she said rising. "It's nearly time for supper, isn't it? I must say, the food has improved considerably. Please give my compliments to the cook."

With that she strode briskly from the room. Lewis scrambled after her, and as they entered the hallway, they both caught a flash of Mr. Gilmour's extravagant orange cravat as he slipped through the doorway that led to the kitchen.

"It appears that I'm not the only one who wishes to compliment the cook," Clementine said, and she swept up the stairs.

Lewis wondered if he should follow Gilmour, confront him about why he had sneaked into the hotel in such a strange way, and why he appeared to be following Mrs. Elliott. Daniel had been curious about the man from the start. As far as he said, he had gained no insight from his many questions, meeting with a polite but intransigent refusal to share any personal information. The man must have put something in the register, though, and maybe that would reveal some line of inquiry.

Lewis opened the heavy leather-bound book that was kept on the table in the hall, shaking his head, not for the first time, at the things his brother-in-law spent money on. A simple ledger would have sufficed to record the names of guests, but Daniel was convinced that more substantial trappings were necessary to attract a better clientele.

There it was: *H.R. Gilmour, New York.* They were no strangers to American travellers, even here in Wellington they would see a number every year, but ordinarily these visitors would stay but one night on their way to some other destination. Gilmour had now been here for several weeks and there was very little reason for him to linger. It was unlikely that he had relatives in the area. If he had family here, surely he would stay with them, not at the inn; it would be viewed as a gross dereliction of the rules of hospitality to let a relative stay in a hotel if there was a bed available for them in the home. In fact, oftentimes, enormous efforts were made to ensure that there was, sometimes to the extent of sending children to sleep at the neighbours' houses. It was one of the things that made inn-keeping such a difficult occupation. Yet, Clementine had chosen to stay here, as well, hadn't she? Perhaps the two decisions were related; Clementine because she needed a place to conduct her business, Gilmour because he needed to keep an eye on Clementine.

Had Gilmour been attempting to eavesdrop on their conversation in the sitting room? Lewis wasn't sure, but he suspected that if he were to go running after him, he would interrupt only some innocuous inquiry about the menu. It would serve no purpose; and besides, he could ask Sophie about the conversation later. He waited for few moments, then wandered into the kitchen as if in search of a cup of tea. There was no sign of Gilmour or of Sophie, although a delicious aroma filled the room — the bread had been sliced and wrapped in a cloth, a pot of soup simmered on the stovetop, and something in pastry was browning in the oven.

The teapot was on the table with warm tea still inside, so he helped himself to a cup. Then he heard laughter, and followed the sound to Susannah's bedroom; he was surprised to find his entire family clustered around his sister.

"No, no, sit," he said, when Daniel jumped up. "It smells like supper is well on the way and there's nothing else needed at the moment."

Betsy was in the comfortable chair by the window, Martha on the floor at her feet, and Daniel on a stool beside her. Sophie and Francis had parked themselves side-by-side on the end of Susannah's bed, although they now shifted away from each other, Sophie blushing slightly as they did so. Lewis supposed there was no other place for them to sit, but it was clear that the current arrangement presented no hardship to the pair. He leaned against the bureau and sipped his tea.

Susannah was looking much better, although she still appeared somewhat flushed. She was sitting up in bed, and Lewis noted with approval that Betsy was knitting, something she couldn't do when her joints ached. It looked as though the womenfolk might be on the mend.

Daniel, as well, had found time for newspapers, and was reading aloud from one, an article about the Cuban "banana," a strange tropical fruit that was selling in New York City at the astounding price of twenty-five cents a finger.

"Did you eat anything like that when you were in New York, Francis?" Martha asked.

"No," he replied. "To tell the truth, I didn't eat a lot of anything in New York."

"You may not eat anything tonight either if I don't get a move on," Sophie said, jumping up. "That pork pie should be done by now."

Lewis made to follow her, but Francis stopped him. "Finish your tea," he said. "I'll help Sophie dish up."

Betsy raised her eyebrows at Lewis, a clear signal that there was plenty to discuss between them at a later time. He shrugged in return. For now, he was more interested in having a conversation with his brother-in-law, and he took Sophie's place at the bottom of Susannah's bed.

"Did you ever find out what that Mr. Gilmour is doing here?" he asked.

"Not from him," Daniel said in a distracted way. He was studying his paper, no doubt looking for more articles to read aloud when next an opportunity arose. Lewis waited a moment before he spoke again. "From whom then?"

"What?" Daniel looked up. "Oh, yes, Mr. Gilmour. The man certainly is taciturn. Every day I'd ask how his business went and every day I'd get nary a reply but 'Very satisfactory, thank you.' It was most aggravating. But then Mrs. Sprung filled us in."

"Mrs. Sprung?" It took Lewis a moment to remember that this was the name of the most faithful of Clementine's retinue. "When did she tell you anything?"

"Oh, one time when she was visiting. We've drunk quite a few pots of tea between the three of us, I'll tell you. Wonderful woman. And so helpful with Susannah, isn't she, dear?"

Susannah nodded in agreement. "She's kept us up to date, all right. She's turned into a real friend, she has. Stops by every day she's here, as soon as she finishes with Mrs. Elliott."

Lewis wondered how many of these little tea parties he'd missed while he was hauling firewood or sweeping the stairs.

"You look like you just ate a sour pickle," Betsy remarked. "What's the matter with you?"

"Nothing," he said grumpily. "So what did Mrs. Sprung say about Mr. Gilmour?"

"Apparently, he's been following Mrs. Elliott around wherever she goes," Susannah said. "Even when she goes to visit her sick father-in-law, he hangs around just down the road a ways. He doesn't think anyone knows what he's doing, but of course everyone's noticed. It's hard for a stranger to blend in around here."

"Did Mrs. Sprung happen to know *why* he was following her?"

"At first everyone thought that he was waiting until she was alone so he could rob her. Then they wondered if he was lurking around waiting to rob the Elliott farmhouse, you know, checking to see when people went in and out, when the coast would be clear, but of course it never was, because somebody's there all the time with the father, aren't they? And he's been such a long time dying that now nobody thinks that's the reason. I mean, if Gilmour was a thief he'd have gone off somewhere else as soon as he realized there was no prospect that the house would be left empty, wouldn't he?"

"Yes, that would make a certain amount of sense. So what is the prevailing theory now? I know there has to be one."

"Oh, Mrs. Sprung and everyone else are convinced that he's smitten."

This statement was so unexpected that Lewis began to laugh. The idea of portly Mr. Gilmour with his tall hat and his gold pocket watch mooning around in the street like a love-struck youth pining for the object of his affections conjured a ludicrous picture.

Susannah defended the proposition. "Why else would he be hanging around all this time with no apparent reason for doing so? He even follows her when she goes into the stores. He's madly in love with her and wants to be Johnny-on-the-spot when she's finished her mourning."

"He'd have to wait for an awfully long time," Lewis pointed out. "After all, it's not certain that her husband is dead, is it?"

"Oh, I think we all know he is ... whatever happened to the body."

"I suppose. But didn't Gilmour arrive before Mrs. Elliott? How does that fit in with the romance?"

But this objection didn't dissuade Susannah a bit. "Maybe he originally had business in the village and fell in love with Mrs. Elliott when she arrived." She leaned forward a little and lowered her voice, "There are some who claim that they were lovers before ever they got here, and that he may have had something to do with Nate's disappearance. Soon as they find the body, he'll skedaddle and then she'll join him."

"That doesn't make any sense at all," Lewis objected. "If he had anything to do with Nate's disappearance, why would he wait around until the body was found? Wouldn't it make more sense to leave town right away, in case he was incriminated somehow?"

"I didn't claim that any of it made sense," Susannah said testily. "I'm only telling you what people are saying. My goodness me, you never told me you wanted it to be sensible."

"Fair enough. Does Mrs. Sprung ever say anything about what goes on upstairs?"

"Are you going to pick an argument with me over that as well?"

"Just tell me."

"All right, but you have to understand that this is just what I was told. Apparently, Mrs. Elliott has managed to contact Mrs. Sprung's dead daughter and they carry on a conversation every day. Mrs. Sprung seems to think that her little Amelia's very happy where she is ... as we all hope one day to be," she added hastily, in deference to Lewis's calling.

"How does she know it's her daughter?"

"Apparently she can see her."

"*What?*"

"I know, I know. She says she can see her, not clearly, there's a haze somewhere between here and the hereafter, but well enough to be convinced that it's really her. Mrs. Sprung said she really only intended to come the once, to make sure that the daughter was all right, but she enjoys the conversations so much that she wants to come every day. She's says it's just like having her little girl back home again."

"But what do they talk about?"

"Oh, Mrs. Sprung fills her in on all the news, what her aunts and uncles and cousins are doing, what the weather's like, what piece of needlework she has in hand, things like that."

"And what does the daughter say to her?"

Susannah's brow furrowed at that. "Come to think of it," she said, "I'm not sure she's ever said anything but 'well and happy.'"

"Interesting," Lewis said, rising. He could hear the clink of dishes coming from the dining room and he supposed he'd better go and help Francis with the supper service. "If she tells you anything else, let me know, will you?"

"You'll have to come and visit me once in a while if I'm to do that," Susannah said, with an impish grin on her face.

Sophie shot Thaddeus a quick glance over her shoulder when he entered the kitchen, then turned and busied herself with ladling the soup into bowls. She seemed a little flustered. He wasn't sure why, but guessed it had something to do with whatever Betsy wanted to talk to him about later.

As he ferried the dishes back and forth to the dining room, he mulled over what Daniel had told him. Poor Mrs. Sprung, desperate for a connection to what she had lost. *How was Clementine convincing her that she was speaking to the little girl?* As he cleared the last of the plates, he made up his mind. He would see this miraculous communication firsthand.

Chapter Fourteen

Each day since she had arrived in Wellington, Clementine had become a little more desperate. She was still uncertain what exactly had happened to her husband, except that he was nowhere to be found. She sorely missed both his company and his advice. She knew she was being watched. She knew that someone had been in her room on the evening of the Orange Lodge meeting, although she had said nothing to the innkeeper about it.

She was sorry now that she had gone to the Elliott farm that day. Perhaps she should have stayed at the hotel. But her options had been to sit in the small, stuffy parlour exchanging banal conversation with the other guests or, God forbid, the innkeeper himself, or to huddle in her room upstairs listening to the nonsense that was being spewed at the meeting across the hall. So she had opted to drive out to the farm and have another argument with Reuben. At least when she went to the farm she had the benefit of some fresh air both coming and going.

She had locked her doors firmly as she left. She was certain that she had. She had checked the locks three times and carefully tucked the keys into her bag. The locks were flimsy and easily forced, but there had been no sign of violent assault on them. They had been picked — easy enough to do if you knew how. She suspected that Mr. Gilmour was the only person at Temperance House who had the necessary talent.

She knew that the preacher was uneasy with her activities. She thought this was probably on the basis of the usual religious grounds, but it was always possible that he suspected something more. She was a little taken aback that her charms had failed to dazzle him in any way, although it did happen occasionally. Every once in a while she met a man who seemed immune to her. It was due to his wife, no doubt, even though she was such a peaked-looking thing and limped a little as she walked, but every time the preacher looked at her the rather harsh lines in his face softened and he appeared to have eyes for no one else. Some marriages were like that, she knew — so solid that not even an earthquake could shift them.

In spite of his seeming disinterest in her, or maybe because of it, Clementine found him the most interesting person in the village. He was obviously intelligent, and seemed to read a great deal. She longed to cast aside the role she had chosen for herself and have a genuine conversation with him — philosophical, perhaps political — it wouldn't matter as long as it was based on well-informed opinion. She had sought him out as he sat reading the papers in the parlour, mostly because she wanted to get some sense of what he knew, but also because she longed for somebody to talk to.

Reuben Elliott's company was driving her mad. Whenever they weren't arguing, he had nothing to say other than observations regarding the state of the farm or comments on his father's health. She had milked more information than she wanted from Meribeth Scully — she found the small-town gossip tedious in the extreme, now that she had used all that she needed from it. The other guests at the hotel were an unexciting group, and she had to be so careful when she interacted with clients outside of her sessions with them. That task was best left to the boy, who could move like a ghost among them. They would all be going home soon anyway — none of them were well-heeled enough to spend an unlimited amount of time and money contacting their dead. There was no golden goose in Wellington, and she could see that the initial deluge of customers was ebbing away into a trickle now that the novelty of it all had worn off. She would have to move on soon. She had no idea where she should go.

Even her son had let her down; whenever she didn't actively need him to help with the customers, he no longer spent much time sitting quietly in the public rooms of the hotel. Instead, he went racing off to find the preacher's little granddaughter. She couldn't blame him, she supposed; he was getting far too old to spend all his time with his mama, and they had moved so often that he hadn't ever had many friends. Martha was a charming little girl, very pretty, with her grandfather's intelligence apparent in her look and speech, but she represented yet another danger — how much had the little boy told her about his life before coming to Wellington? And how much had she repeated to the preacher?

Lewis was unsure of the procedure for joining one of Clementine's little groups, so the next morning he hurried to clear away the breakfast dishes, then waited at the bottom of the stairs until he heard footsteps in the upstairs hall. He climbed the steps and arrived at the Elliotts' sitting room just as her customers were shuffling one by one through the doorway. Horatio was waiting just inside, taking the money for his mother. His eyes widened when he saw who the last visitor was, but he made no remark as he held his hand out. Lewis was embarrassed. He had somehow forgotten that this was essentially a financial transaction, and he had only two pennies in his pocket.

"That's all right, dear, this one is on the house." Clementine seemed not the least surprised that he had decided to join the group.

It took a few moments for Lewis's eyes to adjust to the dimness of the room. Heavy curtains had been hung across the window wall and the little light that filtered through the damask cast an eerie greenish glow that made everything shadowy and indistinct.

Similar drapery covered the door that Lewis knew led into the Elliotts' bedroom. The other two walls were bare, the plaster also appearing greenish in the poor light.

"Please, sit down," Clementine said, gesturing to a chair that was set at the small round table in the centre of the room. "My goodness, Mr. Lewis, you're the seventh at the table. Seven is a lucky number, you know." The others looked at him enviously.

The table was covered in a heavy brocade cloth with tassels along the edge, and some of these had been caught under the foot of his chair. When he pulled it out to sit down, the tassels travelled with the chair and disarranged the cloth. Clementine grabbed it to prevent it going any farther and when Lewis knelt to free the tangle, he peered underneath as long as he dared. But the room was too dark for him to discern whether he was seeing anything other than the legs and feet of the people already sitting. When he stood again, he carefully pulled the brocade back into position. Clementine shot him a venomous look, or so he thought, but it might just have been the heavy shadowing around her eyes.

"Are all here?" Her voice was sepulchral, deepened substantially from the high, irritating conversational voice she normally used.

There was a sticky heaviness in the air and a whiff of smoke. He detected another smell underneath the perfumed air, something that he knew was familiar but that he couldn't quite place. It was very hot in the room and it seemed very crowded.

"We are set to begin," Clementine said. "Please join hands. Now, I must warn you that, no matter what happens here today, no matter what you see or hear, you must not let go. It would be dangerous for the spirits to sever the connection in so abrupt a manner."

Lewis clasped the hands of the plump woman to his right and a red-faced man to his left. He wondered at the presence of the man; he looked like a farmer or a labourer, not someone he thought would subscribe to nonsense easily. The woman, on the other hand, had probably lost someone, a son, perhaps, or a husband. She looked excitable. She would be much more susceptible to the idea that one could contact the dead, he figured.

"We seek enlightenment," Clementine intoned. "We seek the spirits of those who have left us." She swayed slightly as she spoke, and in order to maintain a uniform distance between them, everyone else at the table swayed as well. "Concentrate. Everyone must concentrate. It is helpful, sometimes, to close one's eyes."

The man and the woman on either side of him dutifully closed their eyes, but Lewis had no intention of following that particular instruction. He needed to keep his eyes wide open.

"Come to us," Clementine said. "Come to us and give us news of our beloved ones." A rhythmic knocking began, the sound of wood striking wood. It sounded as though someone was rapping on the tabletop, but when Lewis looked around, everyone's hands were still firmly joined.

"Come to us, come to us, come to us," Clementine repeated, and then she stopped swaying and appeared to be in a deep reverie or trance. When she spoke again, it was in a voice that was entirely different from her previous tone and different as well from her everyday speech. Something in the way she pronounced the vowels conjured up thoughts of Eastern Europe — or Egypt or Turkey or somewhere that was definitely not Wellington. "This is Karina. I am the gatekeeper. I will guide you to what you seek."

Lewis watched Clementine closely. Her face was in shadow, but to his astonishment a thin white vapour began to emanate from around her head —steam or smoke. Slowly, the stream spun out and upward, wafting slightly while Lewis looked on in fascination.

"Mama?" The voice was that of a small child and seemed to be coming from the curtains. Everyone at the table jumped, and everyone but Mrs. Sprung gasped.

"Your Mama is here," said the voice coming from Clementine's mouth. "She wants to talk to you." Even in the dim light, he could see the tears rolling down Mrs. Sprung's face. "She never stops thinking of you, Amelia, you can be sure of that."

Lewis had leaned his forearms against the edge of the table and now he felt it shift slightly underneath them, then rise an inch or so from the ground. No one else seemed to notice. They had all opened their eyes and were staring at a spot somewhere behind his back. He craned around and nearly let go of the hands he clasped. There, on the wall, was the figure of a young girl with long yellow hair. The apparition was indistinct, blurry at the edges, and inverted, its head pointing at the floor. The ghostly girl seemed not to notice her peculiar position, and every strand of her hair stayed in place, as did the collar of her dress, nothing trailing toward the floor as one would expect of someone who was hanging upside-down.

"Amelia, honey, it's your Mama. How are you dear?" Mrs. Sprung called out.

"Mama? I miss you, Mama. You should come and see me soon."

"Oh, I will, darling, I will. I miss you, too."

"I have lots of friends here."

"Yes, I know that," Mrs. Sprung said. "Who are you playing with today?"

"Mary."

Lewis felt his heart thumping. Mary had been the name of his first daughter.

"Mary who?" Mrs. Sprung asked.

"I don't know. She's too little to say."

Karina's voice asked, "Is there anyone from Mary's family asking for her today?"

"She's nodding her head yes," Amelia said. "But she doesn't talk very much."

Lewis's Mary had been in possession of only a few words when she had died from the terrible burning scald that had covered her body. There had been no words that day either, only the child's screams. It had been his fault that Mary had died, his carelessness, and a burden would be lifted from him if only he could tell her how sorry he was and how much he missed her. One guilty part of him wanted desperately to believe in this charade.

Yet he knew that he could not be seeing what his senses recorded, for he was sure that the dead did not come back; they did not communicate with the living. If they did, all his dead daughters would have been carrying on conversations with him long since, he had wished it so often. Mary was such a common name. There must be any number of Marys who had met with accident at a young age. Why was he correlating what he heard with his own experience? And yet he had jumped when he heard it, as if the child were, at last, speaking to him from beyond.

And then he realized how clever Clementine was. Somewhere, someone must have told her that he had lost a daughter named Mary. He suspected Daniel, who continued to behave like a blushing schoolboy in Mrs. Elliott's presence. She had taken this one piece of information and inserted it into the fantasy world she had constructed for Mrs. Sprung. Blindsided by the presentation of this one slightly relevant fact, he had for a moment reacted the same way that all of her victims must react — he had believed what he wanted to believe. This was not witchcraft or treating with the devil as the church would have everyone believe. This was nothing more than a confidence game. He resolved to turn the rules to his advantage.

"Is there anyone else there?" Karina asked.

"There are lots of people here, but I don't know all of their names," said the Amelia voice.

Lewis took a deep breath and spoke, watching Clementine's face as he asked "Is there anyone there called Nathan?"

Clementine's trance-like composure slipped a little, he could see, her eyes widened and her face seemed to sag, but she recovered herself quickly.

"Mama, I want to go play with Mary," the Amelia voice said. "Come back and talk to me tomorrow."

"Oh, but wait," Mrs. Sprung said, but the upside-down apparition faded before she could say anything more."

"I am the gatekeeper. Who is it you seek?" The mysterious Karina spoke again, but Lewis was sure he could detect Clementine's normal timbre underneath the voice.

"We're looking for Nathan," Lewis said. "Is he there? Can he talk to us?"

"There is no Nathan," Karina said.

"What do you mean?" Lewis said. "You must have millions of spirits there, and not one single one of them is named Nathan?"

"There is no Nathan who wishes to communicate. I am the gatekeeper. I open the gate only to those who wish to peer through it."

Clementine appeared to be coming out of the trance she had been in. Her eyes were no longer rolled back and the tension around her mouth faded. The ethereal white stream that had come from her ears had dissipated while they had been watching the figure on the wall. She bent her head slightly and panted as she let go of the hands she had clasped. After a moment she looked up at them. "I'm sorry. The spirits stay for only as long as they wish to. We'll have to try again tomorrow."

"I won't be here tomorrow." It was the ruddy-faced man. "I came all this way and I didn't get a chance to ask anything." He looked accusingly at Lewis. "This one chased them all away."

"I truly don't believe Amelia or anyone else will return today," Clementine said. "If you push too hard they get very shy for some reason." She appeared to be deep in thought. "There are other ways to discover the secrets of the afterlife. With your permission, we can try another method."

The man nodded his agreement. Clementine got up from the table and went to a small chest that had been placed against the wall. From it she produced two large sheets of paper that looked to Lewis like blank newsprint. She returned to the trunk for two inkwells and pens that she placed in front of her. She sat and unfolded the newsprint. She picked up the pens, grasping one in each hand. "I must ask you once again to concentrate. You needn't hold hands this time, but please do not speak, do not interrupt. It would be very dangerous for me if I were disturbed in the middle of this."

They dutifully stared at the tablecloth. The heavy scent grew even heavier and suddenly the room seemed full of grey mist. Clementine had resumed her trance-like state, but said nothing. Her head swung from side to side, first slowly, then quicker and quicker, then with a jerk her hands sprang into action.

To Lewis's astonishment, she began to write with both at the same time. Her hands flew across the pages of newsprint and the room was filled with the scratching of the pens. In unison they wrote, in unison they dipped the nibs into the wells, but it was as if they were mirror images of each other, each starting in the centre of the page and working outward, the right from left to right, the left from right to left. Then, as abruptly as she had begun, she stopped and fell against the back of her chair, seemingly exhausted.

"Water, please, some water."

Horatio appeared out of nowhere and hurried to a side table, where there was a pitcher of water. He filled a glass and took it to Clementine, lifting it to her lips and cradling her shoulders while she drank.

"Let us see what was revealed," Clementine said finally, pulling a candle close, so that they could all see what was written. Lewis leaned forward as far as he could. The writing on the paper was nothing but a scrawl on one side. He could make out only a few words here and there. There was a similar scrawl on the other side of the page, but he could read none of it. Then he realized that the writing was truly reversed, not only had it been set down on the page in an opposite fashion, but the words themselves were backward.

"I read of two men and two horses." The man nodded.

"There is a storm, great cracks of lightning and sheets of rain."

"Yes, but..." the man said.

"Sssh! All will be revealed.... Yes, a great storm and the men in great peril. A river is rising. It flows over its banks. The water washes away everything in its path."

The man groaned.

"There is a maelstrom, a great whirl of water from the river and a great deluge from the sky. The men are unaware of the danger they are in, until the earth gives way under their feet."

"So that's it, then. They're dead, right?" the man asked, ignoring his previous instruction.

"Three are left, one passes. I see a cave or a nest. It is warm. It is safe." —A long pause — "That is all."

"But how can there be three left? There were only two to begin with."

"Three are left. One passes. Look for a safe place."

"Look for a safe place?" the man muttered. "What's that supposed to mean. What a waste of bloody money." And he abruptly rose from the table and left the room.

Clementine seemed unruffled by his sudden departure. "Non-believers will soon believe," she said, smiling.

The others stood, as well. Obviously, the session was at an end. Clementine remained in her chair. Mrs. Sprung and two of the women lingered in the hall for a moment, all of them expressing dismay that the session had been so short. All three looked at Lewis accusingly as he walked past them.

Chapter Fifteen

Lewis now understood why Clementine's customers were so willing to believe that she possessed magical talents, but the mechanisms whereby she produced her apparitions eluded his best analysis. These were details that he decided to ignore for the time being. For now he was determined to collect whatever evidence he could find that would prove double-dealing, for the cruel appropriation of his dead daughter's name into her schemes had transformed his moral objections into something far more personal. He was deeply offended by her attempted manipulation of his grief.

The spiritualists that had been mentioned in the newspaper report from New York had manipulated, as well, and the man they had hoodwinked was so offended by it that he was offering a reward as an incentive to bring them to justice. Lewis did not subscribe to any of the popular theories as to why Mr. Gilmour was in Wellington, or why he appeared to be following Mrs. Elliott. It seemed unlikely that so dignified a gentleman would conduct a love affair on the streets of a small village or lurk outside houses with thievery on his mind.

What if the Elliotts had operated in New York under the name LeClair? If they suddenly needed to go to ground, Lewis could think of no better place than Nathan Elliott's old home in provincial Canada. Their arrival would be easily accounted for, especially since Nate's father was dying. And it was a possible explanation for Gilmour's continued presence — he was here to collect the reward. Lewis turned this theory around and around in his mind. Parts of it fit together neatly. But he was left wondering about Reuben's role in the affair. Was it merely a coincidence that Hiram Elliott became so ill at such a convenient time? Or that Nate had so conveniently vanished? And why had Clementine continued to stay on in Wellington? Why had she bothered coming here at all?

He wondered if there were any subsequent newspaper articles that would provide more information about the LeClair couple and what had happened to them. He searched through the papers that had arrived at the hotel recently, but could find no mention of the story, or any more articles reprinted from the *Tribune*. Newspaper delivery was irregular at best, dependent on someone deciding to pass an issue along to the next person, so it was possible that the appropriate paper had never arrived in Wellington, or that one of the

Elliotts had spirited it away. He needed to visit a reading room where there was a better chance of finding the news in chronological order, but there wasn't such a place in Wellington. The nearest was in Picton.

Francis had picked up the routine of the inn quickly. It must have seemed easy after the heavy work he had been doing. Sophie continued to reign in the kitchen, surpassing the most exacting of standards, and Betsy was free to spend a large part of the day in the sickroom drinking tea and reading to Susannah. Lewis could reasonably assume that the entire arrangement would not fall to pieces during an absence of an afternoon, but he would need some excuse for his little jaunt if he hoped to avoid some comment from Daniel or Betsy that might travel back to Clementine or Mr. Gilmour.

As it turned out, his timing couldn't have been better. The deficiencies of the kitchen at Temperance House had been made apparent with the sudden influx of guests and the unexpected rental of the meeting room. Daniel had read in one of the weekly papers that a Picton merchant named Morrison was offering sets of blue-edged stoneware "at a very cheap price" and Sophie put together an order for two or three lined pots.

"If you could manage some that are lined with tin they wouldn't turn the apples so dark," she said. "And they're easier to clean."

After a huddled conversation with Susannah, Daniel decided he could afford not only Sophie's pots, but a dozen dinner plates, another dozen soup bowls, some glassware to replace several that had been smashed by rowdy Orange Lodge members, and an extra meat platter.

"I'll fetch them tomorrow," Lewis offered. "Francis and Sophie can manage dinner between them and I can be home before dark if the livery has a decent horse available."

That evening he prepared a letter. If he found nothing at the reading room, he would send his inquiry about the LeClair story directly to the newspaper in New York.

He set off early the next morning. Although it was really the season for sleighing, the heavy snow that had fallen had been quickly packed down along the road-way and formed a hard, frozen base that made travel easy. The stable boy had assured him that the going would be as easy with a cart.

Lewis had barely reached the outskirts of Wellington when he realized that it had been too many weeks since he'd gone anywhere, and once again he felt the lure of the circuits. He had spent many long hours on the trail alone, riding from settlement to settlement to preach the Word. He was used to solitude, for the most part, and he missed it. Temperance House was a large building, but even so it seemed that there were people constantly underfoot and the public rooms in particular seemed small when everyone gathered in them. He found the dwellings in town alternately too hot or too cold, depending on how well the fire was fed, and in the wintertime windows were never opened, as once the cold air entered, it was far too hard to get rid of. But this practice made the rooms stuffy and stale and induced a state of near-trance at times. Lewis's clearest thinking had always taken place in the open air on the way to somewhere.

The last months seemed odd to him, and he wasn't sure that he quite had the knack of staying in one place, when new horizons so often beckoned. He shrugged. This was his life now, and the pleasure of spending more time with Betsy and Martha compensated a great deal for the lack of variety in the scenery.

But, as always, the frosty air cleared his head and the lack of company left him free to ruminate. As he considered the investigative task he had set for himself, he realized that the facts he was so eager to consider were few and far between. Nate Elliott was missing, that was fact number one. He had no way of knowing whether he had vanished deliberately or had been injured, as Reuben claimed, and wandered away in a dazed state to expire somewhere in a thicket. Either that or he had died in the clearing and his body had been moved for some reason. *But what reason could that be?* He could think of none. The only other fact he had established was that one of the Elliotts had taken a New York newspaper from the parlour and had appeared to hide it. He was fairly certain that it hadn't found its way between the mattresses by accident; the rest of the room was routinely tidy, with clothing hung up and belongings packed away.

Everything else was nuance; his conviction that Clementine was not what she claimed to be; his suspicion that the Elliotts might well be the LeClairs mentioned in the article; his feeling that Horatio was just a little too practiced at looking innocent and fragile. And why was Clementine so insistent that Horatio be present every time she communicated with the so-called spirits of the afterlife? And had it really been Gilmour who had searched her room on the night of the Orange Lodge meeting?

Lewis hoped he had not fallen into the trap of seeing a pattern where none existed. He had, in the past, allowed his own particular leanings to influence his conclusions about the actions of others. It was one of the things that had hindered the search for his daughter's killer. He had been far too ready to attribute the murder to his son-in-law, Francis Renwell, simply because he didn't like the man.

He didn't like Clementine Elliott either, but it wasn't clear to him if his distaste sprang from her deception or if his determination to unmask her came from his dislike. She was making good coin from her sessions in the upstairs rooms, and this sat uncomfortably with him. Then again, was he himself not paid to spread a message of hope? It was easy enough to argue that he wasn't paid nearly as well and that it was a different thing entirely — after all, he had to have some means to keep body and soul together, and unless he was prepared to become some sort of tattered, wild-eyed holy man dependent solely on the providence of God and nature, he had needed his salary from the Church, such as it was. And then he realized that Clementine could claim the same thing. She brought comfort to the bereaved and charged for it, in order to put food on the table and keep a roof over her head. This would be especially important now that her husband had disappeared, for she would have no other means of support. No, if he were entirely honest with himself, he couldn't point a finger at her for that.

With surprise, Lewis looked around and discovered that he had already reached the town of Picton. The main street was full of traffic — wagons, sleighs, horses, pedestrians — all of them determined to reach their destinations via the most direct route and in the shortest time possible, jostling and in many cases nearly colliding with others as they made their way. Picton was the County seat, and a great deal of Prince Edward's business was conducted here, both at the new court house and because of the town's spectacular harbour.

Lewis went to Morrison's first. The shop was located in a low frame building in a row of similar buildings on a side street that intersected with the main thoroughfare. He carefully consulted the list he had made, for he was sure that he would never remember all the items that he had been instructed to look for. It was a peculiar thing — he could recount by heart numerous Bible quotations and could recall almost every sermon he had ever given, but his memory had never seemed to be equipped to keep track of the more mundane things like grocery lists or errands to be run.

Morrison's stoneware was indeed being offered at an excellent price, and he chose the dish pattern that most closely matched the service that had been included with the other appointments at the hotel. Quite a lovely pattern, he thought; blue transferware, showing an exotic tree and, off in the distance, pagodas, birds, and boats that spoke of faraway Cathay. He would like to go there someday, to see for himself the landscape that was so different from the wooded tract that was Canada. He knew he never would. He was too old for such a journey, but the thought contributed to his wanderlust.

Morrison had glassware, as well, and the tin-lined pots that Sophie had requested. These last were more money than they had counted on, but the china had been so cheap that he cheerfully handed the cash over. Buying everything in one place would give him more time for his investigations.

The reading room was busy, when he finally found it tucked along another back street. Several men, labourers by the look of them, were seated at the long oak tables, leafing through the newspapers. *Probably reading the advertisements*, he thought, trying to gauge who might need an extra hand for a few days or a few weeks, or best of all, a few years. He could read the banners of these papers without appearing too obvious about it. They were all local publications. He looked through the table of remaining newspapers. None of them were from New York; in fact, none of them were American. He would go ahead and mail his letter.

Sitting at another table, carefully away from the rude workmen, were two well-dressed men, their suits brushed and their shoes polished. One of them was holding a book, the other a periodical. Lewis decided he might just as well take the opportunity to see what other reading material was available; after all, he had ridden some way already and had been wanting to visit this place for some time.

Lewis scanned the titles of the books lining the shelf. To his disappointment none of them looked as though they would hold information on the movement and mechanics of stars, something that he would have been very interested in perusing. There were several Bibles offered, a couple of books on religious topics, an atlas that he almost picked down from the shelf — geography was a subject that fascinated him almost as much as the skies. But it was the cover of one of the several pamphlets that caught his eye. It depicted a woman who had obviously succumbed to a bloody and violent fate. She was lying in a cobbled courtyard and he could tell from the architecture of the buildings around it that it was European — France, perhaps, or maybe Spain. The woman's head was lying at an angle that was strangely askew from her body. "The Murders in the Rue Morgue," he read. Ordinarily such a lurid and sensational tale would not have appealed to him. He considered these sorts of stories fit only for the morbid appetite, or for those with too little to keep them occupied — those who revelled in the details of horrific events from elsewhere. His experience with murder, however, made him curious.

He carried the pamphlet to an unoccupied table, well away from the gentlemen and the labourers. He realized that he was reluctant to have anyone notice him reading such a thing. To his surprise, he discovered that it was fiction; he had expected it to be some journalist's overblown account of a real murder, as had happened in the aftermath of his apprehension of Isaac Simms a few years back. The story of Simms's confession to multiple murders had been recounted and exaggerated until he could barely recognize any resemblance to what had actually happened.

According to the information in the front of the pamphlet this was a "work of imagination" written by one Edgar Allan Poe, an editor of *Graham's Magazine*. The story had originally appeared in the magazine, but had then been bound separately and was now circulating as a stand-alone work. Intrigued, he began to read, and was immediately swept into the author's argument regarding analysis: "To observe attentively is to remember distinctly." Lewis could only concur. Had he been a little more observant of the details surrounding the deaths of the young women murdered by Simms, he might well have stopped him sooner. As to Poe's small treatise on chess, checkers, and whist, he could make no judgment. He played no games of chance and was unfamiliar with the rules.

But Lewis was quickly hooked in by the story, fascinated by the abilities of C. Auguste Dupin, who observed his surroundings so carefully that he seemed almost able to read minds. The murders themselves, as he expected, were described in grisly detail, and he commiserated with Dupin's friend, who was able to make neither head nor tail of it. He attended carefully as Dupin examined the apartment and one by one eliminated the means of egress from the murder scene.

"So, what is impossible is impossible and that leaves only the improbable," he muttered as he read. One of the gentlemen looked up and glared at him for violating the rule of silence.

At first he was unsure what other clues the scene might provide. Observation in itself was fine, he thought, but what if there was so much to observe that none of it made any sense? And then, almost as if he had heard, Dupin answered his question. "The necessary knowledge is that of what to observe." He was not surprised when Dupin revealed that he had discovered a tuft of non-human hair clutched in one of the dead woman's hands, but he was surprised that the police had not thought to examine the corpse as closely. The only one of Simms's victims Lewis had had a chance to look at carefully had been the woman he had found in the cabin near Prescott, and repugnant as it had been, at least he had known enough to observe the details carefully, to pry her hands open and to look closely at her neck. The Paris police (for he had been correct and the setting of the story was in Europe) had gone off on the wrong track altogether and had arrested the clerk who had delivered a sum of money shortly before the murders, an apprehension that seemed ludicrous to Lewis. *But then, he himself had behaved ludicrously, too, hadn't he, when he had suspected Francis Renwell?*

In the end he was disappointed by the resolution of the tale. The presence of an exotic beast like an Ourang-Outang in so citified a setting seemed a little far-fetched, except that it reinforced the idea that improbable and impossible were two different things entirely, and perhaps that was the point.

He replaced the pamphlet on the shelf and left the reading room. He could see many parallels between Dupin's solving of the Rue Morgue murders and his own role in the capture of Simms; he, too, had attempted, albeit belatedly, to eliminate the impossible. He wondered if he could apply the same technique to the disappearance of Nate Elliott. No one was suggesting that this was another murder case, but perhaps elimination and careful observation could solve this mystery as well.

It was impossible that Nate's dead body had risen and walked away, and besides, his brother Reuben was certain that he had been alive when last seen. But if Nate had been merely wounded and had wandered into the swamp in a daze, why could none of them follow his trail? The best tracker in the neighbourhood had failed to find any sign of him and no hunter or woodsman had discovered him since. It was as if he hadn't been there at all, and Lewis turned this possibility over in his mind. Not impossible, but highly improbable. And if that were the case, why had Reuben led them to the clearing in the first place? Lewis shook his head. This was nonsense. His mind had been infected by the story he had just read. Nate's body would turn up one of these days, he was sure, and as soon as it did, his widow would be on her way. Lewis's objections to her occult activities would leave with her, as would the money she had collected from her unsuspecting followers. He wondered if Gilmour would depart, as well, since his only interest seemed to be Clementine.

No Ourang-Outang was going to magically appear out of nowhere and neatly answer all of his questions, he realized. He wasn't even sure that the questions were related in any way.

Lewis drove a little more slowly on the way back to Wellington, mindful of the delicate nature of his cargo. As he passed through Bloomfield and continued west, the road followed a high ridge that gave him a commanding view of the rolling countryside around it. To the right a row of prosperous farms marched all the way to Wellington; to the left the farm fields seemed to melt into the vast reedy marsh of West Lake until it, too, gave way to the open water of the lake.

He had been idling along, glancing only occasionally from side to side as he drove, noting the state of the barns and whether or not some building was in need of a coat of paint. His attention was on nothing but his wandering thoughts and his enjoyment of the day. Then, just at the periphery of his vision, he caught a flash of orange to his left. There was someone moving around down in the marsh. As Lewis watched, the figure moved first to the right for a few feet, then to the left, as if it was looking for something.

Lewis slowed his horse even further and squinted. In his younger days he could have seen the figure clearly; now he could only just make out enough detail for a tentative identification. His waning eyesight notwithstanding, he was almost certain that it was Mr. Gilmour, and that the flash of orange he had seen was the man's colourful cravat.

What was he doing in the marsh? It was hardly the place for an afternoon stroll. Even if the water was frozen, it would be hard to walk through the mess of tough cattails, and Lewis was by no means certain that it had been cold enough for long enough to freeze the ice solid. Gilmour was looking for something, that much was certain, and given the fact that he appeared to be intensely curious about Mrs. Elliott, the only conclusion that Lewis could draw was that he was searching for Nathan Elliott's body.

It was a long way from the clearing in the woods to the marsh. When Lewis had been searching with Martin Carr, he had briefly wondered whether or not a dazed man might have wandered into the morass and disappeared, but he had dismissed the idea. He would have left some trail that could be followed or been seen as he crossed the road. And yet there had been no trail, nothing that would lead to the marsh or to anywhere else for that matter.

Had Gilmour spent these past weeks combing the woods and, finding nothing, turned to the marsh for lack of anywhere else to look? Or did he have some piece of information that led him there? In either case, he had yet to turn up any evidence of Nate Elliott's fate — or at least, none that he was sharing with anyone else.

As Lewis passed the Elliott farmstead, he noted that a horse and cart were standing in the dooryard unattended. Clementine appeared to be visiting her father-in-law, and as was apparently quite usual, Gilmour must have followed her there.

Sometime later, as Daniel helped him unload the boxes of fragile china back at Temperance House, Lewis noticed Mrs. Elliott's wagon rumbling past in the direction of the stable, and by the time they had unpacked his purchases she had returned to the hotel. She must have departed from the farm shortly after Lewis passed by.

Not long afterward, Mr. Gilmour returned, as well.

Chapter Sixteen

Hiram Elliott had finally died, Francis announced at suppertime. He had heard the news when he went to pick up a barrel of oysters that Sophie had ordered. The doctor had been to see the old man the previous night and had given his opinion that he couldn't last much longer. Hiram had slipped away quietly in the early afternoon.

"Clementine was at the farmhouse when I went past," Lewis reported. "Reuben must have summoned her. I expect it's a relief after all this time."

The old man had lingered many months longer than anyone had expected, and in these cases the family often became tired with the waiting, Lewis knew, so that it came almost as a surprise when the loved one finally passed.

"Loved one" was perhaps an inappropriate phrase, according to Sophie. Her mother knew the family well, she said, and her mother's opinion was that Hiram was "the meanest man alive." She had added, "Now I guess he's the meanest man dead."

Lewis had to object to this, if only on theological grounds. "You shouldn't speak ill of the dead, you know. He may have repented his sins before he passed."

But Sophie was unapologetic. "He spoke ill enough of everyone else. I don't see why that fact should be overlooked just because he's passed on. We can only hope he's met his just reward."

Lewis was curious about the details of Hiram's meanness, but he had no opportunity to question Sophie further, as Daniel asked with an anxious look on his face, "Do you suppose one of us should call at the viewing tomorrow? After all, Mrs. Elliott is a guest here."

This hadn't occurred to Lewis. He had never met Hiram Elliott and had had only brief encounters with Reuben, but he supposed Daniel was right. It wouldn't hurt them to show their support at a difficult time.

"I could call on our behalf, if you like," he said. "It would be a decent enough thing to do. And I suppose Martha should go as well. She and the boy are such good friends."

Daniel looked a little put out at this, and Lewis realized that he had had a picture of himself squiring the elegant Clementine along, offering a sympathetic arm to her grief.

"Or you could do it," Lewis added hastily. "It's just that I'm probably the least missed. After all, the hotel is still full of other guests."

Daniel agreed, albeit reluctantly. Lewis thought that it wouldn't hurt Daniel a bit to stay back and attend to business. It was his hotel, after all.

The next morning after breakfast, Betsy supervised the scrubbing of Martha's face and hands and marshalled her thick hair into two tidy braids in preparation for their visit to the Elliott farm. Lewis owned only one coat — the old black shadbelly that he wore every day — but he carefully sponged away any stains that he could see, and brushed the dust from his flat-brimmed hat. The farm was close enough that they could walk to it. He was reasonably sure that Martha could easily manage the first part of the journey, but he thought that it might well be slow-going on the homeward leg unless they could beg a ride from one of the other callers. Martha took his hand as they walked, and he was grateful that she was not yet too old to do such a babyish thing. Although the breeze was brisk, it was not too cold and the sun shone brightly.

"You know why we're going to the Elliotts', don't you?" he asked her.

She nodded. "Horatio Joe's grandpa died, and we're going to say how sorry we are. I already told him I was sorry, though, this morning at breakfast."

"That was good of you," Lewis said. "But it's important to do it officially, as well. It's a sign of respect."

"He didn't seem sorry at all."

"He didn't know his grandfather very well, and Mr. Elliott was pretty ill when he arrived. I expect Horatio thought he was just a sick old man."

"I didn't know him at all."

"No, but Horatio's your friend. I think he'll be pleased that you're there."

"Was Mr. Elliott really, really old? Older than you?"

"I don't know for sure, but I would think that he was."

"So it will be a long time before you die?"

He squeezed her hand. "We never know what Providence has in store for us. That's why it's important to be good every day, because we never know what will happen on the morrow. But if it's a case of old age, then I'd say, yes, you're right, it's likely to be quite some time before I go."

She seemed satisfied with this answer and walked along without saying anything for several minutes, although she hummed a little tune to herself as she walked. It was sadly off-key, but an indication of her good spirits. Lewis was relieved. As a minister, he was never one to shy away from discussions of impending death, even his own, but it was a topic that had occupied his thoughts in light of Betsy's illness. He had wondered what would happen to this little girl if they were both to expire before she was grown? He had supposed that one of his sons would take her, or maybe even Daniel and Susannah, but now that her father had unexpectedly returned, the question was answered. Still, the thought of not seeing her reach womanhood saddened him.

His thoughts were interrupted by the sound of a cart approaching from behind. To his surprise, the driver pulled even with them and stopped.

"Could I offer you a ride?"

It was Archibald McFaul. He was driving a trap, not the usual cumbersome hay wagon that normally did double duty as transportation. He was one of the few men in town who was prosperous enough to keep such a vehicle.

"Why, it's the preacher-turned-innkeeper," he said. "I expect you're on your way to the Elliotts' as well. Please, get in. I'm going there myself."

"We'll gladly accept," Lewis said and lifted Martha up to sit next to McFaul. "This is my granddaughter, Martha, who lives with us. Martha, this is Mr. McFaul."

"How do you do, Martha." His eyes narrowed a little before he smiled at her and Lewis was left to wonder if this man knew the whys and wherefores of Martha's history. She smiled back shyly, however, and said, "Thank you for giving us a ride, sir," demonstrating the good manners that Betsy demanded at all times.

McFaul nodded, then turned to Lewis. "And how are you getting on in the hotel business?" he asked. "I'd have thought it a rum do, waiting tables and emptying chamber pots, after the glory of fighting for men's souls."

"I've had to give that life up," Lewis said. "My wife isn't well. I can't say I'm particularly enamoured of innkeeping, but I haven't been able to find anything else for the time being. It was good of my brother-in-law to offer us a place, though, so I won't waste my breath complaining."

"You're an educated man? Forgive me for asking, but I've always heard a lot of nonsense about how ignorant saddlebag preachers are, and yet you're well-spoken enough."

Lewis wondered how McFaul knew so much about him, for he had never spoken more than a few words with the man, and had certainly never vouchsafed the fact that he had been an itinerant minister. But being such an important man, he supposed McFaul had his thumb firmly on the pulse of the village and made it his business to know about everybody. Besides, Lewis carried a certain degree of notoriety, he supposed, as a result of his role in the capture of a murderer; but he had the impression that McFaul's knowledge went beyond the sensational details that were repeated so often about the case. Not for the first time he wondered at this man who had so kindly offered them a ride. How had a poor Catholic boy made such a success of his life surrounded by a large community of staunch Protestants? For McFaul was without question a leader in Wellington.

"Yes, I'm educated," Lewis said in response to the question. "In fact, I taught school for a number of years and have tried as much as I could to continue my education, although this has, of necessity, been an informal process."

"Well, that should help. I'll keep my ear to the ground, and if I hear of any occupation that might suit, I'll certainly let you know. And what about you, young lady?" he said, turning to Martha. "What do you do for a living?"

She giggled. "I go to school and I help Uncle Daniel at the hotel."

"Well, of course you do," McFaul said. "I could tell just by looking at you that you'd be an enormous help. I wish I had a Martha to assist me."

During the course of the conversation they had covered the distance to the Elliott farm. The yard was full of wagons and horses. Hiram Elliott might not have been popular, but the people of Wellington would nonetheless observe the proprieties.

The family had laid Hiram out on a table in the parlour. The mirror over the fireplace had been covered in black cloth and Lewis noted that the clock had been stopped at quarter to two, marking the time of death. Reuben greeted them. "Good of you to come," he murmured, a refrain that he would repeat many times over the course of the afternoon.

Clementine was seated in a chair by the casket, Horatio at her side. The boy brightened when he saw Martha, but before Lewis would let her go to her friend, he insisted that they take their turns to file past the deceased. He noted that although Clementine was dressed in black, as befitted her status as a mourner, she had not been content with plain crepe. The material she had chosen was far finer, and cut in what Lewis supposed was the latest fashion, trimmed with lace and small jet buttons. She must have acquired the dress in New York, for he had seen nothing like this locally. But then, she had been expecting a death, hadn't she? That was why Reuben had gone to find his brother, after all.

"Thank you for coming, Mr. Lewis," Mrs. Elliott said when they finally reached her. She then turned to her son. "Why don't you show Martha where the refreshments are?" Horatio accepted this suggestion with alacrity, and Lewis nodded his permission.

"Had you met your father-in-law prior to this visit?" he asked when the children had tiptoed out of the room.

"No. Nate never spoke of his family, and I didn't even know they existed until Reuben arrived to say that his father was dying. I knew only what I've seen in the last few weeks — a poor old man on his deathbed. It's difficult to maintain the appropriate air of grief under the circumstances."

There was a queue of people behind him waiting to speak with her, so Lewis moved on. A table of tea and cakes had been set up in a smaller parlour near the rear of the house, and he was directed to help himself to refreshments. Martha and Horatio were nowhere to be seen. He assumed that they were playing somewhere in another part of the house. It would be the same for the boy as it was for his mother, he reflected — Hiram Elliott was nothing more to him than an old, dying man. It was no surprise that his look had brightened when Martha appeared.

The conversation in the parlour revolved around the perennially favourite topic of the disposition of the deceased's assets.

"Most peculiar will, most peculiar," said one portly

gentleman who seemed to have inside knowledge of the arrangements.

"That's Hiram's solicitor," whispered the woman standing beside Lewis.

"The property will go to Reuben, surely. After all, he's worked the farm for years, and I don't expect Hiram was any too generous in paying him for doing it." — This from a man whom Lewis recognized as a local cooper.

There was a general murmur of agreement, and it was apparent that nearly everyone had the same unflattering opinion of the recently deceased.

"Well," said the solicitor, "it may or it may not, but there were conditions laid down that had to be satisfied before the property could pass."

"Isn't that just typical," muttered the woman beside Lewis, "old Hiram being difficult even in death."

The solicitor beamed at the people standing around him with the smug smile of one who enjoyed having inside knowledge. "Apparently, Hiram was determined to bring Nathan home one way or the other."

The room erupted in comment.

"… so that's why he went to so much trouble to fetch Nate."

"… figured Nate wouldn't come back unless there was money involved."

"… old man still pulling the strings."

Lewis had heard enough. He gulped down the last of his tea and went to find Martha. He hated the squabble over wills that seemed to attend so many deaths. It was Hiram's property, after all, so why shouldn't he leave it any way he liked? At least this was a point of contention that was unlikely to arise within his own family. He had nothing. There was nothing for them to fight over.

Lewis found the children in the kitchen, where one of the neighbourhood ladies had given them each a cookie and a glass of cider. He buttoned up Martha's coat and shooed her out the door, but they had barely reached the gate when Archibald McFaul emerged from the front door and noticed their departure.

"You've had enough, as well?" he called. "Wait and I'll take you back."

He brought the horses to where they were waiting, and lifted Martha into the buggy himself.

"Well," he said, settling himself into the seat, "duty done. Now it's back to business."

"There was a great deal of jabber about Mr. Elliott's will, wasn't there?" Lewis said.

McFaul chuckled. "Yes, Hiram has apparently taken one last shot at his boys. I wondered why Reuben was in such a lather to get Nate back home, and now it looks as though it had something to do with the will. It's my best guess that the terms are so convoluted that it will end up with the courts deciding. It would be just like Hiram to make sure the whole thing was tied up for years."

"Will it really come to that?"

McFaul nodded. "Oh, yes, I expect so, especially now that Nate appears to have disappeared again. And then there are dower rights to consider. Mrs. Elliott would have to be given some consideration, even though Hiram didn't know she existed. Or the boy could well inherit on behalf of his father, if, indeed, his father inherited anything at all." He shook his head. "Old bugger. Pardon my language, but I can't think of a better term for Hiram Elliott." He fixed Martha with a stern stare. "You didn't hear me say that, did you?"

She giggled and shook her head.

"Ah, I thought not. You look exceedingly deaf to me." McFaul spent the rest of the short drive letting the little girl help him drive the trap, and then most obligingly deposited both her and Lewis at the doorstep of Temperance House.

Chapter Seventeen

Lewis's day still started at dawn. In his long years of riding the enormous circuits assigned to Methodist ministers, he had nearly always been saddled up and ready to set off each morning just as the rays of the rising sun were lightening the eastern sky. There was no reason to jump out of bed with first light now, but he found it hard to shed a habit that had been so firmly entrenched.

His first task for the day was always to feed the stove so the room would be lovely and warm when Betsy and Martha woke. He would soon have the kettle boiling and he would take a cup of tea to Betsy while she was still in bed. This slow and gentle easing into the task of getting up and dressed gave her stiff joints a chance to limber up, and as a result her limp was far less pronounced, during the morning hours at least. When again they inevitably began to protest, Betsy now had the option of spending the afternoon in a comfortable chair, passing the time of day with Susannah. It was a soothing rhythm they had fallen into, and Lewis could see the benefits of it in the gradual improvement in his wife's colour and the lessening of the tight lines at the corners of her mouth.

Often he poured two cups of tea and took a few minutes to sit on the edge of the bed before he roused Martha. He began to realize that he had missed the gentle companionship of everyday living in all those years he rode the trails, and now he prized this morning time, when he could simply be with his wife before the duties and tasks of the day called him away. Some mornings few words passed between the two; sometimes they had particular items to discuss.

Today Betsy was already wide awake by the time the water had boiled. Today was a discussion morning, he realized. It was Saturday – he could let Martha sleep awhile so his wife could have her say. Betsy waited until he had perched beside her and taken the first few sips of his milky tea.

"Have you noticed anything between Sophie and Francis?" she asked him.

"Like what?" As far as Lewis was concerned, the two of them seemed to be getting along just fine, and the work went all the smoother for it.

"Well, it's just a feeling I have, but they certainly seem to go out of their way to be in the same room at the same time."

He was puzzled for a moment, and then he realized what Betsy was hinting at. "Do you really think so?"

"They always sit side by side and Sophie blushes a little when I catch them doing it."

Betsy had always been far handier at reading these sorts of signals. It was Betsy who had known that Rachel Jessup, the girl who had been murdered in Demorestville, had decided on her choice of husband, although poor Rachel didn't live long enough to realize a marriage. He thought back over the last week or so and realized that Betsy was right. Nearly every time he happened upon Francis in an idle moment, Sophie was nearby, and vice versa.

He wasn't sure how he felt about this. He hadn't liked Francis Renwell much when he was courting his daughter Sarah. His dislike continued when the two were married, and only intensified after his daughter's tragic death. He had warmed to the young man since, but this was guilt more than anything else. The notion that he might be thinking of courting Sophie seemed like an act of treachery, a dishonouring of a daughter's marriage that had been a love match from the beginning, no matter the dreadful things that had happened afterward. But Francis was still a young man, and when Lewis stopped to count up, he realized that it had been seven years since Sarah had been taken away — a very long time for anyone to be alone. Perhaps it was time to let go and let things take their natural course.

"Well, I must admit, I'm a little taken aback," he said. "But Sophie seems like a nice girl, and, as you know, I've completely changed my opinion of Francis."

He could tell by the look on Betsy's face that he had somehow completely missed the point of what she was trying to say.

"Oh, I agree, Sophie's a grand girl," she said. "And it would be nice to see Francis settled down somewhere. But have you thought about what this might mean to Martha?"

He hadn't. Trust Betsy to go directly to the heart of what was important for her nearest and dearest.

"Sometimes she seems more like my child than my own did. I'd hate to lose her now."

"So would I." Just the thought of it caused a choking sensation in his throat. The little girl was so much like her mother that losing her would be like losing Sarah all over again. "Do you think they would take her, if what you suspect is right?"

"Francis would take her in a minute. You can tell by the way he looks at her. He desperately wants to be a real father to her, to make up for all the time he's lost."

"And Sophie?"

"Sophie seems to be very fond of Martha, as well, and I'm sure she'd go along with whatever Francis wants. The problem is that I don't see how we could object. He's Martha's father, after all, and if he finds himself in a position to make a good home for her, I don't think there's anything we could do about it. We're both old, Thaddeus, and I'm sickly. How could we argue that Martha's better off with us? Sophie would make a wonderful mother for her, but that doesn't mean I want to see it happen."

It was a conundrum, and Lewis realized that if he were honest, he would have to admit that Martha would be far better off with her father and, apparently, a new mother. Perhaps even a new family, with brothers and sisters and the bustle that attends the households of the young. But he didn't want to be honest. He wanted to be selfish and keep Martha forever.

It was too bad that Francis Renwell was nothing to them, really. Just an in-law. Related not by blood, but my marriage, and now that the marriage no longer existed, they had no claim on him. If he had been one of their own sons, Lewis might have been able to engineer a solution that included him and Betsy, although his one previous attempt at putting all of his family under one roof had ended in acrimony. He could scarcely ask Francis to assume that kind of responsibility, especially since Lewis's ability to contribute to the household was limited.

But that could change, and it was high time it did anyway. The hotel was running smoothly now, and it wouldn't be too long before Susannah would be up and about again. He had no illusions about his effectiveness as an assistant innkeeper — Sophie, and even Francis, were far more help than he, and it wouldn't take Daniel long to realize it. Lewis had earned his keep so far, but if he and Betsy were to stay in Wellington, he would at some point have to offer his brother-in-law at least some kind of nominal rent for their little house. That had been the plan from the beginning, but it had been derailed by Susannah's accident. It was time to start looking seriously for a job.

Preaching was the obvious choice, but all of the nearby Methodist meetings already had ministers they were quite happy with. They would not be likely to turf someone out on his behalf; nor, he thought, should they. School teaching was an option. It had been his first career, and he had gone back to it when he was recovering from his plunge through the ice, but it demanded regular attendance for a large part of the day, and he couldn't leave Betsy alone on her bad days. He couldn't ask Susannah to step in; once she was well again she would have her hands full at the hotel. He needed something with more flexibility. He resolved that he would find something to do in the village. He would build up his funds as much as possible. And then, if Francis took Martha somewhere else, he would have the wherewithal to follow.

Chapter Eighteen

Horatio had become fascinated by the Holey Man. After he'd got over his initial fright at the unexpected meeting, he had wanted to go back the next day and find the strange being; and every afternoon since, whenever he and Martha were deciding what they should do, his first suggestion was always that they should play down around the shore.

Martha didn't mind catering to him at first. A couple of times they had taken the homemade sled back to the dunes and tobogganed again. Once they walked along the lake, kicking at the thin ice that had formed along the shore. Once they had played hide and seek in the warren of fishing reels and dry-docked boats that clustered around the wharf. But all the time they played, Horatio would sneak glances out over West Lake, and Martha knew he was hoping to catch a glimpse of the shuffling creature that had scared them so.

As the year grew old, daylight faded quickly in the afternoons, so on schooldays Martha and Horatio stayed closer to home and amused themselves by playing marbles or tag with the other neighbourhood children. But that Saturday Horatio's mother didn't need his assistance in the afternoon, so after the noon meal they headed straight for the shore.

They ventured farther along the sandbar than they had ever been before, nearly reaching the place where the shore started to curve around the lake and the sand hills spread into a wilderness of cedar forest. At one point there was a narrow channel that connected the two lakes, but this seemed frozen enough to walk on if they went carefully. It was here that they caught a glimpse of the Holey Man off in the distance.

"What is he doing?" Horatio asked as they spotted the raggedy figure rowing a skiff slowly around one of the small islands that dotted West Lake.

"I think he's checking his traps," Martha replied. "I'm pretty sure those are muskrat lodges along the shore there. I bet he's a trapper and that's why his clothes are so funny-looking. He probably just tans the hides at home and makes them into clothes."

"But where is his home?"

Martha shrugged. "I don't know. I didn't even know he was here until he scared us that day."

"Do you think your grandfather would know where he lives?"

"I don't think so," she said. "We haven't been here long enough to know stuff like that."

"What about your uncle?"

Again Martha shrugged. She hadn't mentioned the Holey Man to her grandparents. She wasn't sure why, but she had a feeling that if she did, she might be forbidden from going down to the sandbar, and since that was just about the only thing Horatio ever wanted to do, she had no doubt that he would simply go without her.

"What do you suppose he eats?" Horatio asked.

"Well, there's lots of fish. And squirrels and rabbits. And if you can catch beavers, their tails are good roasted. I guess that would be enough food for anybody."

"Let's go look at his traps."

Martha hesitated. "He might get mad if he thinks we're fooling around with his traps."

"I just want to look at them, that's all." He scanned the horizon for a few minutes, but the Holey Man had moved on and was no longer visible. "Let's go across to the island."

What appeared like a very short distance when you were just looking at it suddenly seemed much farther with the prospect of walking it, and Martha was uneasy about going so far on the ice.

"I don't think we should. I'm not sure the ice will hold us. Why don't we just look along the shore here? There's plenty of muskrat here, too."

"There's nothing here but a bunch of reeds and grass," he said.

"No, those mounds are where the muskrats live," Martha said, pointing to what appeared to be nothing more than a jumble of vegetation. "Down underneath. And you can see where he put a stick to mark where the trap is."

Horatio went to where she was pointing and scuffed away the snow. A trail of air bubbles frozen in the ice betrayed the entrance to the animal's den. They could just see a small piece of chain above the surface. Horatio grabbed it and started to pull.

"Be careful," Martha said. "It's probably set. You don't want to get your hand in the way."

The trap, when Horatio finally hauled it to the surface, proved to be little more than a few wires twisted together, but it was enough to have caught and drowned a fat, glossy muskrat.

"I thought it would have bigger teeth," he said, "Don't they gnaw on stuff?"

"You're thinking of beaver," Martha said, "Their teeth are a whole lot bigger," although she wasn't by any means sure of this.

Horatio held the trap high and let the muskrat corpse twirl in a dripping circle. "How does the trap work?"

"I think it catches them by the leg and then they can't get away."

"It doesn't kill them?"

"I don't think so. I think it drowns or the trapper has to come along and bash it over the head or something. That's why they check the traps all the time."

"Well, don't that beat the Dutch," Horatio said. "I'd like to see that!"

Martha wouldn't, and she hoped that the occasion would never arise. In fact, she hoped that now that they had had a chance to look at a trap closely, Horatio's fascination with the trapper would wane.

They lowered the trap back into the water and tried to brush the snow back around the foot of the den, but at this they were not very successful. Martha was sure that the Holey Man would know that someone had been at his traps.

When the pair headed back toward the harbour, it was already starting to get dark. It would soon be suppertime. As they wandered along the path, Horatio tried to imitate the Holey Man, shuffling and snuffling along, but he stopped when he saw someone standing by one of the boats. It was Mr. Gilmour from the hotel.

He nodded at them as they went past, but continued staring across the water toward the marsh.

Chapter Nineteen

No business near 'em, no business at all. The Holey Man mumbled to himself as he shuffled along checking his traps. He had seen the two kits haul the trap up. They hadn't seen him, not then, even though he knew that they had been watching him. *They're only kits, young 'uns and you leave those alone.* Old Man had beaten that into him — *don't trap when the critters have kits and don't take the young 'uns.* Old Man had told him a lot of stuff, but he'd never been able to remember all of it. *Don't eat anything unless it's in the trap or you seen it die. Don't eat dead stuff you just find lyin' around in the woods.* He remembered that one. He'd found the remains of a fawn that the coyotes had taken down. Something must have scared them away — they'd probably heard him coming — and only the crows were there when he'd arrived in the clearing. He'd been hungry, oh so hungry, although he didn't know the word for the gnawing ache in his belly that happened when Woman hadn't filled his bowl for a few days. He'd grabbed a haunch and begun to gnaw. He liked venison. But then Old Man had been there, coming along behind him and had ripped the meat out of his fist and smashed him across the face with it. *You don't eat dead stuff, boy.*

He'd thought that maybe the young 'uns he'd seen were hungry, too, but they hadn't taken the fat, glossy she-muskrat that had been in the trap. They'd looked at it and poked it with a stick, but then they lowered the trap back down into the hole they'd made in the ice, muskrat and all. He'd gone and retrieved it later, after they'd gone, and he'd taken the carcass back to the shack. There he had carefully peeled off the pelt with his hands, the way Woman had taught him, so there wouldn't be any nicks or cuts in the hide. He'd pegged it down and set it to dry in the wind. Sometimes, when Old Man had taken down a deer, Woman would do something different with the hide. Something that needed a lot of grease mixed with the deer's own brains, but he'd forgotten what it was exactly that she did. He saved all the grease he could anyway, in a big tin, just in case he someday remembered what it was he was supposed to do.

He had quite a big stack of rawhide pelts, muskrat mostly, but some mink, as well. Now that Old Man was gone, he didn't know what he was supposed to do with those either. Old Man had taken them to where the big shacks were, crowded along the water opposite his woods, but he had never gone along to see exactly which shack you were supposed to go to. After Old

Man came back there would be flour and sugar and tea, and sometimes potatoes; he remembered that all right, but he had no idea how you went about turning pelts into potatoes.

He set the dark red muskrat meat to soak overnight in some salt and water, just like Woman had always done. He'd boil it up the next day if he didn't catch anything nicer. He didn't like muskrat much, but he'd used up all of the good meat from last winter. He didn't know what this good meat was called, but it had a lovely sweet taste and there was a lot of fat under the skin. The pelts were difficult to get off, but they were easy enough to dry. It had been cold enough by then to freeze meat solid, so he had simply chopped the carcasses up and put the pieces in the meat barrels. He'd rolled the barrels back behind the cabin to the stone hut built into the side of the dune, and made sure the heavy door was firmly shut so the coyotes couldn't get at the meat. The coons had somehow got in anyway and gnawed at the sides of the barrel, but he'd set traps for them. The big ones, Old Man had told him, were for bears, even though he'd only ever once seen a bear, but Old Man said they were plentiful once. He'd caught three coons. The traps kept his meat safe, but he'd eaten it all up before winter's end, and then there was nothing but muskrat and rabbit, squirrel and fish, for a long time.

He'd found good meat again in the marsh, not long ago, on one of the little hummocks of solid ground that stuck up here and there among the cattails. *Don't eat stuff you find dead in the woods*, Old Man said. *Only if you seen it die.* But he'd eaten the other sweet meat and it had been good. Maybe dead sweet meat was different from other dead meat.

He'd tied a rope around the critter's feet and hauled it into the skiff. When he got it back to the cabin, he skinned it and cut it into pieces just like before, but he knew that it was not yet cold enough to keep for any length of time. He knew that Woman had packed salt all around the pieces she put into barrels, but he had hardly any salt left. He'd packed it anyway, but after a week or so he could tell from the smell that he'd done something wrong and that it was turning already. He'd only really got a few good meals from the whole carcass and now he was back to eating muskrat again.

He wished he could take some venison, but he would need the gun for that, and he wasn't sure how to use it. Old Man had always done the shooting. There was no powder left anyway; Old Man hadn't got any more and then the shack had fallen on him.

Most of his traps were empty, the bait still rotting in them. He wondered if the smell of the young kits had scared everything away. He sniffed the air. The wind was shifting around a little to the north, and that always brought colder air. Maybe that would blow the smell of them away.

He shuffled around the shore of the island that was closest to the woods, and then rowed the skiff across to the sandbar. It was a good place for traps. The muskrats liked to burrow into the sandy banks.

The first trap he checked yielded only a mink. It, too, had been looking for muskrat. He tossed it aside. Old Man would have treated it carefully, its pelt a prize, but it was no good for eating, so he didn't bother with it.

He pushed farther along the shore. Nothing. And nothing again. The gnaw in his belly grew as he worked his way along. He had circled the lake and was nearly back at the cabin and still he had found nothing. He would row back out into the lake and try for some fish, he decided, despite the fact that his net was full of holes and his hands didn't seem to have the knack of fixing them. The best he could do was to fish with a pole, but it took a long time to pull in only a fish or two. He would use some of the spoiled sweet meat as bait.

He pulled the skiff up on shore and shuffled past the cabin to the clearing behind, panting heavily as he climbed over the dune that screened the root cellar from view. As he crested the hill his eye caught a glimpse of something that was a strange colour, a colour that didn't belong here in the woods. He didn't know what it was called, just that it belonged to no critter that he knew of. He crept closer. It was a piece of cloth and it was lying beside a bear trap that he had set underneath one of the bushes that screened the door to the stone hut. Whatever had been caught in the trap had managed to free itself and had left the cloth behind.

The critter had made a distinct trail as it left the clearing, easy enough to follow, up over the dunes and down again. At the top of the third rise it must have fallen and gone sliding down the sandy slope. It would be hard walking these dunes with an injured leg. The trail led toward the smaller lake, but the critter had never reached the shore. There, lying face down in a small clearing, was more sweet meat.

He approached cautiously, but the critter didn't move. He could see that it must have hit hard when it fell down the hill. There was a large gash on one side of its head and quite a lot of blood in a pool underneath it. He found a largish branch to poke it with. It moved then, and opened its eyes, and when it saw him it tried to scramble away, but it was too weak to move far. This would be very good meat, he could see. The critter was fat and, most important, it wasn't dead yet. *Don't eat the dead meat. Just what you find in the traps or what you seen die.*

He settled back on his haunches. He would wait patiently until it died, just like Old Man said to do, and then he would eat well again.

Chapter Twenty

Custom remained brisk at Temperance House. Guests continued to arrive in order to consult with the famous Mrs. Elliott, and there were a few farmers and tradesmen who were of a temperance persuasion who came to Wellington for business reasons and needed a place to stay. Now, however, they also had occasional guests who arrived not for the rooms, but for the dinners, as word of Sophie's talents spread. And the meeting room had been booked again for that evening.

The master of the Orange Lodge had been correct; the members did indeed grumble about the lack of spirits at their meeting, and he had quickly made arrangements with the Wilman Hotel for the use of their ballroom the following Saturday night.

Daniel hadn't expected the Lodge to return to Temperance House, but it seemed that the Orangemen had managed to turn the tables on the Agricultural

Society — the society was now forced to look for other premises for a lecture they had planned for the same evening. They approached Daniel and asked if they could hold it at Temperance House.

"Well, this is all right, isn't it?" Daniel had said when he gleefully reported the news to Lewis. "It'll keep us hopping, what with all the guests right now, but we're in much better shape than we were for the first meeting."

Chairs were not an issue this time. The Agricultural Society lectures nearly always drew a reasonable crowd, but they appealed mostly to farmers, and any of those who also belonged to the Orange Lodge would probably opt to go to the livelier gathering at the Wilman instead.

Nor was Lewis instructed to stand in the hall until refreshments were called for. The society president made it clear that any of the hotel guests and staff were welcome to sit in. Their guests were duly informed of this at breakfast, but none of them seemed particularly interested when they discovered that the subject of the evening's lecture was to be the latest improvements in farm implements. It was a specialized subject, to be sure, but Lewis, ever-thirsty for whatever knowledge came his way, found that he was looking forward to the talk.

The guest lecturer was a fussy little man with a huge handlebar moustache who spent most of the afternoon setting up a magic lantern with which to illustrate his comments.

Lewis's prediction that the lecture would be lightly attended proved to be accurate. Only twenty or so people filtered into the room, but to Lewis's surprise, Clementine Elliott was one of them. Maybe he shouldn't have been so surprised — no doubt her evenings were dull. She seemed disinclined to sit with the group of guests who commandeered the sitting room every night after supper, instead keeping herself to her room. Probably any diversion would be welcome, even one that had so dry a topic.

The lecturer reported breathlessly that he had received reports of a new, improved hand-powered threshing machine — the esteemed manufactory of Barrett, Exall and Andrews of Reading, England, were poised to introduce this wonder to the North American market. He discussed this miracle of modern agriculture for a full twenty minutes before moving on to the next topic, which was the advent of a portable steam engine designed for farm use.

"This is used mostly for belt work," he reported. "Threshing, winnowing, chaff cutting, root pulping, cake crushing ..." On and on he droned, outlining in detail how the engine could be used for a myriad of farm tasks.

The farmers in the audience appeared to find the information fascinating, but Lewis soon found his attention wandering from the subject of zigzag harrows and new kinds of seed drills and he began to pay closer attention to the lecturer's manipulation of the magic lantern. Any of these types of shows Lewis had seen before had used glass plates through which the light shone the image onto the wall across the room. The images could be made to appear to move using this method, but only from side to side and in a jerky, unrealistic manner. This man, however, had mounted his device on some sort of roller behind a screen, and he moved the entire lantern back and forth, a technique that gave the projected pictures a more lifelike sense of movement. Lewis resolved to ask him about it after the lecture.

He had been kept busy with serving the refreshments immediately after the man had finally finished talking, so there were only a handful of people left in the room by the time he got the chance to ask his questions. To his surprise, Clementine was still there, sitting in the same chair she had been in all evening.

The lecturer was only too happy to explain how his lantern worked.

"Yes, many magic lanterns use glass frames, and you can make the image seem as though it's moving, but as you noted, it's not a very realistic movement, because there is no depth of field."

Lewis must have looked puzzled at this, because the man explained further. "In real life, objects don't just move from side to side." He demonstrated by picking up one of the wine glasses that had not yet been cleared away. He moved it from right to left in front of Lewis. "Real objects also move up and down and toward and away." Now he held the glass out to Lewis, as if offering him a drink, then pulled it back toward himself, as if to take a sip. "You see? With the rollers you can vary the size and pace of the pictures and make them seem more lifelike."

"What are the mechanics of the lantern itself?" Lewis asked.

The lecturer was only too happy to open the back of the device for Lewis to examine.

"This particular *camera obscura*, or should I say more properly *laterna magica*, uses a double-image device. It is this, combined with the rollers, which allows manipulation of the camera itself. A skilled operator can then more closely imitate the movement of real life. So, the light from the lamp" — here he pointed to the oil lamp that had been set on a table directly behind the camera — "enters the box, providing the illumination of the glass plates. The light shines through them and exits the camera," — he indicated the aperture at the front of the box — "and shines onto a flat surface, in this case the wall, some feet away from it."

"What is the mirror for?" Lewis had practically stuck his head inside the box to look at it.

"Oh, if you don't have a mirror, the image comes through reversed," the man said. "Everything would appear to be backward and upside-down. This, like so many things we don't understand, was originally ascribed to some sort of natural law and was thought to be an insurmountable problem. Then as time went on, someone realized that if the image was reflected in a mirror, it would project in the correct manner."

"I hadn't realized that," Lewis said. "Upside-down you say?"

"In the old days, of course, the only source of light strong enough to effectively project pictures was the sun, so magic lanterns were used only in the daylight. Now, with our superior lamp oils, it's not only possible to operate them at night, but in some respects it's better, as you can more effectively exclude other light sources. The roller system is a vast improvement in terms of making the images move more realistically, but we have a long way to go, I'm afraid, before we can ever match the effect of projecting a real object."

"It's possible to do that?"

"Oh, yes." The man chuckled a little. "When the camera obscura first came into use, many unscrupulous people used it to dupe the unwary. Some scoundrel would set up in a darkened room and when he had assembled an audience, a confederate would move around in front of a pinhole light and it would appear that a ghostly image was in the room. The unwary audience could be convinced that spirits were being called back from the dead."

Lewis was aware of someone pushing back a chair, and then of someone walking away. When he looked around, he realized that Clementine Elliott had abruptly left the room.

"Is it possible to make an image that would be life-size or something approaching life-size?" Lewis asked.

"It all depends on the focal length of the lens used," the lecturer replied. "With a portable camera like this one, the pictures remain fairly small. The longer the lens, the larger the enclosure would be the rule of thumb. Not terribly practical for casual use, I'm afraid."

Lewis thanked the man for his trouble in explaining the inner workings of his contraption and bade him goodnight.

He lay awake a long time that night, digesting the information he had gathered at the lecture. It was now clear to him how Clementine had produced the ghostly image on the wall. The curtains she had hung across part of the room obviously concealed a camera obscura, and she required Horatio to be present for her sessions, not as a chaperone, but as a living image, projected on the wall by the natural light from the window. She had been unable to solve the problem of the reversed image, however. The size of the mirror required to correct a life-sized image would present far too many difficulties for a travelling show. The camera itself must fold down somehow, in such a manner that it would fit easily in a trunk.

Somewhere she must have come by a general description of Mrs. Sprung's daughter, and by designating Amelia as the conduit through which the other spirits spoke, she was able to convince any other questioners that contact had been made. Lewis didn't know if Horatio assumed other disguises — he had only attended the one session — but he assumed that by wearing various wigs and hats and varying the pitch of his voice, the boy could represent almost anybody, depending on what Clementine had been able to find out about the circumstances of the questioner. He wondered where she had discovered Mrs. Sprung's recent loss, and then he realized that she seemed to be on excellent terms with Meribeth Scully — Meribeth, who heard everything that went on in the village, and passed the information on without a second thought.

There were other aspects of Clementine's performance that still puzzled him, however. He had no explanation for the wispy streams of matter that had emanated from her ears or for the strange mirror-writing she had exhibited. Her voice had changed dramatically as she spoke, as well, but this could be a theatrical trick, easily acquired with a little practice.

His conviction that it was all just a parlour trick now became a certainty. He wondered if there was any way he could sneak inside Mrs. Elliott's sitting room to examine the camera she had obviously set up there. He was already sure of the method, but he was keenly curious about the mechanics of the device, and perhaps closer examination would reveal the answers to his other questions, as well.

But the sitting room doors were always firmly locked. He supposed he could attend another session, but the deceptive tricks would already be in place for the willing victims. He could scarcely bluster in and start tearing down curtains or rummaging under the table. Daniel would consider that a gross violation of his guests' privacy and the rules of hospitality, and it was, after all, Daniel's hotel. The alternative was to break into the room somehow.

He wondered if he was being obsessive again, like he had been when he suspected Renwell of murder. It certainly seemed within his character to become so, and it was a trait that he had vowed to guard against. Breaking into a room in order to satisfy his curiosity would definitely fall into the category of obsession, he decided. Then he wondered if he should bother doing anything at all. Now that Hiram Elliott had died, it remained only to settle his estate, and no doubt Mrs. Elliott would soon be on her way to somewhere else, taking her outrageous activities with her. As he drifted off to sleep that night, Lewis resolved to put the entire matter out of his mind.

Chapter Twenty-One

Mr. Gilmour did not appear at breakfast the next morning. This was odd, as he had yet to miss a meal, and had appeared to enjoy his food even on the days when it was poorly cooked. There was still no sign of him long after the rest of the guests had drifted in and taken their seats, and when the breakfast hour had come and gone without him, Lewis remarked to Daniel how unusual this was.

"Did he say anything about going out early?"

"No," Daniel said. "Of course, he doesn't say much about anything, so I suppose it's possible that he had an early appointment, although I don't know where, since I've never been able to discover his business here in the first place." It remained a sore point with Daniel that Mr. Gilmour had refused to confide in him. "I wouldn't worry about it. He'll probably be back in time for dinner."

But he wasn't, and none of the other guests could recall when, exactly, they had last seen him.

"I'm sure he was here for supper last night," Daniel said. "I distinctly remember him remarking on the excellence of the pumpkin pie."

"Perhaps we should go and knock on his door," Lewis suggested. "He may be ill and in need of assistance."

But there was no answer when they knocked. When Lewis tried the handle, the door was unlocked. He swung it open tentatively.

"Mr. Gilmour? Are you here?" Lewis called. "Are you all right?"

There was no reply. The room was empty. Gilmour's valise was on the chair, however, and his hairbrushes were neatly lined up on the washstand.

Lewis looked at Daniel and shrugged. "I don't know where he's gone, but he must be intending to return. He's not lying here in distress of any sort, so I don't see that his whereabouts are any of our business, do you?"

"I guess not. It just seems so odd."

They closed the door and descended to the kitchen, where Sophie had begun to serve the family dinner. She dished up the main course and passed the plates. Lewis noted that Francis had taken care to sit down last, so that there was room for Sophie beside him at the end of the table.

"I don't suppose there's any of that pumpkin pie left, is there?" Daniel asked.

"What pumpkin pie?" Sophie's brow wrinkled in puzzlement.

"The pumpkin pie you made for supper last night. It was excellent, and I was hoping there might be a sliver left."

"We didn't have pumpkin pie last night. We had apple cobbler."

Now it was Daniel's turn to be puzzled. "Well, we had it one night this week, didn't we?"

"Yes, we had it Friday night."

Lewis looked at Daniel. "Are you sure it was the pumpkin pie Mr. Gilmour liked so well?"

Daniel nodded.

"That means he's been missing for more than a day."

"What do you think we should do?" Daniel asked.

"I'm not sure." A guest was well within his rights to go off and do whatever he wanted and was under no obligation to inform anyone when he did so, but it was generally considered a courtesy to let the inn-keeper know, especially where meals were involved. But supper the night before had been a hurried affair, because of the meeting upstairs, and Lewis could not recall with any degree of certainty whether Gilmour had been present in the dining room or not.

"You don't suppose he's taken a powder?" Daniel said anxiously. "He's run up quite a bill."

It was possible, Lewis supposed. It was true that some of Gilmour's personal belongings were still in his room, but they had no way of telling whether or not everything was there. What were a set of hairbrushes and a valise against the amount that was owing for the room? And they hadn't even looked inside the valise.

For all they knew, it could be sitting there empty, a decoy to cover his departure.

"Let's look around his room again. We'll be a little more thorough this time."

But the valise was full of clothing, along with a number of letters bundled together with string. In the drawer of the washstand they found a tin of moustache wax and a container of hair pomade. There was no sign of his overcoat or the tall hat he wore when he went out, but as far as Lewis could tell, the rest of his effects were still there. It appeared as though Mr. Gilmour had had every intention of returning at some point.

"Should we inform someone?" Daniel asked. "I mean, I know it's only been a day or so, but what if something's happened to him? Should we let the constable know?"

"Why don't we talk to the other guests first?" Lewis said. "Maybe one of them can shed some light on his whereabouts."

He and Daniel discreetly canvassed the guests during the supper hour. Everyone was aware of the gentleman, they said — he was difficult to overlook, what with his brightly-coloured accessories — but no one could recall having seen him during the last two days.

"I'll ask around town tomorrow morning," Lewis said to Daniel. "If no one's seen or heard from him, I'll talk to the constable then."

* * *

The next morning Lewis went up and down the street asking about their missing guest. No one had much helpful information, except the postmaster, who informed him that Gilmour hadn't been to collect his mail since Wednesday or Thursday of the previous week.

"He gets quite a lot of it, you know," the man said. "And it's all from New York."

Lewis stopped in at the livery stable on the way back, but Gilmour had hired neither horse nor cart, nor, as far as anyone there could tell him, had he boarded any of the coaches. Wherever he had gone, he had apparently gone on foot. Up and down the main street Lewis asked everyone he met, and although most he asked could remember seeing Gilmour at some point within the last week, no one had any recollection of setting eyes on him within the last two days.

Lewis began to wonder how such a striking figure had managed to disappear without anyone noticing. Not even Meribeth Scully could shed any light on Gilmour's whereabouts. In fact, she seemed a little put out that she had no information for him.

Lewis decided it was time to report the disappearance to Constable Williams.

"Are you sure he hasn't just skipped out?" the constable asked.

"I can't rule it out," Lewis replied. "But his things are still in his room. I'm just a little concerned, that's all, and my brother-in-law and I both feel we would be remiss if we didn't say anything, and then subsequently discovered that he had met with an accident."

Williams nodded. "I'll ask around town about him, but I'm sure he'll turn up. If he returns to the hotel in the meantime, could you please inform me?"

Lewis wasn't sure what else he could do. Gilmour might well have gone out of town for a day or two and forgotten to let them know. But he couldn't get rid of a nagging suspicion that the disappearance might have something to do with Mrs. Elliott. Apart from the fact that Gilmour seemed to have been spying on her, there was no apparent connection between the two — unless Clementine Elliott really was the Madame LeClair from the New York newspaper, and Gilmour had followed her to Wellington, hoping to collect the reward that had been mentioned. But if that were the case, why would he have disappeared before he had a chance to collect it?

So much for putting the matter entirely out of mind, he thought ruefully.

Clementine wasn't at all sure what her next move should be. It was clear that the preacher had deduced the means by which she summoned the "spirits" that so enthralled her clients. She had no idea what would he do with the knowledge. He had been skeptical from the first, she knew, and had made no secret of his disapproval. In ordinary circumstances, his detection of her methods would have been a clear signal that it was time to leave, to pack up and carry on to the next place where there was a ready supply of bereaved relatives. But these were anything but ordinary circumstances.

More than ever, she missed her husband. They had always listened to each other's advice, plotted each move as a team, played to each other's strengths. She understood the importance of playing her role, of improvising only within the boundaries of the story that had been agreed upon, but this plot had unravelled somehow, and she was no longer sure what her role was. But she had been left no message, no instruction, no indication that the plan had changed. She had questioned Reuben closely, had made him go over the details many times, but he could shed no light on what had happened.

Sometimes in the dark of a sleepless night she wondered if her husband had deliberately abandoned her. She was no longer the young girl she had been when he'd scooped her off the streets of Boston. She'd not been on her own for very long when he found her, and she had not yet honed the skills she needed to survive. She'd picked the pocket of a prosperous-looking mark, but she had been clumsy and the man felt a tug as she removed his purse. He'd spun around and accused her. Suddenly there was a second man at her side, who proffered the purse to its owner.

"This fell from your pocket, sir, as you were walking," he said. "It's fortunate that I saw it fall. You should be more careful."

She had no idea how the purse had made its way from the sleeve where she had tucked it to the hand of the second man, but she was grateful that he had managed it. The owner of the purse glared at them, as if he knew that something was not quite right, but then he went on his way with a nod and a muttered thank-you.

Her saviour, who she now realized was quite a fine-looking young man, had taken her by the elbow and marched her down the street.

"If you're going to be a common cutpurse, you need to be better at it," he'd hissed in her ear. "I was able to remove only half the coins from his wallet before I had to hand it back. I'll split the take with you if you like, but you'll make far more if you come with me. I could use a pretty accomplice."

He'd introduced her to less risky methods of generating funds and she discovered that she had a talent for discovering secrets that were used to good effect in his schemes. They worked well together, and the partnership was further cemented when she fell in love with him. He had always seemed to return the regard.

But now there were fine lines gathering at the corner of her eyes and every day it was becoming more of a struggle to corset her body into the hourglass shape that showed her expensive dresses to best advantage. Perhaps her husband had tired of their partnership and had found opportunity to get away cleanly. But in her waking moments she couldn't take this explanation seriously. He would never have willingly left the boy behind. He doted on his son.

Perhaps he truly had met with an accident and she really was a widow. But if that were the case, where was the evidence? His body should have been found by now, somewhere, and then maybe she and Reuben would be able to come to some sort of arrangement. The way matters stood, however, she was in limbo, with no definitive proof of what had happened and no definite indication of what path she should follow. She knew that the sensible thing to do was to cut her losses and leave, but even that would be far from simple. Gilmour had been dogging her closely, but in some respects that made him easier to deal with. At least she had known who he was and why he was following her. Now, apparently, he had disappeared and she had no way of knowing if he had given up or had merely been replaced by someone new — someone she wouldn't immediately mark as a bounty hunter.

She had denied any knowledge of Gilmour's where-abouts when the innkeeper asked at supper the previous evening, but before the final dishes were cleared away she had sent the boy upstairs to Gilmour's room, with instructions to look for any correspondence that might shed some light on the situation. By the time she had finished her meal and retired upstairs, her son was back in their bedroom with a fistful of letters, some of them personal, but many of them from the old man in New York. These confirmed that Gilmour was a hired detective, but there was nothing to indicate that he had been instructed to give up the case. One letter noted that Clementine's husband had been tracked to Wellington, and another that he had vanished shortly thereafter. She found that the date of her arrival had been reported, but there was no hint that Gilmour had been replaced. Maybe he had changed his tactics. Maybe he was hoping that his absence would provoke a move on her part.

Until she knew for sure what he was up to, the safest place, and the one with the most promise, was Wellington.

In the meantime, she would destroy the letters and find some way to silence the preacher. She could try the time-honoured method, she supposed, one that she had used successfully before in order to get out of a tight spot. To be sure, he was religious man, but in her experience that sometimes made it all the easier. She would have been surer of this approach if he had been one of those men who scrambled to tip his hat to her. But she knew that her charms had so far failed to enchant him in any way, and she wished she hadn't seen the way his face softened when he looked at his wife. She had no idea what else to do.

Upon his return to the hotel, Lewis reported his conversations of the morning to Daniel, who appeared to be somewhat relieved that the constable was unconcerned.

"Well, I guess Gilmour will turn up," he said. "So, do we hold his room in the meantime?"

"I don't think we can do anything else until we have a more definite idea of what has happened to him, do you?"

"No, I guess not. As long as we're not stuck for the money he owes us."

Just then Sophie announced that they could begin serving dinner. She continued to conjure miraculous meals out of the kitchen, this noontime serving up a succulent chicken stew with fat floury dumplings. Daniel, in the meantime, headed upstairs. He had lingered too long over his morning tea break with Susannah, apparently, and had not yet finished cleaning the rooms. That left Lewis and Francis to manage the service by themselves, a task they performed adequately, if not efficiently, and they briskly cleared away the plates from the main course as soon as the diners had finished.

For dessert, Sophie had concocted a savoury pudding from the plums that Susannah had preserved in jars at the end of the summer. This was served hot, with a dollop of heavy cream poured over it. It was met with enthusiasm by their guests, but in an effort to appear efficient, Lewis balanced too many plates on his arm at once, which forced him to stand very straight and awkwardly lower each serving to the table. With all of his attention focused on making an uneventful delivery, Lewis failed to notice that Clementine was reaching for the plate at the same moment he was placing it in front of her. Her hand and the plate collided slightly in mid-air, sliding the dessert forward and causing a thick blob of the cream to land on the front of her dress.

Lewis apologized profusely as she leapt up and dabbed at the mess with her napkin.

"It's of no matter," she said. "But I wonder if you might bring me a jug of hot water after the meal, so that I might sponge the stain."

Lewis agreed and left Francis to serve the rest of the dessert as he scurried off to fill a jug from the reservoir at the side of the sink-room stove. He had assumed that Clementine meant him to take it to her in the dining room, but when he returned, she was nowhere to be seen.

"She's gone upstairs," Horatio said through a mouthful of pudding. He must have taken what was left of his mother's dessert as well as his own, for there were two plates in front of him. "She said to tell you to take the water up there."

Lewis was annoyed at having to climb the stairs. The carrying of pans and jugs up and down was one of the things that aggravated his aging knees, and he avoided it whenever he could. He had caused the current problem, however, and he supposed it was incumbent on him to deliver the means of rectifying it.

Clementine called to him as he crossed the hall. She was not in her bedroom, but in the sitting room next door, and the heavy scent of the herbs she burned during her spirit sessions still hung in the air. They would have to leave the windows open for weeks to get rid of the smell, Lewis thought, for no one would want to sleep in the room until it was gone.

Clementine had made no effort to hide any of her paraphernalia, although he noted that she quickly closed the door behind him. He could see a corner of what appeared to be a closet jutting out from behind the dark curtains. It was a much larger camera than the one the lecturer had used. That stood to reason; she needed to project a nearly life-like image in order to convince her patrons. There were wads of gauzy material on one chair, no doubt the materials that streamed from her ears when she assumed her trance-like state. How she made them move was still a mystery, but one that he needn't concern himself with. It was enough to know what it was.

He set the jug on the table and was preparing to leave her to her cleaning when she asked, "Did you bring a cloth?"

He hadn't. "I'll go and fetch you one."

"That's such a lot of trouble for such a small stain," she purred. "Perhaps if I could just borrow your handkerchief it would save you all those steps."

He dug in his pocket. Fortunately, he had grabbed a fresh one that morning and it was still pristine. He held it out to her, but she didn't take it as he expected.

"Just dip it in the water and bring it here," she said.

He moistened the cloth and again held it out to her. She had undone the top few buttons of her bodice and held the stained area away from her undergarments, which were plainly visible underneath.

"If you'll just rub it here," she said, "that should take the stain out."

He hesitated.

"Go on," she said, "I need both hands to hold the material taut. Otherwise the water will leak through underneath."

He stepped closer and dabbed tentatively at the stain. "Rub a little harder." She breathed the words in a husky voice and removed her hand from her bodice.

He stepped back. There was no mistaking the invitation she was extending, and he wanted no part of it. Surprisingly enough, he had found over the years that attempted seduction was almost an occupational hazard. Too often some lonely woman had misinterpreted his interest regarding the state of her soul as an interest in something else entirely. He had several times been the object of some unhappy woman's designs, and although he was often hopeless at discerning the nuances of courtship, he was adept enough at recognizing the signals of enticement. This was a trouble he didn't need.

Clementine stepped forward and closed the distance between them. "What's the matter?"

He noted that she no longer spoke with the high-pitched twang that irritated him so, but rather with the rich contralto voice that she had evidenced when calling spirits.

He knew he should turn and leave immediately. He had no intention of falling victim to her wiles, and the situation was compromising in the extreme, but this could also be a golden opportunity to gain some information. Curiosity won over caution.

"You're not really from the American south, I take it?"

She laughed. "Of course not. It's just a way to sound a little more exotic for my customers. It's one of many personalities I can conjure up. I can be anything you want, you know."

"Including a spirit guide?"

"Especially a spirit guide." She shrugged. "People see want they want to see. I just make it easier for them." She reached out and laid her hand on his arm. "And what could I make easier for you? It must be so hard for you, having to be so circumspect all the time. Wouldn't you like to let go for once?"

He grasped her hand and removed it from his arm, then let it drop by her side.

She changed her tactics at this rebuff. "I know you've been suspicious of me ever since I got here," she said. "Fair enough. Now you know you were right. It's all trickery. So the question is, what do you want in exchange for your silence? You can have anything you want, you know." She unfastened another button and pushed her bodice down over one shoulder. "Anything. You're a man in the prime of life, but your wife is an invalid. That must be difficult."

So she was prepared to offer a straight bargain, he realized. He would keep his knowledge to himself and she would offer up her body in exchange. It was no bargain as far as he was concerned. Had he been inclined that way, there had always been far more attractive women who put themselves in his path. He had never even been tempted. He had always known that Betsy was there for him and he wanted no one else, not even now when her ailing body had aged her beyond her years. He began to laugh.

"You're going to have to give me something besides that," he said.

Clementine was taken aback; he could see it on her face. She had been so sure that she could reel him in with desire that he wondered if there had been other preachers in other places who had fallen victim to her charms.

Her face grew hard. "What is it you want then? Money? I don't have much, you know."

"No, I don't want your money. Just information."

"Go on." She was wary and he was sure that she would divulge only what she had to. Never mind, it was a start anyway.

"I know how you produce the image on the wall. You do it with the magic lantern and I'm guessing Horatio assumes some sort of disguise for the projection. Wigs, hats, anything that will change his appearance?"

She nodded.

"How do you know what he should look like?"

"It boils down to the art of listening," she said. "If you listen hard enough you can discover almost anything about anyone."

This was true enough. In his role as a comforter of the soul, he had often been privy to the most astounding confessions.

"It helps to have a gossip handy," she went on. "The little woman at the dry goods store was an excellent source."

Of course. Meribeth Scully knew everything that went on in the village, and would be happy enough to impart it all in that breathless, conspiratorial way she had, especially to so exotic a confidante as Clementine Elliott. It was a technique he had employed himself when he tried to discover who had murdered so many young women, and he had pumped the voluble Mrs. Varney in Demorestville for information on more than one occasion.

"How does Horatio manage when someone is hoping to contact a grown man?"

Clementine sighed. "It's been difficult. My husband used to do those. We've had to be very careful without him and use whoever Horatio is playing to simply relay information."

When Lewis thought back, he realized that it had been "Amelia," now revealed as Horatio in a wig, who had mentioned the name Mary. It had all seemed so real, even though he hadn't spoken with her. People did, indeed, see what they wanted to see.

"And the emanations? I take it you do something with that gauze over there."

"Yes. There's a rather complicated network of strings attached to them. I can manipulate them to make it look as though they're streaming out from me."

"I deduced as much. I can't figure out the mirror writing though."

She smiled. "I've been able to do that since I was a small child. I have always preferred to do things with my left hand, but so many tasks are designed for the right. My parents insisted that I must learn to use my right hand as much as possible. I ended up being able to write with both. It's quite a party trick, you know. It's the one thing I do that is truly impressive."

It was so easy to see now how the trickery worked. It had even worked, for a few moments anyway, on Lewis.

"So is your name really LeClair?"

Her eyes narrowed. "It was foolish of Horatio to take that newspaper. He thought he was helping me by hiding it, but all he did was draw attention to it.

I destroyed it as soon as I found it. Was it you who searched my room then?"

"No. I found it by accident when I was turning the bed one morning. I'm not certain who searched your room, but I suspect it was Mr. Gilmour. How does he fit into this?"

"I don't know who he is. I know only that he's been following me."

"And you don't know where he might have gone?"

Clementine shrugged. "I have no idea."

Just then the door flew open and Horatio ran into the room. "Mama, Mama," he cried. "I waited for you downstairs, but you didn't come back." The boy stopped, a look of confusion on his face. Whatever he had expected to see, it obviously wasn't two people having a conversation. So that was the game, Lewis realized. Clementine had been prepared to go only so far, and had arranged to have her son interrupt them before she had reached her limit. He could hear other guests coming up the stairs and heading for their rooms. He had no wish to be discovered closeted with Clementine, or to be questioned about why his errand had taken so long.

"I'll leave you for now, but there are still some things I would like to know. Perhaps we can speak later?"

Clementine nodded, but he was uncertain how much more of the truth he would be able to force out of her.

* * *

There was still no sign of Mr. Gilmour the next day. Constable Williams had asked around the village, he said, but no one had noticed the man leaving. Lewis suspected that the constable hadn't overly exerted himself. After all, Gilmour was a stranger, and strangers have strange ways. His suspicions were confirmed when Williams said, "It looks to me as if he's skipped out and left your brother-in-law stuck for his lodgings," an opinion that was echoed by Daniel.

"Well, we'll just gather up his things and clean out his room," Daniel said. "I hope there's something of value there that can be sold if he's truly gone. Just goes to show you, someone may appear to be a gentleman, but appearances can be deceiving. After this, I'll ask for payment before the bill gets so high."

"I wonder if we might learn something from that bundle of letters he left," Lewis said. As much as he disliked the notion of reading someone else's correspondence, the fact that no one even appeared to be looking for Gilmour sat uneasily on his conscience. "At the very least there might be an address of someone we could notify."

"Or send a bill to," Daniel pointed out. "Excellent suggestion."

But when they went to Gilmour's room, the letters had vanished.

Lewis was certain he knew who had taken them, although he had no way of proving it. There was a connection between Gilmour's disappearance and that of Nathan Elliott's, he was sure, but unless he could persuade Clementine to confess to more than being a charlatan, he had no idea how to go about discovering what had happened to either of them.

Chapter Twenty-Two

Martha wondered if you always had to give something up in order to gain something. In spite of the fact that she still felt a little shy around him, she had been delighted when her father returned so unexpectedly. She loved her grandparents fiercely, but the sudden appearance of the long-lost father she had been told of made her feel more normal, like the other children she sat in a row with at school. Their conversations centred on what their pas had done or said, how strong they were, or how mad they had been over some misbehaviour. There were one or two who reported at times that they had been "whupped good," but they said this almost with pride, as if being "whupped" was proof of their father's regard.

When Francis had turned up at the hotel, Martha had been afraid that this meant that she would now be "whupped" on a regular basis. Her grandfather never laid a hand on her. He hardly ever even yelled at her, and she wasn't sure that she could bear being hit. Francis had seemed very gentle, though, and took no part in any decisions that affected her. She suspected that this might change soon. She knew that Sophie really liked Francis, and that he liked her in return. Maybe they would get married. That was all right with Martha because she liked Sophie, too, but she wondered if that would mean that she would have to live with them instead of with her grandma and grandpa. And she would be a "step" if that happened. Margaret Robison, who was two years older than Martha but still in the primary class, was a step, and she said it was awful.

"My stepmother makes me work all the time, and she whups me if I don't do it fast enough," she reported. "She's got all these little babies now and Pa makes an awful fuss over 'em. Me and Harry have to sleep in the shed out back and we have to get up early every morning and get the fire going and cook the breakfast so she don't have to do it. Harry says he's leavin' as soon as he's fourteen."

Martha privately felt that Harry's departure would be a welcome event, as he was one of the meanest bullies in the schoolyard. But Margaret's account worried her. What if Sophie married her father and had a whole lot of babies and she had to sleep in the shed? She thought that perhaps Grandpa could prevent this from happening if he was close by, but what if Sophie and Francis moved away and made her go, too?

She hadn't told anyone but Horatio that she had lost the coral necklace that Francis had given her. The last time she could remember having it was Saturday, the day they had found the muskrat trap. Grandma would be annoyed. She'd told Martha to put it away safely and only wear it for good so it wouldn't get lost. Grandpa would help her look for it, but he wouldn't do it without telling Grandma first, and then Francis would probably find out. She couldn't imagine her mild-mannered father getting angry with her, but all of the other children in her school seemed to think that getting angry was a father's primary function.

Horatio helped her look at first, but he became bored and impatient and wanted to hunt the Holey Man or go off and play with some of the boys instead. So Martha stopped looking. Maybe if she were willing to forego the necklace, she could keep Horatio. But if she didn't have the necklace, would Francis be so mad that he'd go away again? If Francis went away, did that mean that she could stay with her grandparents? But then she'd be fatherless again. She went round and round the argument dozens of times, but couldn't decide what the best bargain was. She only knew that somewhere along the line, she would end up losing something.

The wintry weather had abated over the previous few days. Although the temperature plummeted at night and made everyone grateful for the warmth of their stoves, the sun shone brightly and mid-afternoon temperatures had crept upward past the freezing point. The snow melted away entirely in the well-travelled areas. Where no one walked, it collapsed into sullen grey mounds against fences and buildings. The sun softened the ice, and open holes began to appear near the wharves and along the edges of the shore. Farther out into West Lake the surface glistened with puddles of melted water.

Lewis knew that Martha and Horatio often played down near the shore and realized he should caution them about venturing too far out onto the ice. He decided to bring the subject up that night at the supper table. This meal had become a pleasant evening ritual for them all, a time when they shared the events of the day and discussed their plans for the morrow. They were all far less hurried than they had been, and not as tired, now that Sophie had taken over in the kitchen and Francis had proved eager to earn his keep. The addition of the two made the mealtime conversation livelier, as well, although they often seemed to be addressing their remarks to each other rather than to the room in general.

Frequently it was Martha who amused them the most, with accounts of her adventures at school or with Horatio, but today the child had been uncharacteristically taciturn. Lewis was sure something was bothering her, and was surprised that she hadn't confided in him. She had always been so open and quick to spill out whatever was on her mind. Perhaps she was just growing up, but the thought that their old, easygoing relationship might be changing made him sad.

"So, what have you and the famous Horatio Joe been up to?" he asked.

Martha gave a little shrug of the shoulders. "Not much. We went down to the lake, but there wasn't much to do."

"I've been wanting to talk to you about that," Lewis said. "The ice is pretty punky with the mild weather. I hope you're careful and stay on the shore. In fact, it might be a good idea if you didn't go down there at all until it freezes up again."

She looked at him with alarm. "But we don't go on the ice unless we know it's safe."

"But how do you know it's safe until you go on it?" her father asked.

"We look for the footprints," she said. "If the Holey Man has crossed the ice, we know we can, too."

"The Holy Man? Who is that?" *Did she mean some other preacher or one of the priests from Tara Hall?* They were immediately recognizable with their long black robes. But what would one of them be doing at the lake?

"We don't know who he is. Just that he's holey."

Lewis struggled to understand the words from an eight-year-old point of view. "How do you know that he's holy?" He briefly considered halos, wings, or even miracles performed along the sandy shores of West Lake.

"Because of the holes in him," Martha said matter-of-factly.

Not *holy*, but *hole-y* he understood then, but it made no more sense to him than a halo would have.

"Holes? In his clothes, you mean, or his boots?"

"No. Well, yes, he has holes in his boots, but there's a big hole in his face, too. We don't know who he is, so

Horatio calls him the Holey Man. He has traps and he goes back and forth across the ice all the time. We see his footprints in the snow."

Sophie had at last finished dishing up their meal and joined them at the table. "The Holey Man," she laughed, "what an excellent description of him."

"Do you know who she means?"

"Well," she said, settling down happily beside Renwell, "I don't know what his name is, but everybody thinks he's the son of this strange old couple that lives somewhere over in the cedar dunes. They've been there for years. You see them once in a while when they check the traps that are close to this end of the lake. Once in a while the old man comes in with a bale of hides and trades them for sugar and tea, but not often."

Not an angel or a saint then, but an unfortunate, child of unfortunates.

"Does he really have a hole in his face?"

"And in his clothes, he's so raggedy," she said. "But yes, he does. You can see right up into his nose, if you can get close enough. He's like a wild animal."

A hare lip, then, and worse perhaps.

"He tried to talk to us one time," Martha said. "But he wouldn't get very close, and he was all drooly. He said something, but it was hard to figure out what it was."

"Poor thing," said Sophie. "It can't be much of a life back in the woods like that, but I don't expect things would be easy for him anywhere."

"He never comes to Wellington with his father?"

"Never. The old woman never comes either, and nobody ever goes near the cabin. They say there are traps set everywhere in the marsh and on the dunes, and none of them too well-marked. I know Dad always warned Martin and the other boys to stay well away, in case the old trapper decided to take a shot at them."

This was alarming information, and briefly Lewis considered banning the shore as a play area for the children. But then he realized that, other than from treacherous ice, there was probably little danger. The trapper would be unlikely to bother anyone so close to the village and the Holey Man — for Lewis was now unable to think of him by any other name — had proved to be unapproachable, even by the irrepressible Martha. Still, it did no harm for them to be careful.

"I want you to let me know if you're going down to the harbour," he said to Martha, "and you're not to go wandering along the sandbar. Stay close to the village, do you hear? And I think it would be a good idea if you just stayed right away from this Holey Man. In fact, if you see him down there, I think you should just come right back home again."

"Yes, sir," she said. "I don't think I want to talk to him anyway. There was some really icky stuff coming out of the hole in his face." She wasn't sure what Horatio's reaction to this directive would be, but she was tired of his obsessive quest for the odd creature anyway.

Lewis wondered if he should warn her about traps and how to look for them. The trapper would be hoping for muskrat, most likely. The traps would be light, set in the water at the entrance to their dens. It would be an easy matter to avoid them, if you knew what to look for. The trapper would have to mark where he had set the traps; otherwise, it would be difficult to find them again once a heavy snow had obliterated landmarks and drifted into a different landscape. The children most likely played in the open areas along the shore, not near the banks where the muskrats burrowed or in the weedy growth where they sometimes built their small lodges, poor replicas of the enormous mounds the beavers made, but Lewis decided he would take no chances. He would walk along the sandbar and see where they were. And then he would make sure that the children knew, too.

Chapter Twenty-Three

When they had finished washing the supper dishes and left the kitchen for their own small house, Lewis reached down for Martha's hand and gave it a squeeze. She left her hand in his, but there was no returning warmth.

She no longer needed supervision to ready herself for bed, but she always called down to him when she was ready to say her prayers. It was a task he cherished, a time when his granddaughter vouchsafed her secrets and sleepily asked questions about topics that puzzled her. That night, he slowly hauled himself up the steep flight of stairs to her attic room and sat down on the bed beside her.

"What's wrong, Martha?"

"What do you mean?" she asked, but her eyes looked away as she said it.

"I know something's bothering you. You haven't been chattering away like a chipmunk these last few days."

She shrugged.

"I know I tease you because you chatter, but to tell the truth, I miss it, and I have to think that something's wrong when you turn into a clam. Is it something at school?"

She shook her head.

"Is it something to do with Francis?" This was pure guesswork on his part, but Francis's return and its consequences was the thing that was bothering Betsy the most, so it was reasonable to assume that Martha had reached some of the same conclusions that her grandmother had.

"Sort of."

"Why don't you tell me about it."

She heaved a great sigh. *How awful to have the weight of such a load on your shoulders at such an early age*, he thought. He hoped he would be able to lift at least some of the burden.

"I lost my necklace," she said quietly.

"The one Francis gave you? I thought you had put it away and were only going to wear it for special times."

"That's what Grandma told me to do. But I didn't do it. I wore it all the time — underneath so nobody could see. And now I've lost it. I've looked and looked everywhere, but I can't find it." A tear rolled down her cheek. "If Francis finds out, do you think he'll be mad? Do you think he'll go away again?"

Lewis had forgotten what it was like to be a child, how easy it was to add two and two and come up with five, and to interpret the actions of adults in the light of schoolyard logic. He folded the little girl into his arms.

"No, my darling, he won't be mad, and if he goes away again, it won't be because of you, but for some other reason. Is this what's been bothering you all this time? You should have told me, so I could help you look."

She snuffled. "I know, but I thought you'd tell Francis. And I thought Grandma would be mad, because I didn't do what she told me."

"Well, you should have listened to her, but I promise you, she won't be mad. I'll tell her not to be, all right?"

"Yes, sir." There was a hesitation, though, and Lewis knew there was more.

"You like Francis, don't you?" he asked.

"Yes. And I like Sophie, too. But what happens if Francis and Sophie get married?"

What indeed, he thought. But he was astounded that even Martha appeared to have noticed the chemistry between the two.

She went on. "One of the girls at school has a stepmother, and she says it's horrible and she has to sleep in the shed and do all the work. If Francis and Sophie get married, will I have to go with them? I don't want to sleep in the shed."

Lewis had to fight to suppress a chuckle, but he could see that Martha was extremely worried by this prospect. "Listen, sweetheart, Francis travelled a very, very long distance to come back and find you. He loves you very much. I don't think he would make you sleep in the shed after going to all that trouble, do you? And Sophie is a lovely, lovely girl, and she's very fond of you, so I don't think she'd be mean to you either. And we don't know for sure that they'll get married, do we? After all, they haven't known each other for very long. Maybe they'll decide they don't like each other that well after all."

Even as he said it, he knew that there was an element of wishful thinking in his argument.

"But if they do, will I have to go with them?" she asked. "Because I'd rather stay here with you and Grandma."

"I don't really know, Martha. It's something I've been wondering about, too. But I have decided one thing — if Francis moves away and wants you to live with him, your grandmother and I will move with you, so we'll always be close by. We won't ever be so far away that you won't be able to see us whenever you want to. Would that make it better?" He hoped that what he told her was in fact true, for he couldn't imagine a life without her.

The smile that had been so elusive over the last days returned to the child's face. "Yes, sir." Then her face fell again. "But I still can't find my necklace."

"I don't like secrets very much. I think we should tell everybody, and then everybody can help look for it."

"Horatio helped for a little while, but then he got bored and wanted to look for the Holey Man. I think I lost it when we were playing down by the lake."

"Well, we'll have a good look around the hotel first, and make sure it didn't just slip off here."

"I was going to ask Mr. Gilmour to keep an eye out for it, but he never came back."

"Mr. Gilmour? Why would you ask him?"

"Because he was there. At the lake."

"When was this?"

"Saturday afternoon. I saw him down by the wharf. I'd have asked him then, but I didn't know it was lost then."

"Did he walk back to the hotel with you?"

"No. I said hello and he nodded at us, but then he just stood there looking at the lake."

What would Gilmour have been doing down by the lake? Probably, Lewis thought, the same thing he had been doing in the marsh — looking for something. And now someone needed to look for *him*.

He tucked Martha in and kissed her good night, but his mind was only half on what he was doing. The other half was wondering what exactly could have happened to their guest.

The next morning, when Francis heard the reason for Martha's listlessness, he did what he had wanted to do ever since he'd returned — he scooped her up in his arms and hugged her.

Lewis had not totally excused Martha from responsibility for her actions. He made her tell both her grandmother and her father herself. Betsy's eyes narrowed and her lips tightened when she heard that the necklace was lost, for after all, she *had* warned Martha, and the girl had disobeyed her. But Lewis forestalled her with a glance.

"Well," Betsy said finally, "I hope you understand now why you should have saved it for special."

Martha nodded, relieved that she was to receive no tongue-lashing to add to her misery.

She approached Francis right after the breakfast rush was over, when everyone else had left the table.

"I thought you would be mad."

"Oh, sweetheart, it's just something I thought you would like. I'm sorry you've lost it, but I'm even sorrier that the losing of it has made you so miserable. We'll see if we can't retrieve it. Don't ever be afraid to tell me things, though. I'm not sure what you could tell me that would ever make me angry with you."

She had hugged him back then, and the look on Francis's face made Lewis wonder how he had ever suspected this man of any crime.

Sophie and Daniel both promised to give the hotel a thorough search. Francis was still needed at the hotel in the mornings, but as soon as dinner had been served and the dishes cleared away, he and Lewis set off for the harbour. They had questioned Martha carefully about where she and Horatio had been playing, but when they reached the lake, Lewis realized that the children had roamed over a huge area, and the prospect of ever finding an object so small as a coral necklace was remote. Gilmour would be easier, if he were truly out there somewhere.

They picked their way along the sandbar, Lewis searching on one side, Francis on the other. They found nothing but a few glass bottles and a wooden spar that had washed ashore.

When they reached the channel that separated West Lake from Ontario, beyond which the scrubby poplars and marram grass began to give way to more substantial cedars and thicker underbrush, they realized they would have to cross water to go any farther. But the state of the ice made Lewis profoundly uneasy. There were puddles lying on the surface and he could see two big cracks that ran nearly all the way across. Granted, this time he could be sure of aid if he fell through — it was broad daylight, not a bone-shuddering cold night; there was little current here, not like the fast-flowing waters that had nearly sucked him down between Kingston and Wolfe Island; and it was such a small distance to cover, no more than a few steps, really, and in all probability it was only a few feet deep. Still, only with a supreme act of will did Lewis force his legs to take the first steps out onto the frozen surface. Francis waited until Lewis had reached dry land again, then skipped across in a few easy strides.

"Are you sure they came this far?" Francis asked. "Martha didn't say anything about crossing the channel."

"No, she didn't," Lewis said. "But she did say something about seeing Mr. Gilmour down by the wharf. I'm just wondering if he wandered this way for some reason. Let's climb this hill. We may be able to get a better view of things."

The two men clambered up the sandy slope until they crested the dune. From this vantage point they could see almost all of West Lake. Off to the right, Lewis spotted a plume of smoke drifting in the air, but it was impossible to tell where, exactly, it was coming from, although it was most likely chimney smoke from one of the farmhouses across the lake. Wellington lay over to their left, the village seeming small from this distance, its buildings huddled along the shore. As they looked to the northeast, the structures became fewer and were punctuated by the barns that belonged to the farms that fronted the lake. Lewis could just make out the Elliott house, a short field away from the water.

From this perspective, he realized that West Lake was, in fact, nearly two inland lakes, bisected almost entirely by the islands and the long point of land that thrust out from the mainland opposite them. The marsh filled the part of the lake between the peninsula and the mainland, with the islands spilling out into the open water from there. He wondered if the entire lake would be filled in after a hundred or so years. Or perhaps it would take a thousand, he didn't know; but even now, if the ice was solid enough, it would be but a short distance from the Elliott farm to the peninsula or to one of the islands.

When they had been looking for Nate Elliott, he had dismissed the notion that the injured man had headed south toward this lake. He would have been spotted, they had all thought, if he had crossed the main road. But what if he had somehow got as far as the marsh, or staggered across to one of the islands and finally succumbed to his injuries there? But no, the lake had not been frozen then. It would have to have been the marsh. If so, it could be months, or maybe even years before anyone found his body.

It seemed impossible that he could go so far unremarked. Except that it really wasn't that far at all when you got out here and saw the geographic relationships from a different vantage point. And what if he hadn't wanted to be seen, if he had for some reason taken advantage of the opportunity to slip away? Lewis knew that Clementine was a fraud and Nate had been her partner in it. What if there was more chicanery involved here? He wondered if Gilmour had reached the same conclusion.

"I don't see much of anything," Francis said. "Should we head back?"

Lewis hesitated. If Gilmour had come out here, something had certainly happened to prevent him from getting back. They could at least go on a little farther to try to find out what it was.

"Let's keep going for a bit," he suggested.

The sandbar was wider and the hills taller on this side of the channel, and cedars thrust their way up through the tough grass. These grew thicker as they progressed, and in places the overhanging trees forced the men out over the water. The ice underneath their feet was brittle and apt to crack suddenly. Here and there they could see markers that signalled traps and the piles of brush that served as dens. Muskrats would find the sandy soil here to their liking, and the marshy areas would provide plenty of food.

As they worked their way along the shore, they could see evidence of human presence, as well, in the form of an occasional footprint that had been frozen in the mud and patchy snow cover. The marks were too large to have been made by Martha and Horatio, who claimed not to have ventured this far anyway. Perhaps they were the tracks of a hunter or trapper, or maybe the mysterious Holey Man, who, according to the children, wandered this way regularly. There were no returning prints to indicate anything but one-way traffic.

The men stopped to rest for a moment when they reached a clearing — an area of springy grass that had held its own against the cedars.

"Why is it that every time I go somewhere with you, there's ice involved?" Lewis grumbled, wringing out the bottoms of his pant legs. They had become soaked when the ice had given way in their trek along the shore.

Francis laughed. "At least it's nicer weather today. That was a raw night at Wolfe Island. And, by the way, why would Mr. Gilmour have come along here? It's not exactly the place someone would choose for a casual stroll."

Lewis realized that he needed to set aside any lingering reservations he had about his son-in-law and tell him at least a little of what he suspected.

"I think he's been following the Elliotts. I'm certain he's been trailing Mrs. Elliott at any rate, and he may have thought he could find out what happened to her husband."

"Out here? But why?"

Briefly, Lewis outlined what he had discovered so far — his knowledge that Clementine's contacting of the dead was a trick, and his suspicion that the

Elliotts were, in fact, the LeClairs mentioned in the newspaper.

"If so, there's a reward offered by the man they bilked in New York. I'm wondering if Gilmour decided to collect it. The only thing that puzzles me is why he hasn't turned Mrs. Elliott in long since."

"Because American law has no jurisdiction here," Francis replied. "And none of her Canadian customers has put in a complaint. As long as she stays on this side of the border, Gilmour wouldn't be able to touch her, short of kidnapping her and hauling her back to New York." He reddened a little. "It sort of works both ways, you know."

Of course. Lewis should have realized that. But then he had little experience with the ins and outs of border crossings or international crime. Francis, who had fled across that same border as a rebel would understand much better the implications.

"If what you think is correct, maybe Nate knew Gilmour was on his trail and arranged his own disappearance."

That was exactly what Lewis was beginning to think. Gilmour had arrived at Temperance House two or three days before Nate Elliott had gone missing. The timing was certainly right. And then Clementine had arrived, just at the point when Gilmour must have considered the whole thing a lost cause. Why had she come to Wellington, if her husband had gone to such pains to cover their tracks? Surely, if their theory was correct, her husband would have arranged to meet her somewhere, after the fact of his death had been assumed, and they could have gone merrily on their way. There was a piece missing somewhere in this puzzle, but Lewis couldn't find it.

He rose and stepped away from the clearing, but with the first step his right leg plunged through the ice, soaking his boot and leg to the knee.

"Why is that when we're on the ice together, you're always the one to go through?" Francis commented mildly. "You seem to have a real talent for it."

Lewis's retort died on his lips. There was something in the water. He had kicked against it when he pulled his foot away. As he broke a little more of the ice away around the hole, he discovered it was a small leg-hold trap, of the sort used for muskrat, fully baited and unsprung.

"You're lucky you didn't step into that," Francis said when he saw it. "It wasn't marked at all. It wouldn't be much fun out here with an injured leg. Somebody would have quite a time getting back home again." Then he stopped to consider what he'd said. "You don't suppose that's what's happened to our missing Mr. Gilmour, do you?"

"Maybe."

It was an old trap that Lewis had found, covered with algae, and it had probably been there for a long time. That would explain why it wasn't marked — it had been set and forgotten. He wondered if there were even deadlier traps scattered around the lake. Maybe he wasn't the only person who had stumbled upon one.

After the discovery, the two men continued more cautiously, testing each step before committing their weight to it. The trees were thick here, and at times they were unable to see more than a few feet into the woods. It was little wonder that they nearly passed right by the clearing without noticing it, but Francis suddenly missed his footing and slid across the slick surface, almost going down entirely. At the last moment, he stuck out a hand to save himself from a soaking. From this low angle, he could see through the lower branches of the thick cedars that masked a small gap in the growth.

"Let's check up in there," he said, and they pushed their way through.

There was no question that someone had been there. Vegetation was broken and smashed and the snow was stained a reddish brown. Something heavy had been dragged to the opposite end of the clearing, where a trail disappeared into the woods.

"Someone's taken a deer, maybe?" Francis suggested warily, but he sounded unconvinced.

"I hope so," Lewis replied, "but somehow I don't think so."

Francis was about to follow the trail that led away, but Lewis hesitated. "Just a moment," he said. "Let me take a look around." *The necessary knowledge is that of what to observe*, Dupin had said in the Rue Morgue story. Lewis would observe, and hope that he would find the knowledge he needed. He followed the marks on the side of the hill up to the top of the dune. They appeared to be a long skid that ended abruptly at the stain on the ground. There was no blood — for Lewis was sure that was what it was — on the hill itself, just at the bottom. Something, or someone, had fallen, landing against a broken cedar stump, for there, too, he could see a stain that darkened the wood. A few feet away he discovered a boot print, but this was well away from the skid. Did whoever fell manage to rise and walk away? Or had there been a second person in that clearing?

Lewis looked more closely at the print. If it had been made by the trapper who supposedly guarded these woods, he would have expected him to leave the mark of a heavy, irregular tread of a homemade boot. This print was smooth, with very little tread at all — *a city boot*.

Had Nate Elliott been hunkered down here in the wilderness all this time? Had Gilmour somehow figured this out and been ambushed for his trouble? Suddenly, Lewis was profoundly uneasy at what they might find if they followed the trail that led away through the trees, and he wondered if they should return to Wellington for help. But he wasn't sure how he could persuade anyone that help was needed. A footprint in the snow and a brown stain wouldn't be enough to propel Constable Williams out of his lassitude. He and Francis would have to go ahead, but they would need to be very, very careful, regardless of whether it was Nate Elliott or the trapper waiting for them at the end of the trail.

The drag marks were easy enough to follow. Here and there, spots of blood marked the way. Then, on a low branch, Francis spotted a small jagged piece of cloth — the same brown tweed as Mr. Gilmour's overcoat. Lewis had walked right past it. *So much for making the necessary observations*, he thought.

"It looks like the branch caught on whatever was being dragged and ripped it away," Francis pointed out.

"Whatever or *whoever*," Lewis agreed. They moved even more cautiously after that.

The trail seemed to lead them deeper into the forest, following the contours of the great sand hills that Lewis knew lay underneath. In many places the soil was loose and tree roots lay in a tangle just beneath the surface, waiting to snag his foot and trip him up. He could see how easily someone might have fallen. He became winded as they climbed and then descended the dunes, and his left knee pained him with every step.

"Do you smell smoke?" Francis asked. Lewis sniffed the air, but could detect nothing until they had travelled another difficult hundred feet.

I'm too old for this, Lewis thought. *My body aches and my senses have all dwindled away.*

The trail appeared to be leading them away from West Lake and toward the windswept shores of Lake Ontario, an area that was unsettled and seldom visited.

The forest suddenly opened up to reveal another small clearing. In it stood a ramshackle structure that appeared to have been built of old cast-off boards and pieces of log. One side of the structure had collapsed, but a thick plume of smoke rose from the chimney on the side that remained standing.

The drag marks led straight across the clearing to the cabin door.

"I think we should be very careful here," Lewis said in a low voice. "I'm not sure who, or what, we're dealing with."

"Do you think it's Elliott? Has he been holed up here the whole time?"

"I don't know. But whoever it is either attacked Gilmour or at the very least dragged him off. Neither action speaks of anything but a desperate man."

"Why don't we circle around behind and see if there's another way in? I don't fancy bursting in the front door."

There was no back dooryard, as a small dune pressed its sandy bulk against the rear wall of the cabin.

"If we can get up on that, we should be able to see the whole clearing," Lewis whispered.

Francis nodded and they crept around the edge of the clearing as silently as they could. As they reached the top of the dune, they realized that it sloped sharply down on the other side into a small ravine before it rose again in yet another mound of sand. Stones projected a foot or two from the steep side, and as he slid down the bank, Lewis realized that a heavy oak door had been set into these stones.

"A root cellar?" Francis whispered.

Lewis was aware of a nauseating stench that seemed to emanate from behind the door. Something foul was hidden there.

There was no lock to bar entry; instead the door was held shut by two iron bars that slotted into brackets on either side. Lewis lifted these out and, holding his breath, jerked the door open. A disgusting odour rushed out, making his eyes water, and it took a moment for him to register what was inside. Two wooden barrels, homemade from the look of them, stood against the back wall. A third had fallen over and spilled its contents over the bone-littered floor of the cellar. Crudely butchered hunks of meat strewed from the mouth of the open barrel.

Lewis stepped inside for a closer look. The bones crunched unpleasantly under his feet. Some of them were very old, picked clean by the insects that no amount of stone wall could keep out. Some had bits of flesh still clinging to them.

Francis tied his handkerchief over his mouth and nose in an attempt to protect himself from the worst of the stench, and inched into the cellar behind Lewis.

"My God," he said, "some of this is human." He used his foot to flip over one of the chunks of flesh. At one end was what appeared to be the remains of a human foot. Lewis backed away from it hurriedly and slipped on the unstable footing beneath him. He fell squarely on his knee, the one that was already sore from their long trek, and he couldn't suppress a yelp at the pain.

"*Sshh!*" Francis said, but it was far too late for silence to save them. When Lewis looked up he was staring straight into the muzzle of an ancient musket.

Martha had described the Holey Man, but her childish account had not prepared him for the reality of the man's appearance. His mouth was a gaping hole and Lewis wasn't entirely sure that he had any jaw at all, for his flattened, fish-like face seemed to merge with his neck. His eyes were odd in some way, and full of his fury at their trespass. But none of these strange details could divert Lewis for long; most of his attention was claimed by the gun that was pointed at his head.

He sensed that beside him Francis was shifting his weight cautiously, as if he were making ready to spring. Lewis's knee protested with a stabbing pain when he moved, but he did the same, preparing to rise at the same moment. They could not both be shot, for it took time to reload the gun. Lewis thought he was most likely to be hit, being the most directly in the line of fire, and he steeled himself for the shock. He hoped that he could move fast enough to avoid injury to anything vital.

Even though he was ready for it, he was still a second or so behind the younger man when they moved. With a leap, Francis crashed into the Holey Man, knocking him down and sending the musket flying. Lewis rolled to his right and crashed into the corner where a small cascade of bones brought him face to face with yet another horror.

The skull had been scraped clean and the dome of the braincase had been cleaved in two, but it was still recognizably and unmistakably a human head.

Lewis had no time to consider the ramifications of his find.

His first impulse was to locate the gun, which had landed a few feet away from the doorway. He scrambled over to it. It had not been cocked or loaded. He threw it down again and went to help Francis, who was attempting to subdue the Holey Man, who howled and spat and kicked in a frantic effort to get away. Lewis pinioned the arms while Francis gained a stronger hold on the man's feet. As soon as his limbs were immobilized, the Holey Man stopped struggling and went limp. His howls subsided to a whimper. Francis flipped him over so that he was lying face down, wrenched his arms behind him, and held him immobile with a knee in the small of his back. In one part of his mind, Lewis wondered where his son-in-law had learned such manoeuvres, but it was a question that would have to wait. Right now he had other, more pressing questions to ask.

Gingerly he picked up the skull he had found and set it down in front of the Holey Man.

"Oh, my God," Francis said. "Did you do this?" and he gave his prisoner's arms a wrench.

"Found it," the Holey Man whined. "Old Man say dead meat no good. Not in woods, in marsh. Belly hurt. Not dead long." But with his horrendous and deformed mouth, this statement was unintelligible to his questioners and sounded like nothing more than a long nasal whimper.

Lewis cautioned Francis with a glance. "We won't get to the truth of the matter by frightening him."

He crouched down in front of the Holey Man, whose features were truly monstrous, a twisted parody of a normal face, the eyes lash-less above the deformed nose and mouth. The ears were wrong, too; tiny and set forward in a peculiar way. In fact, everything seemed peculiar, and Lewis suspected that the horrendous hare lip was only a part of what was wrong with this poor creature. A number of pelts of varying origin — muskrat, beaver, fox, coon — had been haphazardly sewn together into a sort of cloak that he wore over his shoulders, and a hat of similar design lay nearby. But Lewis did not see much evidence of the "holey" clothing that Sophie had described. His pants were of good quality and intact, and under the furs he sported a brown jacket of very familiar design. The boots he wore were too small for him, but the caps had been sliced so that his feet would go in, and his bare webbed toes stuck out through the slits. Before they had been mutilated, the boots had been first-quality — city boots. Lewis began to get a very uneasy feeling about where these articles had come from.

"What's your name?" he asked softly.

There was no answer. Lewis wasn't sure if he had been heard so he reached out to turn the man's face toward him, so that he would understand he was being addressed, but the Holey Man flinched at his hand's approach, so he let it fall. His gesture did, however, gain the man's full attention, and he repeated his question in a louder voice.

"What's your name?"

"*O-ee.*" Lewis struggled to understand the words. He realized that the Holey Man's lips had difficulty closing over the gaping hole that was his mouth. "*O-ee. O-ee.*" And finally with an enormous effort, "*Bo-ee.*"

"Boy? That's your name? Just Boy?"

The Holey Man peered at Lewis through the shaggy mass of hair hanging in front of his eyes.

"Old Man call me …" he seemed to have to think a little, "Old Man call me Idiot."

Lewis understood only the last word, and felt a twist of pity for this poor malformed creature.

"May I call you Boy? Is that the best name?" The Holey Man obviously understood him, for he nodded his assent. "Where did the head come from, Boy?"

"Ra." He jerked his head to the right to indicate a place away from the cabin.

"Are there any more?"

The Holey Man didn't answer, but his eyes darted back toward the cabin.

"I wonder if Gilmour's in the shack."

Francis heaved the Holey Man to his feet and half-dragged him up the dune and down the other side to the cabin. Now that they were closer, it was evident to them that the shack was in the process of falling down. When a portion of the roof had collapsed, it had smashed most of one wall beneath it, causing the entire structure to lean alarmingly. It wouldn't take much, Lewis thought — a heavy snow load and it would come tumbling down.

When they went inside, it took his eyes a few moments to adjust to the dimness of the interior, but his awareness of the stench was immediate. It was the smell of half-cured hides and offal and of bedding and pots gone unwashed for a very long time. There was a richer and more immediate odour, as well, one that was far more pleasant, although not nearly strong enough to mask the essential fetor of the room. It seemed to be coming from the iron pot that steamed on the crude hearth in the corner.

The wall beside the fire was a jumble of broken logs, boards, and bark shingle. No attempt had been made to clean it up or repair it in any way, and there were a number of gaping holes in the rubble where the wind blew through. This would be a sad place to spend a winter, Lewis thought to himself.

"Oh, my God. Look." Francis was staring up at the ceiling. There were several joints hanging from the rafters of the shack. Most of them were unrecognizable as anything but hunks of meat, but one shoulder still sported most of an arm and Lewis thought that one piece might be a buttock.

Francis began to retch. Lewis himself felt the bile rise in his throat. He had seen many terrible sights in his time — from the dreadful wounds inflicted on the bodies of soldiers to the white and bloated dead in the aftermath of battle; he had seen young women strangled and mutilated by an insane murderer and he had seen that same murderer struggle and kick as the life was choked out of him — but he had never seen anything quite like this deliberate degradation and destruction of human flesh.

He drew his handkerchief to cover his nose, and continued his inspection of the cabin. The fireplace was a crudely built pile of fieldstone with a wooden chimney that had been twisted askew by the fallen roof. A large homemade wooden ladle lay on the hearth beside several stone jars that appeared to be full of a greasy fat. Lewis grabbed the ladle and stirred the contents of the iron pot that had been set to simmer over the fire. Its principle ingredient rose to the top. Like the grisly

relic he had discovered in the root cellar, the top of the
skull had been cracked in two, but the eyes were still
intact and yellowed teeth protruded from underneath
a bristly moustache. It was, without a doubt, the missing Mr. Gilmour. Gagging, Lewis quickly withdrew the
ladle and the head sunk back into the simmering stew.

The Holey Man had been watching without
expression during this survey of the cabin. It was only
when Lewis neared the corner opposite the fire that
he seemed to become agitated again, and Francis was
forced to restrain him once more.

There were a jumble of items in a pile against the
wall — a ragged pair of man's trousers and the filthy
remains of a woman's dress. The trousers were gigan-
tic, far too large to have ever fitted The Holey Man. It
made no sense for him to have kept the dress. And then
a possible explanation struck Lewis — these must be
the relics of the trapper and his woman — the people
with whom the Holey Man had lived. His parents, he
supposed. He wondered how they had died. Killed
when the roof collapsed, maybe, and the poor raggedy
creature had been left behind to fend for himself?

There were other pieces of apparel, as well,
Gilmour's orange cravat, some men's underthings, a
pair of leather boots, and another pair of trousers, the
leg torn and covered in dried blood — trousers that
matched the coat now worn by the Holey Man. No,
not the Holey Man, for that was the name others had
given him, this was Boy.

As Lewis shifted the clothing to one side with
his foot, Boy began to howl again. There were more

treasures underneath the clothing — Gilmour's gold pocket watch and Martha's coral necklace. Lewis's stomach turned at the thought of his granddaughter coming anywhere near this fetid hole, but then he realized that, in fact, she hadn't. She had lost it when they were playing by the shore. The Holey Man — Boy — must have found it and brought it here to add to his hoard. Lewis hesitated for a moment; he knew he should leave things as they were. Everything was evidence. But the necklace had no bearing on what had happened here, he judged, and so he palmed it and put it in his pocket. He hoped Boy hadn't noticed.

There was more — three red buttons, a child's toy soldier, a marble — things that might have been lost by others along the shore and found by Boy on his trap route around the lake. In addition, there was a brown calfskin folder. Inside was a sheaf of documents, legal papers from the look of them, but Lewis recognized none of the names on them, save one — a handwritten agreement that had yet to be signed. It was a conveyance of property, assigning Nathan Elliott's share of his father's estate to his brother Reuben "in exchange for agreed services." There was no indication of what, exactly, these services consisted of.

Puzzled, Lewis returned the papers to the folder. Had all of them belonged to Nate Elliott, or only the one? If so, had Boy found it and, unable to read it, stuffed it into the folder with the others? If that was the case, where had the others come from? And did this mean that the skull and rotting meat in the root cellar was all that was left of the missing Nate?

Lewis was about to replace the papers when he realized that one side of the folder felt much thicker than the other. He pulled at a strip of leather along the side. It slid back easily, revealing a pocket underneath the flaps that had held the papers in place. Inside was a handful of banknotes, all of them American in origin.

"What do you think we should do?" Francis asked. "Should one of us go for the constable or should we try to take him in ourselves?"

"Maybe we should try to take him. I don't think either of us wants to have to stay here and wait."

As Francis turned to speak, the Holey Man saw his opportunity. One hard shove and Renwell went crashing to the floor. The Holey Man scrambled toward the door. Lewis threw himself in that direction, and only just closed his hand around the fleeing man's foot. The Holey Man kicked and Lewis lost his grip, but by this time Francis had regained his feet. He knocked the shaggy figure flat and blocked his escape route. The Holey Man slithered away from them, and seeing his exit barred, lunged toward one of the gaps in the rubble of the caved-in wall. Clawing at the broken logs, he tried to force himself through.

Francis slammed into him again and the Holey Man went flying toward the hearth. For a moment Lewis was sure he would land in the fire, but, arms flailing, he managed to avoid the flames, crashing instead into the iron kettle that hung above. The greasy contents spilled over the side and splashed over one of the man's arms. He spun round and round the cabin holding his hand and howling from the scalding pain.

Lewis tried to stop him. "We'll help you," he said. "Just stop and we'll put some cold grease on it. It will stop hurting so much then."

Francis and Lewis were so occupied with trying to calm this hysterical outburst that they failed to notice that the Holey Man's wild scramble had knocked one of the stone jars into the fire and dislodged part of the rubble wall. The flame flared as it found the grease, then the tinder-dry cedar shakes from the roof exploded in a flashover that ignited the wooden chimney.

They had not thought that the Holey Man could make more noise than he had already been making, but now he rushed forward with an ear-splitting scream and began trying to put out the fire with his bare hands. Lewis grabbed him by the shoulders and pulled him away.

"Get some water. Is there a bucket?"

There was, just outside the door, but by the time Francis located it and filled it from the lake, the fire had engulfed the entire wall of the cabin.

"This is useless, it's gone," he said. "Let's get out of here."

Together they hauled the Holey Man through the door. They thought he would calm down once outside, but he continued to struggle with them, and then in one frantic, twisting motion pulled away. He went straight back into the cabin, his howls still audible over the roar of the flames.

Lewis tried to go after him, but by this time the smoke was thick and the heat intense, and Francis pulled him back just as what was left of the roof fell in a storm of flame.

"You'll burn, too, if you go in there."

The Holey Man's screams ended abruptly and they knew there was no point in continuing to fill the bucket with water or to throw it on the burning cabin. They could do little but wait a safe distance away until nothing was left but a smouldering heap of charred wood. It was best to leave the constable to sift through the debris and retrieve what was left of the body, Lewis decided, if anything at all remained of Gilmour's head or the grisly meat that had been hanging in the cabin.

"We should go."

Lewis knew Francis was right. The fire was burning itself out and there was nothing more they could do. Wearily, they began the long trek home.

Chapter Twenty-Four

Clementine found the courtroom stiflingly hot. Picton Court House itself was a handsome enough building and she admired the solemn Greek-inspired portico that guarded its entrance, although she was disappointed to discover that the pillars were constructed of wood painted to look like stone, and not the real thing. From the outside, the courthouse appeared massive, as though it should have numerous spacious rooms dedicated to the pursuit of justice, and as the county seat, she supposed Picton was where all trials and inquiries were held. The room set aside for the hastily-called coroner's inquest, however, was small and airless, and grew increasingly uncomfortable as more and more people crammed in to hear the lurid details of the preacher's discovery. The choice of rooms had been deliberate, she realized; an attempt to limit the number of spectators who could be counted on to disrupt the orderly proceedings of the inquiry. She wondered that so many people had so little to do on a weekday morning that they would willingly attend a hearing whose details were already so well-known.

Whatever evidence had survived the fire, along with the contents of the root cellar, had been gathered up and taken into the village by Constable Williams and the group of men he had gathered to assist him. They had been prepared to find Mr. Gilmour's head. Although well-boiled, it had survived the fire. The preacher had told them about the other skull he had discovered, but to the constable's astonishment, the cellar yielded two more, well-buried at the bottom of the mound of bones. Dr. Keough had examined the find and notified the coroner. The coroner had then directed the constable to pack up all the bones and take them to Picton for examination.

Reuben had been asked to look at the skulls, in the hopes that he could confirm one of them as his brother's. He had been unable to do so. Clementine was grateful to him for at least sparing her that disturbing task, for there was no doubt in her mind that her husband, or at least his head, had somehow ended up in the bone pile in that cellar. Accident or misadventure was the only plausible reason she could think of to explain his failure to meet her at their rendezvous point at Niagara. Something had gone terribly wrong. She hoped the inquest would explain what.

Reuben had accompanied her to the courthouse as well, as befitted a brother-in-law, but she found no comfort in his presence. She sat, as impassively as she could, while the facts were presented, all the time wondering what she should do next.

Besides the skeletal remains, little evidence was discovered in or near the root cellar, other than a tall hat that had been found under a bush near a sprung bear trap. The only identifiable items taken from the cabin's debris were a marble, a toy soldier made of lead, and a gold pocket watch.

The innkeeper testified that he had often seen Mr. Gilmour in possession of a similar watch, and that in all probability the one found in the cabin was one and the same, although he couldn't be absolutely sure, he said, not having examined it closely while it was still being used by Mr. Gilmour.

Then the preacher took the stand. Clementine tensed. This man was too canny, by far, and knew too much already. Had he had time to search the shack before it caught fire? Who knew what he had found, or how much of what he knew he would disclose to the court?

He stated that he and his son-in-law had been looking for his granddaughter's necklace, which she had lost while playing along the sandbar. His granddaughter mentioned that she had seen Mr. Gilmour by the lake just prior to his disappearance, and so Lewis was alert to any evidence that the gentleman might have explored the same area. They had stumbled upon a clearing that showed clear evidence of a mishap, and had followed a trail which took them to the cabin.

Lewis described the root cellar they discovered and gave a brief account of their struggle with the gun-wielding creature who had confronted them. Another man would have made much of this, Clementine mused, but the preacher was very matter-of-fact, mentioning only those details necessary to give the jury a full picture of what had occurred.

Several people left the courtroom when he recounted the scene in the cabin and one woman fainted when he described the contents of the iron pot. The other spectators hung on his every word, eager to have the more sensational aspects of the case confirmed.

"And what led you to believe that the head was that of the missing Mr. Gilmour?" the coroner asked. "Is there any likelihood that it could have belonged to someone else?"

Clementine found it an inane question, but then she supposed that this was such a bizarre case that the coroner was anxious to do nothing that would attract criticism later.

Lewis replied that he had frequently seen Gilmour at his brother-in-law's hotel, and was familiar not only with his appearance, but with his effects, most notably his watch, his distinctive cravat and handkerchief, and his outer clothing, one piece of which had been appropriated by the man who had threatened them with a gun.

"Even though it was somewhat mutilated, there is no doubt in my mind that the head I found was the same one that had once been attached to Mr. Gilmour's body," he said. "It was of the right appearance, and I can't imagine that he gave up his possessions voluntarily."

There was a titter from the onlookers at this.

"And, apart from Mr. Gilmour," the coroner asked, "did you recognize any of the other remains that were discovered in the vicinity?"

"At the time, I was aware of only one other skull, and it was not identifiable as any particular individual," Lewis replied. "I discovered a sheaf of documents in a leather folder, and one of the papers bore the names of both Reuben and Nathan Elliott, but I didn't recognize the names of anyone else listed there, so although it's possible that the skull was Mr. Elliott's, the document was the only piece of evidence that would point to that conclusion."

Clementine jumped as Reuben clutched her arm.

"Shush, stop it," she hissed at him. "He can't know what it was about." She hoped she was correct.

"There were a number of other articles in the shack," Lewis went on. "Some buttons, the marble, for example — items that might have been discovered by anyone who rambled along the shore. I don't know if the folder is indicative of Elliott's presence or if it was merely something that had been found and added to the collection of trinkets."

Had Clementine been conducting the inquest, the next question would have been about the substance of the piece of paper with the Elliott name on it, but the coroner seemed little interested in this.

"And did the man you apprehended give any indication of who any of the skulls belonged to?"

"The man who occupied the cabin had a number of severe deformities, including a hare lip. This made him nearly impossible to understand, but he seemed to indicate that he had found the older of the skulls at some distance from the cabin."

"And this individual was already dead when he was discovered?"

Clementine wondered if she was the only one to notice the look of impatience on the preacher's face.

"I don't know. There is no way of telling what happened. As far as I could make out, he found both Gilmour and the other individual somewhere near his traps and he appeared to have processed them both in the same way that he dealt with the wild animals he caught. I suspect he thought that was the proper procedure. I don't believe he had any contact with civilized society and in all probability was unaware of our usual distinction between dead animals and dead people."

Clementine found this statement very odd. Lewis seemed to be defending the wild man in some way, giving him a rationale for his actions, as if he were sorry for him. There were depths to this preacher that she had usually found lacking in others of his profession, but then he had had much to deal with in his life, according to Meribeth Scully, whom she had pumped for information. He had tracked down a murderer and seen him hanged. He had testified once before to the unthinkable.

"How did the fire start?" the coroner asked.

"Having realized the extent of the degradation in the cabin, Mr. Renwell and I attempted to remove the man, with the intention of taking him to Wellington. He managed to free himself briefly and in his effort to exit the cabin, he apparently knocked some of the debris from the collapsed roof into the fire. I don't know how long the cabin had been there, but the wood was old and extremely flammable, and by the time we realized that it was burning, we had little chance of putting the fire out. We dragged the man to safety, but again he freed himself and went running back into the flames."

"And why, in your opinion, would he have done this?"

Clementine realized that this was one question the preacher hadn't expected to be asked, for he hesitated for some time before he finally said, "I don't really know why, but you must understand that this man lived in the manner of a wild beast. As well, his physical limitations may well have been matched by mental disabilities that were equally profound. I doubt that we would be able to understand his motivations even if he could somehow have communicated them to us."

The coroner thanked Lewis and dismissed him. Renwell, the son-in-law, was called to the stand next. He confirmed the story the preacher had told, and the coroner had only one other question for him.

"It was you, and not your father-in-law, who managed to wrest the gun away from this man?"

Francis nodded his agreement with this statement.

"Was that not a very courageous act? To rush an armed man?"

Francis grinned. "Not really. From my vantage point, I could see that he hadn't pulled the hammer back. Afterward, I discovered that the gun wasn't even loaded. I don't think the poor thing knew how to shoot it."

After that, Wellington's constable described his inventory of the cellar, and gave his opinion that the extra skulls must have once belonged to the old trapper and the woman who had lived with him.

"It was generally accepted that the deformed boy was their son," he said. "You'd see him checking the trap lines once in a while, but the old man kept him away from the village. Now that I've had a chance to think on it, I hadn't seen the trapper for some time, but he kept to himself anyway, so it didn't occur to me that something might have happened to him."

In a dry, clinical voice, Dr. Keogh next confirmed the details of what the constable had found in the cellar. The group of onlookers appeared bored during his long description, but the coroner's next question caused an uproar.

"In your opinion, what would have been the reason for the barbaric splitting of the skulls?"

"I believe that splitting the skull is part of the generally accepted procedure for making head cheese."

There were screams from the women still present, and it took several minutes to restore order to the room.

At that juncture, the coroner seemed content with the evidence presented and directed the jury to retire for deliberation.

Clementine was glad of the chance to exit the stuffy room, as, apparently, was everyone else, judging by the way they rushed for the door. Outside, the witnesses and the curious mingled together on the steps of the portico discussing the case while they waited for the jury to return.

Lewis thought that it might take some time to reach a conclusion in light of the evidence that had been presented.

"I think they'll rule that it was Gilmour in the cabin," he said to Francis as they stood a little apart from the mob that was milling around. "After all, we both identified the head and his watch was there. I don't know what they'll make of the others."

"There's only one piece of evidence to connect with Nate Elliott, and that's burned up," Francis said. "It's hard to say which way they'll jump on that."

"By the way, you might have told me the gun wasn't cocked. I hurt my knee rather badly when I rolled out of the line of fire."

"I wasn't completely sure."

"You were, too."

Francis just grinned. "I'm going to go look for a cup of tea. There's an inn just down the street. We can see the courthouse from there, so we'll know when the jury comes back in."

Many others had the same notion, among them Reuben and Clementine Elliott. There were no unoccupied tables, so the two men stood as they sipped their tea. The Elliotts had managed to find a seat at a small table set away from anyone else. They appeared to be in a deep, and to Lewis's eye, somewhat rancorous discussion. Curious, he edged closer, hoping he could discover what they were talking about, but Clementine noticed him long before he was within earshot.

"I'm so sorry, Mrs. Elliott," he said. "If there is anything we can do to ease your burden, I hope you'll let us know."

"Thank you," she said. Her face, which Lewis had never found attractive, was now pinched and pale and she looked more like a cat than ever. "I do appreciate you keeping Horatio occupied while I'm here. Little Martha has been a good friend to him."

Betsy had offered to keep an eye on the children while the inquest was being held, and Sophie had promised that they could come into the kitchen to help her make cookies.

"It was the least we could do," Lewis replied. "I know this is a difficult time for both of you."

Clementine nodded her gratitude, but it appeared that neither had anything else to say. Lewis tipped his hat and wandered back to Francis's side.

"I wonder what that was all about," Francis said.

"I'm not sure we'll ever know," Lewis replied. But he was determined to find out.

After an hour, they were finally called back in. The jury agreed without question that Mr. H.G. Gilmour had suffered "death by misadventure" and that his remains had been cremated in the cabin fire. They agreed equally that the individual who resided in the cabin had been guilty of cannibalism, and that he, too, had perished in the flames; however, they could come to no determination as to whether or not he was guilty of murder. Nor could they come to any conclusion regarding the other remains that had been found.

"It is our opinion," the foreman said, "that one of the human skulls found in all likelihood belonged to the trapper who was known to take his hides to Wellington, and it is probable that one of the others was his female companion — whether wife or otherwise, we have no way of knowing — but we cannot determine this with absolute certainty."

The coroner nodded. The jury had confirmed his opinion.

"As for the fourth head ..."

Lewis was watching not the foreman but the Elliotts, and though he saw Clementine stiffen, Reuben appeared unconcerned.

"...there has been conjecture that this belonged to the missing Nathan Elliott, and it is tempting to accept this explanation as the easiest and kindest conclusion for the family. However, we have no positive identification and no evidence in hand to suggest definitively that this is the case. Therefore, we have to conclude that these remains belong to a person or persons unknown."

A gasp went up from the crowd. This was a source of gossip and speculation that would occupy them for months to come.

The coroner officially endorsed the jury's verdict and dismissed the hearing, leaving the crowd in a hubbub. It was the finding that Lewis had expected. But he hadn't expected Reuben Elliott's lack of reaction to it.

Chapter Twenty-Five

The village was preoccupied with the true fate of Nate Elliott and rife with stories about the old trapper and his wife, although no one knew where the woman had come from and most claimed that no official joining in the eyes of God had ever taken place. Only a few people had ever encountered the Holey Man personally — those who worked near the docks or children who played near the shore — but it now seemed that nearly everyone had known of his existence, or so they claimed. It had not occurred to any of them to inquire after his well-being when so many months went by without a sign of the trapper.

Perhaps it was just as well, Lewis thought, for what would they have done with him if they had? No family would have invited such a wild thing into their home. Had he not perished in the fire, he might well have been sent to prison to pay for his cannibalistic acts, even though to Lewis's way of thinking these had not been deliberate transgressions on his part. He had not been flouting the strictures of civilized behaviour; he simply hadn't known any better. Other than that, he had shown no criminal tendencies, and how could you lock someone up just because you didn't know what else to do with him? Nor did Lewis subscribe to the notion that the Holey Man was mad, as some in the village claimed. Shunned and neglected, yes, but any derangement of thought he had shown had been the result of the bizarre circumstances in which he had obviously been raised. Besides, even if he had been insane, there would have been no place to send him other than to the grim, grey cells of Kingston Penitentiary. There were plans for the construction of a Provincial Lunatic Asylum in Toronto, but this had not yet begun, and again it would be a case of shutting away behind bars and stone walls.

No, the Holey Man was not mad, nor was he a criminal in the true sense of the word. Marked at birth, it was a miracle that he had survived at all. Raised in squalor, his life had been reduced to mere subsistence. It was as well that he was gone, for he would not have understood why he could no longer wander the lake at will, or why he must submit to a regime so foreign to him. It would have been like locking away a wolf and expecting it to understand the reason.

The village gossips had less to say about Gilmour. No one knew anything about him, really, other than the fact that he was an American and had appeared to follow Mrs. Elliott everywhere. No doubt he was unfamiliar with the area, they said, and unused to the woods. It was easy enough to understand how he could have become lost or suffered some mishap, but no one seemed to question why he had ventured along the sandbar in the first place.

But what of Nate Elliott? He had grown up in Wellington, and as a boy must have frequented the lake and its shores. The marsh and the dunes would have been familiar territory.

Unless of course, he had been in a dazed state from the tree branch that had fallen on him and had somehow wandered into the wilderness unaware. This was circulated as the most likely explanation, but Lewis heard others as well. Some claimed that it hadn't been Nate's skull at all, but that of some other poor soul, and they pointed to the jury's verdict as proof. These people speculated that Nate had merely become fed up with his family again and decided to leave in the same abrupt and enigmatic way in which he had disappeared so many years ago, and that his wife and son would no doubt hear of his whereabouts in short order. There were darker rumours, too — that Nate had taken whatever money he could find at the Elliott farm and absconded into the night; or that Reuben and Nate had quarrelled and one brother had chased the other across the marsh to his doom.

It occurred to no one but Lewis that there might be a more profound connection between the victims. He was certain that Gilmour must have been after the reward mentioned in the newspaper clipping. He had been watching Mrs. Elliott and trying to figure out where her husband had disappeared to. Like Lewis, he had wondered if Nate was hiding somewhere in the dunes. It seemed possible that the accident that Reuben had reported had never occurred, and that it was a distraction manufactured in order to let Nate slip away unnoticed. *But why?*

Gilmour must have been hoping that the Elliotts would at some point reunite and attempt to cross the border, at which point he would pounce. But all the Elliotts really had to do was settle down on the family farm and wait for Gilmour to go away. After all, he couldn't wait forever.

The only document in the leather folder Lewis had found that connected Nate Elliott to the unidentified skull had been the unsigned letter of conveyance, a document that continued to puzzle him. There had been no papers with the name LeClair. He struggled to remember what he had seen. There had been a number of calling cards similar to the one that Clementine had scattered around Wellington, one or two with foreign-looking names. There had been a letter of introduction and a baptismal certificate with an Irish name. He should have looked more closely, paid more attention. But Francis had been struggling with the Holey Man, and Lewis had assumed that there would be plenty of time to examine the papers later. So much for Auguste Dupin's advice to "observe what is necessary" — Lewis hadn't had time to observe much of anything at all.

* * *

As soon as the inquest was over, the skulls were gathered up with the mass of bones and flesh from the root cellar, along with whatever charred remains could be salvaged from the cabin. These relics were all taken to the undertaker's, but no one was willing to hazard a guess as to which bones belonged to whom. No one was sure who should be notified of Gilmour's death, and there was no one to claim the bodies of the Holey Man or his family. The undertaker suggested that everything could be buried in a mass grave as soon as the soil thawed in the spring. In the meantime, they would be held over for the winter in the dead house, where a short service, deemed to do for all, was to be held.

To Lewis's surprise, Sophie asked for time off to attend the tomb-side service to be held the next day.

"It's not on my account," she said. "I barely knew the Elliotts, but my mother's youngest sister was close to Nate at one point. In fact, I think he was a beau, but she decided in favour of Albert Chance instead. In any event, Mother remembers Nate well, as he was at their house a great deal of the time before he left. She needs some help in the graveyard, though, as the ground is so rough and she's afraid she might stumble."

Daniel grumbled a little, but agreed that Sophie could go after she promised to prepare the bulk of the noontime meal before she left.

The next morning, Sophie asked Lewis to go to the store for her. They were running low on butter and she could use a lemon, she said, if one were available. He decided to make one trip do the work of two, and drop in at the post office as well, as one of the guests had arranged for his mail to be forwarded to Wellington, and was apparently expecting an important communication.

To Lewis's surprise, there was a letter waiting with his own name on it.

"New York City," said the postmaster, "You owe me a penny for the postage." And he hesitated for a moment before he handed it over, an invitation to discuss the reasons for correspondence from such an important source.

Lewis merely scrounged in his pocket with the hopes that he might find a penny there, and when he found it, held out his hand for the letter. He waited until he was well down the street before he peeled away the wax seal and unfolded the sheet of paper.

The letter he had written to the New York newspaper had been forwarded to Mr. Van Sylen, the man who had been bilked of his money by the LeClairs and had offered a reward for their apprehension.

Sir,

Thank you for your recent inquiry regarding the man and woman who call themselves LeClair, although they also go by many other names, I have discovered. My information is that they have at various times used the names

Beauregarde, Sonderburg, and Guiseppe in their duplicitous activities.

As you are aware, they have claimed to be in communication with the spirit world and by this device have fraudulently extracted large sums of money from those, like myself, who were desperate to know the fates of loved ones. This reprehensible practice has resulted in considerable added anguish for families who were already laboring under a burden of grief.

I have hired a private detective by the name of Horace Gilmour, a man who is most highly recommended, to discover the whereabouts of the LeClairs and to return them to justice in this jurisdiction.

My latest correspondence from Mr. Gilmour derived from your vicinity, but I have not heard from him for several weeks. If you have information regarding his activities, or that of the LeClairs, I would appreciate your sharing of this knowledge. If Gilmour has moved on to another locale, I would also appreciate knowing this.

I am,
Most respectfully yours,
Augustus Van Sylen
New York, New York
Dec. 14, 1844

Beauregard, Sonderburg, Guiseppe — Yes! Those were names Lewis had seen on some of the calling cards that he had found in the folder at the cabin. Apparently, they had not ever used the name Elliott in their deceptions, or the Irish surname that had been on the baptismal certificate. And Gilmour had not been just a bounty hunter, but a detective on hire. No wonder he had been so persistent.

But what to do with this information? Lewis supposed he should inform Constable Williams that Gilmour had been in the employ of this Mr. Van Sylen, who would presumably be able to provide a means of contacting the next of kin. But even should he pass on the intelligence that the Elliotts were also known by a number of pseudonyms, he could well imagine the reaction of the phlegmatic constable. He would be completely uninterested — not only had these events taken place outside of his jurisdiction, they had occurred in another country, and, after all, no crime had taken place here.

Lewis returned to Temperance House, but once there realized that he had forgotten his other errands. Rather than face Sophie's disappointment, he made an about-face in the front hallway and was about to leave again when Clementine and Horatio descended the stairs. Again she was dressed in the elegant black of mourning, an ostrich plume on her hat and a silk veil folded round the brim, ready to mask her grief at the graveside.

He stepped forward and opened the door for her, tipping his hat as she went by.

"Good morning, Mrs. Beauregard."

The smile that had been on her face as she turned to the greeting quickly faded as she realized her mistake.

"Pardon me," Lewis said. "I thought you were someone else."

"Think nothing of it." She had recovered quickly, but Lewis knew his salutation had rattled her. She pushed Horatio through the door and quickly followed.

The errands would have to wait as Lewis made an abrupt decision to accompany Sophie to the funeral. Perhaps Mrs. Carr could shed a little light on how Nathan Elliott of Wellington had somehow turned into M. LeClair of New York.

"It's been many a year since I've had the pleasure of escorting a pretty young woman down the street," Lewis joked as he and Sophie walked along to the Carr house.

"You be careful now, Mr. Lewis," Sophie returned. "You know this town — there will be rumours flying about us in no time."

Lewis liked Sophie immensely, not in the least for her ready wit. Francis continued to seek her company whenever he could make an excuse to be close to her, and if events culminated in the direction they appeared to heading, Lewis thought the two might be a good match. It gave him a pang, of course, and reminded him once again of the loss of his daughter. But Sarah and Francis had been too much alike, impetuous and headstrong, the both of them. Sophie's good nature was paired with a down-to-earth attitude that brooked little nonsense and made short work of the practical business of life. She might be a steadying influence on Francis — and on Martha, as well.

The Carrs lived in a small cottage at the edge of Wellington. Lewis noted with approval the general tidiness of both the yard and the house. It was clear where Sophie had learned her housekeeping skills.

Mrs. Carr was delighted that Lewis was to join them.

"Sophie's a good girl," she said, "but she's just a slip of a thing and I need a strong arm to lean on. Martin couldn't get away from the mill today, so you'll do very nicely instead, Mr. Lewis."

"Sophie tells me you knew Nate Elliott well."

"I did, I did. He courted my sister Jane for quite some time. She wouldn't marry him, though. She decided to go west with Albert Chance instead."

"Is that why Nate went away?"

"Oh, no. It was never so serious as that. It was the old man drove him away, and come to think on it, the old man may have had a lot to do with Jane choosing someone else."

"What do you mean?"

"Oh, she would never have met with Hiram's approval." She chuckled. "I'm not sure that any girl would have."

"No, I mean, about why Nate left."

She looked at him closely for a moment. "I'm not sure it's seemly for me to ramble on about that. I only know what I heard, and what Jane told me, and I don't hold with idle gossip."

Generally, Lewis approved of this attitude. Gossip was a pernicious element in small-town life and was the occupation of small-minded people. But Mrs. Carr might well have knowledge that would help him answer his many unresolved questions about the Elliotts.

"I'm still trying to puzzle out why Nate Elliott came to such an unhappy end," he said. "I thought that it might help if I understood why he left in the first place."

Mrs. Carr nodded. "Of course, of course, you were the one who found him, weren't you? Or at least what they think is him, no matter what the coroner says. Well, God forgive me for slandering anybody, much less the dead, but Hiram Elliott was probably the most miserable man I ever met in my life. Now, you wouldn't know this, being from away, but Hiram's wife died young. He wasn't too bad while Alice was still alive, but after she went he made life miserable for those two boys. That's why Nate was always at our house."

"Miserable in what way?"

"He was nasty to both his boys and he did his best to turn them against each other, as well. When they were small, he'd often whip both of them for something one of them did. Or he'd lock them in the sty with the pigs until they screamed themselves hoarse. Once, he kept the pantry locked and refused to feed Nate when Reuben misbehaved. Things like that. When they got too big to whip, he'd lock all the doors so they couldn't get into the house. I don't know any of the details of why Nate finally lit out, but I don't think anybody was surprised. The surprise was that Reuben didn't leave too."

"What did you think when Nate came back? If he was on such terrible terms with his father, why would he hurry back just to be at the deathbed?"

"My guess is that Nate did it mostly for Reuben. I don't think he ever hated his brother, in spite of the way they used to fight. They say Hiram managed to tie everything in knots before he died and that was why Nate came back. He wouldn't have done it for the money, you understand. He was never a greedy boy. But he might have done it for Reuben."

"What did Nate say about it?"

"I don't know. I didn't see him when he came back. If he'd been around a little longer, I expect he would have called on us, but after he and Reuben arrived back in Wellington, they went straight to the Elliott farm and no one saw much of him until Reuben reported him missing a few days later." She sighed. "I would like to have seen him again. I always liked Nate."

They had reached the gates of the graveyard. There was a sizeable mass of people clustered around the brick building that was used to hold the dead for burial. Lewis always thought how unfortunate it was when a death occurred in the wintertime and these interim funerals took place. The mourners then had to revisit their grief all over again in the spring once the graves had been dug.

He walked Sophie and her mother to a place in the crowd where he could easily watch Reuben and Clementine. Reuben's face was impassive and Clementine had lowered her silk veil over her face, so he could see nothing of whatever emotion she might be feeling. Horatio stood between the two, and the boy's pale face was tear-stained and tense. One look was enough to show that the boy, at least, believed that it was his father who was being interred here today. But Lewis was beginning to wonder just who that father had been.

A familiar misery settled on Clementine like a pall, and not for the first time she regretted the decision to come to Wellington. Nothing had gone right since Reuben had first appeared at their squalid, third-floor apartment in New York. It had all seemed so simple — come to some arrangement with Reuben, show up at the farm, and bury the old man. She should be sitting in some fine hotel somewhere with her husband and son, not standing in a Canadian graveyard as a pompous country clergyman mangled the Bible verses he had chosen.

No matter what had been decided at the inquest, she knew without a doubt that the remains of her husband were being committed to the vault this day. It had taken her some time to admit to this fact. It had been a slow, agonizing realization that assaulted her in waves, catapulting her from despair to denial and back again a thousand times. She had begun to feel uneasy when he had failed to keep their rendezvous. The bouts of panic had started when the days flew by with no word from him. Her mind had been in a whirl at the inquest. But only now, standing beside his bones, did she truly realize that she was on her own. She sneaked a glance at Reuben, who appeared entirely unmoved by the ceremony, but then there was no reason for him to feel any grief, was there?

What a bastard he had turned out to be. As far as she was concerned, the terms of their original arrangement had been fulfilled, but Reuben obstinately refused to uphold his end of the bargain. He'd laughed at her when she threatened to tell all she knew.

"Are you really willing to risk it?" he sneered. "One bounty hunter is quite neatly out of the way, but who knows how many more there are? That old man in New York has put up quite a reward. I expect there are dozens who would like to claim his money. One story in one newspaper is all it would take and there would be a plague of them following your every move."

She knew now that Reuben had never intended to pay what he owed. His mad scheme had cost her her husband, and in spite of that he was perfectly willing to cut her loose without a penny from his precious farm.

She should leave immediately — every one of her overstretched nerves was screaming at her to get away. The preacher had not exposed her, yet she didn't know why. He had not said a word about the equipment in her sitting room, hadn't even hinted to anyone that all was not above board. She had begun to relax a little when she realized that he was not going to denounce her publicly as a fraud. And then this morning he had made himself clear — he had only been waiting for more evidence before he played his hand. How much did he know?

She could cut her losses and go, but there weren't enough coins in her purse to cover her hotel expenses, never mind set her up in a new town. She glanced at Reuben again, standing lumpenly at her side. He was determined to wait her out; he had made that clear.

"Just give me what you owe me," she'd said.

"No."

She had picked the brains of the fool of a barrister who had drawn up the will, and it was only then that she truly realized how much of the advantage was Reuben's. All he had needed to do was to find his brother and bring him home before the old man died. He could trot out any number of witnesses who would swear that Nate had returned, and after all, hadn't the entire village scoured the neighbourhood for days looking for his body?

But there was one small glimmer of hope, one indication of how she might successfully play this through to the end. The barrister had informed her that under the laws of Canada West, she might be deemed to have a stake in the property. He had also disclosed several other interesting facts; facts that she might well use to her advantage if she had enough nerve left to turn the tables — one last gamble that would see them on their way with a pocketful of money. Reuben was right, though. She couldn't risk the publicity of disclosure — but neither could he, or all would be lost.

She turned her plan over and over in her mind while the minister rambled on, and by the time he intoned the final "Amen," she had reached a resolution. She would try one last bluff and hope it was enough to rattle the smugness out of Reuben.

Clementine felt some of the tension lift away now that she had decided on a course of action. She could give her mind over to playing her role. She put her hand on Horatio's shoulder, clutched her silk-clad bosom and began to sob in a way that was most gratifying to the widow-watchers standing around her.

Chapter Twenty-Six

The funeral had no sooner taken place than Christmas was upon them. The village observed the holiday in many different ways. The Catholic fathers held a special mass at the small church that had been built behind Tara Hall. The Anglicans, as well, gathered for a Christmas service. The Presbyterians and the Quakers did nothing special at all.

The Methodists met for a Christmas Eve Love Feast. This ritual, with its emphasis on strengthening the spirit of harmony and goodwill, had been borrowed from the Moravians in New York and Pennsylvania, and had made its way north with many of the Methodist denominations.

It was one of Lewis's favourite services. There was mellowness to the gathering, a peace that seemed to descend on the congregation — the reading of the Christmas story, the lighting of the candles, the singing of the hymns, always led by a child. One sweet voice would start the first lines and one by one other voices would mingle with it. Martha would not be selected for this honour, which was a profound disappointment to her. Lewis was secretly relieved by this decision. His granddaughter had many talents; music did not appear to be one of them.

Christmas Day itself was a quiet time for almost everyone, a day of reflection and meditation. Boxing Day was generally the time for more secular observances. Most people planned large meals and parties, although the Presbyterians preferred to do their feasting on New Year's Eve.

As was traditional for the head of the family, it fell to Lewis to provide a small Christmas gift for Martha. He had not much money to do it with, but he fished out a few pennies from the crock that Betsy kept their coins in, and that would be enough for a hair ribbon.

As he walked along the street to Scully's dry goods store, he reflected that his attitude toward this annual gift-giving had changed considerably since Martha had come to live with them. His own children had been given utilitarian offerings — bibles, prayer books, leather bookmarks so they could easily find their favourite bible passages. Occasionally they had been given china mugs with their names on them, or if times were good, an orange from faraway tropical climes.

Since moving to Wellington, he had become far more aware of the emphasis that females placed on their appearances. Part of it stemmed from Clementine's arrival, of course, but part of it was just that Canada was falling more into step with the rest of the world. What had once sufficed for a woman living in a log shanty in the backwoods was in no way appropriate for the wife of a respected town man. Even the Quakers, who frowned on ornamentation of any sort, wore clothing that, though plain, was made of the finest materials. He wasn't sure that he should approve of this worldlier attitude, and he could think of any number of reasons to call it foolish, but it was the norm, and he thought that a single hair ribbon was unlikely to turn Martha into a shallow flibbertigibbet who thought of nothing but her clothes. Besides, and in all conscience he had to admit it to be true, he had been just a little jealous at her delight with the neck-lace her father had given her.

"Why it's Mr. Lewis," Scully called when he entered the store. "And what could I do for you today, sir?"

When he explained his errand, he was steered toward a rack of coloured ribbon, "any one of which would be suitable," he was told. It did not take him long to choose — the emerald green would go nicely with Martha's dark hair.

"How much do I need?" he asked. "I have no experience with these things."

"Take an arm's length," Scully advised. "That way there's enough for however she wants to do her hair. I'll cut it for you."

While the shopkeeper scurried away to find the scissors, Lewis went to the table in the corner to say hello to the little humpbacked dressmaker, and to thank her for recommending Sophie.

"Sophie's worked out then, has she?" Meribeth Scully asked, although Lewis knew that she was perfectly aware that she had. "And I hear that she has quite captivated your son-in-law. I expect she'll be calling on me for a new dress one of these days."

"I don't really know," Lewis returned bluntly. This gossipy creature would get no scuttlebutt from him, but he was surprised that the budding relationship between Francis and Sophie was already the subject of speculation around town. The couple had known each other for only a few weeks, after all.

"Mrs. Elliott seems to think a wedding might be in the offing."

So it might not be common knowledge after all. Meribeth was probably fishing on the basis of a chance remark of Clementine's.

Meribeth didn't seem to expect him to answer in any detail, for she went on. "How is poor Mrs. Elliott holding up? My, my, she has had a time recently, hasn't she? Poor thing. And now all that legal business ahead of her, as well."

"I'm not sure what you mean," he said. "I expect she'll just go back to wherever she came from, won't she?"

"Oh no, I don't think so. Old Mr. Elliott's will has made that unlikely."

"What do you mean?"

Meribeth's eyes glittered with the pleasure of imparting the latest news. "Apparently, if Nathan Elliott hadn't come home before his father died, his barrister had instructions to sell the farm and give the proceeds to the Church of England. If he did return in time, the estate was to be left jointly to the two brothers. As you know, there's some question of what exactly happened to Nate Elliott ..." She stopped for a moment to peer closely at Lewis, as if he were withholding some intelligence on the matter. When he didn't reply, she went on. "So now no one is sure what should happen. In any event, Mrs. Elliott intends to claim her husband's share. On behalf of the little boy, of course," she said hurriedly.

"Where did you hear all this?" Lewis asked.

"The will's been filed at the courthouse. It's public knowledge now. Of course, the case could take many years to sort out, but Mrs. Elliott says the value of the property makes it a worthwhile proposition, and in the meantime she'll apply to the courts to uphold her dower rights. I think we'll have the pleasure of her company for quite some time."

Lewis's purchase was ready for him, and as much as he wanted to continue the conversation with Meribeth, he could think of no excuse to do so without looking as though he was as bad a gossip as she was. He thanked Scully and left the store.

Lewis mulled the conversation over in his mind as he walked back toward the Temperance House. He wondered how Reuben would react to Clementine's intentions. Not well, he expected. He must have found the whole thing galling from the start. He had dedicated his life to the farm and his father, but in order to see the reward of this, he had been forced to retrieve a long-lost brother who would claim a share that some might argue he was not rightfully entitled to.

Certainly, it appeared that the first stipulation in Hiram Elliott's will had been met — Reuben had returned his brother to Wellington prior to his father's death. But what was likely to happen now, with Nate Elliott occupying a strange legal twilight between living and dead?

Lewis had puzzled over the letter of conveyance in the leather folder that he had found in the Holey Man's shack, but now the significance of it finally struck him. Nate's "return" had probably been nothing more than an arrangement between the brothers. He'd had a private detective trailing him and needed to disappear in a hurry. How much of his inheritance had he been willing to forego in order to do so? Rather a lot, Lewis suspected, and Reuben would be happy enough to help him if it meant he wouldn't have to share the farm.

Lewis also suspected that the legalities of the transfer would have been far more cut and dried if Nate had waited until after his father's death to disappear again, but unless he wanted to spend the rest of his life in a place he hated, he needed to shake not only Gilmour, but any other bounty hunters who were after the reward. And he needed the distraction of the accident in the woods to do it. Was it just Reuben's bad luck that Nate had somehow stumbled into a real accident before he'd had a chance to sign the necessary papers?

And what of Clementine and Horatio? If no legal transfer of property had taken place, where did they stand? From what Meribeth Scully said, it sounded as though Clementine intended to insist on whatever rights she might have.

He wished, not for the first time, that there was a reading room in Wellington; somewhere he could easily consult the statute books, for he knew little of the ins and outs of the law. He wondered if he could somehow justify another trip to Picton. Once again he felt the suffocating narrowness of his current situation. When he had been riding the circuits, he seldom needed an excuse to go anywhere. The rumour of someone in need of a prayer or two was enough to send him galloping off, and he could easily conduct any other business along the way, without having to explain it to anyone.

He was so occupied with his thoughts that he wasn't watching where he was going and jostled against a gentleman who was equally deep in thought, but going the other way.

Lewis apologized before he recognized who he had bumped into.

"Why, it's the preacher." It was his newfound acquaintance, Archibald McFaul. "And how are you getting on, sir?"

"Splendidly," Lewis replied, "except for a bit of puzzlement, which would explain my lack of concentration."

"Oh, puzzlement," McFaul said. "I'm in a state of puzzlement most days. Is it anything I can help you with?"

Lewis hesitated for a moment. McFaul was a man who owned a great deal of property. Surely, he would know something about this. Furthermore, he could probably be counted on not to broadcast the conversation up and down the street. He'd ask, and see where the asking led him.

"I've just heard that Hiram Elliott's will seems to be rife with complications."

"I did hear something to that effect myself," McFaul said. "All I can say is that Hiram himself was rife with complications, so it's not surprising that his estate is equally so."

"Apparently, Mrs. Nate Elliott intends to stay in Wellington until Hiram's estate is settled, and I've just realized that I don't really know what that means. How long exactly does it take a court to declare someone dead? I'm not asking out of curiosity," Lewis hastened to add. "Mrs. Elliott is a guest at our inn, and we are, of course, concerned with her welfare." He didn't want McFaul to think that he was engaging in idle speculation, although he was fairly certain that the whole village was buzzing with the news by now.

"Yes, of course, you would be. Well …" McFaul considered the question for a moment. "I'm not entirely sure, but my understanding is that if a person has not been heard from or sighted for a period of seven years, a judge can clear the way for remarriages, or any other arrangements of that nature."

"That long?" Lewis said. "And what will happen to the estate in the meantime?"

"In some respects that's an entirely separate question. Under the terms of Hiram's will, the property was to be left jointly. Unfortunately, of course, Nate predeceased his father. The issue will be whether or not his share devolves to his son."

"Wouldn't that happen automatically?"

"Not necessarily," McFaul said. "At the time of his death, Nate had not actually inherited anything, you see. I expect a clever lawyer could argue that Reuben became sole heir the moment his brother died."

"And what about Mrs. Elliott? Apparently, she's asking to have her dower rights upheld. What does that entail?"

"Under normal circumstances a widow in Canada West is entitled to thirty percent of the income from the estate regardless of the terms of the will. Again, it could be argued that those rights died with her husband. I understand your puzzlement. It's a knotty question all right and in the end the courts may well set the will aside entirely."

"What would happen then?"

"We operate under the law of primogeniture in this province. In that case, the entirety of the estate would go to the eldest son. And since Hiram's wife has been gone these many years, there would be no dower rights to consider. The courts tend to look for solutions that will leave a farm fully intact, you see. A judge could well be inclined to rule that way."

"Which is the eldest son?"

McFaul looked at him in surprise. "Oh, yes, I forgot, you're not from here, are you? Reuben is the eldest."

Lewis thanked McFaul for his time and resumed his homeward course with a great deal to think about.

* * *

Lewis went round and round the facts he had at hand, trying to fit the pieces together in a way that made sense. It quite spoiled his enjoyment of the Christmas Eve service. Instead of settling into a peaceful repose as the prophetic words of Isaiah washed over him, Lewis fidgeted as he considered each aspect of what he had learned.

He wasn't sure why it bothered him so. His primary concern had been the fraudulent nature of Clementine's so-called contact with the dead, but events had taken a sinister turn and now it seemed that far more than a little fraud was involved. And now that Gilmour was gone, Lewis was the only one who realized it.

It seemed clear to him that Nate had returned to Wellington only so that Reuben could help him evade retribution for his chicanery in New York. In exchange for fulfilling the condition in the will, Reuben had probably agreed to furnish him with some funds, as well, witness the transfer documents that had been in the folder, but in all probability this would have been considerably less than half the value of the estate. Nothing more than travelling money, perhaps; at the most, enough to set Nate up in a new location.

Come, Thou long-expected Jesus; born to set Thy people free ...

The hymn was led by Charlie Carpenter, who had a fine, high voice. Lewis knew that Martha was still a little upset that she had not been asked to take this role and she squirmed beside him. He reached out and touched her elbow — a signal to settle down — and she subsided, although she still looked a little unhappy.

She would never be asked to perform this ceremony, he knew. *Grow used to it, little mite, you can't have everything you want.*

Born thy people to deliver; born a child and yet a King ...

One by one the others had joined in the words written so long ago by Charles Wesley. Lewis's was amongst them, but even as he sang, one part of his mind returned to the Elliotts.

Nate had never been near the woodlot. If he had waited for cover of darkness, he could probably have left the Elliott farmhouse and walked along the road without a soul seeing him, but there was always the possibility that some late-to-bed might notice him and report the fact after he had supposedly disappeared. He must have chosen to cross the marsh to a deserted section of the mainland at the other end of the lake. Gilmour seemed to have reached the same conclusion. Lewis had seen him searching there on the way back from Picton. It was but a short way across to the peninsula that jutted into the lake. What the plan had been from there was anyone's guess — Nate might well have intended to find a hidey hole in the cedar forest as Lewis had originally thought — or he might have simply kept going until he was well away from Prince Edward. As Lewis mulled this over, he decided that the latter was the most likely course.

He attempted to put these thoughts aside and direct his attention to the service. The old, familiar words of the Christmas story rang out, but they did little to divert him.

By claiming that Nate had been injured while cutting wood, Reuben had gained him travelling time. With all those people searching for him, any questions that Gilmour might have had about the incident would have looked foolish indeed. The fact that Nate had genuinely disappeared served only to reinforce Reuben's story.

He didn't know what to make of Clementine's arrival in Wellington. No one here had been aware of her existence. There had been no need for her to satisfy propriety by attending her father-in-law's funeral. Perhaps she had been the go-between. The transfer agreement had been unsigned. Had Nate arranged to meet her somewhere, at which point he would sign the document? She would return it to Reuben, and the money would change hands. Apparently the brothers didn't trust each other, and the document would have served as insurance for both. Lewis could think of only one reason for Clementine's announcement that she was prepared to wait for however long it took to see the estate settled in her favour — Reuben had reneged on the contract. With Nate truly dead, and in all probability this was the case, there was no chance that he could return at some later date and claim his inheritance. And if what McFaul had told Lewis was true, Reuben had every chance of walking away with everything. He no longer needed the surety of the agreement.

The lighting of the candles had begun. One by one the flames flickered and then burned brightly. Soon the room was bathed in their soft glow.

Hark the Herald Angels sing, glory to the newborn King!

The triumphant words signalled the end of the service, but not of the celebration. Soon hot cups of coffee and rolls would be passed to the worshippers, and Lewis would need to bring his mind to the present in order to convey his greetings to his neighbours. Beside him, Martha was singing loudly and flatly and this was finally enough to put a temporary end to his speculation.

Chapter Twenty-Seven

Temperance House was nearly cleared of guests, everyone having gone home to their families for Christmas. The only two remaining in residence were Clementine and Horatio, who indicated that they would not, as had been expected, spend the day with Reuben. Even Sophie had deserted them — she would spend the day with her family, but would return the next morning to cook a Boxing Day feast.

Martha was delighted with the ribbon Lewis gave her, and demanded that her grandmother fix it into her hair immediately. Betsy unwound the braids the little girl normally wore and let the soft curls spill down her back, held back by a length of the green ribbon. Francis complimented her on her new style when they trooped into the dining room for breakfast — Daniel had decided that the Elliotts would feel less lonely if everyone ate their meals together — and then he brought out his present. Lewis realized with a start that it was no longer his place to provide the Christmas gift — that was up to Martha's father now.

She bubbled over with delight when she saw what she had been given — a beautifully carved Noah's Ark, complete not with camels and giraffes, but with pairs of animals that a Canadian child might be more familiar with — bears and raccoons and foxes — and even two tiny cats that peered out coyly from a window. It must have taken hours to make, and it must have been done in secret, late at night, for even Lewis had been unaware of the activity.

He was further put to shame, for Francis had provided a gift for Horatio, as well. It was a jig doll, in the form of a lumberjack, whose jointed limbs were constructed in such a way as to allow it to do a clattering dance as the board it stood on was pushed up and down. It was not so finely carved as Martha's ark, but Francis had painted it in gay colours and the boy seemed delighted with it.

Clementine thanked him rather tearily and Lewis reproached himself further. This woman had lost a husband, after all, and the boy a father. He had been so focused on her transgressions that he had forgotten her tribulations. Christmas was a time for peace and goodwill and he was glad that he had not taken any definitive action to reveal what he knew. He would let everyone enjoy the holiday and decide his course of action at a more appropriate time.

The noon meal was a simple one of sausages with bacon and cabbage, and again they all shared it in the dining room. The street outside was quiet, the shops closed and shuttered for the day. Little traffic went by — only a handful of pedestrians and a sleigh or two — although Lewis was surprised when the stage rumbled through in mid-afternoon, quite disturbing the quiet meditations each of them had sunk into after dinner. Supper was oyster stew made with cream and served with biscuits. By eight o'clock that evening the hotel was in darkness, everyone having retired to bed.

The serenity of Christmas Day did not survive long into Boxing Day. Sophie bustled in early with a list of orders for them all, for although there were no overnight guests besides the Elliotts, a number of people had inquired about coming to the hotel for dinner, drawn by the glowing reports of the tasty meals served there. The dining room would be quite full, and everyone was fully occupied in attempting to follow Sophie's frequent and precise instructions regarding the preparations for the feast.

Lewis and Martha were put to work setting the tables. They took all of the tablecloths outside to shake them free of crumbs and sponged away any stains they found before the cloths were laid again. Sophie had suggested that the middle of each table be adorned with pine branches and candles, an embellishment that Lewis was dubious about, but which Daniel found appealing.

"Oh, yes," he said, "that would make the room look lovely. This is a first-class establishment, after all, and our guests will expect no less."

Lewis thought Daniel was getting a little above

himself with this description, but when he saw the result of their efforts, he had to admit that the room looked nice and that the greenery added a festive touch.

He and Martha were standing in the doorway admiring their handiwork when the front door was flung open. It was Reuben Elliott, and he appeared to be in an agitated state.

"Good morning," Lewis said, but Reuben failed to make a civil reply.

"Is Mrs. Elliott in her rooms?" he asked in a very abrupt manner.

"Yes, I believe so," Lewis replied, and Reuben went bounding up the stairs.

Something was apparently very wrong, for over the course of the next ten minutes everyone who was downstairs could hear voices raised in argument. Lewis wondered if he should go upstairs and intervene, but he had only just decided to do so when he heard Reuben stamp down the stairs again. He left without a word, and slammed the front door as he went, making the glass rattle and the bell ring crazily.

"I wonder what that was all about," Daniel said.

Lewis shrugged. It had not been possible to hear what was said, other than a word or two here and there, but it was clear that a further complication had arisen in the Elliott plan. He had no time to think about it, though, for at that moment their first dinner guests arrived and he was kept busy taking their coats through to the small parlour and seeing them to their tables.

The meal Sophie had prepared was sumptuous.

The opening course of fish chowder was followed by a salmi of wild duck, which in turn led to the main dish of Christmas ham, which Sophie had drenched in maple syrup and studded with cloves, accompanied by roasted potatoes, candied carrots, and a piquant mustard sauce. Lewis attempted at one point to count the number of side dishes that were presented — the cold room appeared to have been emptied of its contents and he noted everything from coleslaw to pickled beets — but he kept losing count as he passed them to the guests.

For dessert there were several varieties of pie, including mincemeat, but the *piece de resistance* was without doubt an extraordinary plum pudding, served with a choice of either hard or caramel sauce, which was set alight just before it was served to the guests. Lewis decided not to inquire too closely as to the form of liquor required to accomplish this. It was, after all, Christmas. Besides, the flame would have the effect of burning off all the alcohol anyway.

He would not have been surprised if Clementine had kept to her rooms after the upset of the morning, but she and Horatio both appeared at the appointed time and took their places at a table. Horatio dug into his food with great gusto and put away an enormous amount, but his mother seemed pale and distracted, and merely picked at each course.

As he cleared away her unused dessert plate, Lewis leaned in close.

"I don't mean to pry, but we couldn't help but be aware that there was some unpleasantness earlier. Is everything all right?"

The sly, cat-like look appeared on her face. "Yes, you do mean to pry, and no, everything isn't all right, but thank you for asking."

With this rebuff, Lewis shrugged and moved to the next table.

Slowly the dining room cleared out, the guests groaning with a satisfied pleasure. With the customers provided for, it was now time for the family to eat, and Sophie revealed that she had held something back. As well as ample helpings of everything they had served in the dining room, she had prepared a succulent goose pie just for them. Just as she was taking it out of the oven, Francis and Daniel helped Susannah into the kitchen and arranged her as comfortably as they could at the end of the table, her leg supported on a stool with a cushion. It was the first time she had been able to join them for a meal since her accident.

We have many things to be thankful for this Christmas, Lewis thought as he led them in saying grace. Then he settled in to eat, which he did until he was sure he would never want food again, yet he kept reaching for "just another nibble" of the toothsome fare.

Daniel was ecstatic at the compliments he received from their diners, and kept repeating the most flattering of them, but by the time they had finished eating, everyone else was exhausted. Daniel and Lewis helped Susannah back to her room, and by the time they returned, Francis was already helping Sophie with the dishes. Betsy was hobbling and Martha was yawning, so Lewis suggested that they go home for a couple of hours of quiet time, which he sincerely hoped would translate into naps for them all.

"What was all the excitement this morning?" Betsy asked as they walked across the yard.

"I'm not sure," Lewis replied. "Mrs. Elliott didn't want to discuss it. Something was certainly amiss though, wasn't it?"

"Something always seems to be amiss with that woman," Betsy replied. "I don't know if she makes it so or if it just happens all on its own, but she appears to find herself in one difficulty after another, doesn't she?"

Betsy didn't know the half of it, Lewis thought, but he was too tired and full to think much more. As soon as they reached the house, Betsy went to lie down on the kitchen bed while Lewis fed some wood into the stove. When he had stoked the fire to life, he turned and discovered that Martha had climbed in beside her grandmother and they were both sound asleep. Yawning mightily, he, too, went to bed.

It was dark when Lewis awoke. He had neglected to draw the curtains before his nap, and the full winter moon had climbed quite high in the sky, shining through the window upon his face. This must be what had pulled him from his deep sleep. He had completely missed the supper serving, he realized, but then he remembered the Boxing Day feast they had had earlier and that Sophie had intended to simply lay out the left-overs and let everyone pick at what they most felt like eating. He stretched and sat up, not sure if he wanted to get up and go for a walk or indulge himself in the luxury of throwing another log into the stove and going back to bed. Years of hard habit won; he would go out. A little exercise would make it all the easier to go back to sleep later.

Betsy and Martha were still curled together on the kitchen bed. As silently as he could, he tended the stove, then slid his feet into his boots, put on his coat, and slipped outside into the crisp, starlit night. The cold air bit deep into his lungs as he stood on the stoop and located his old winter friend, Orion. He had never managed to find a book about the stars, as he had intended to do so many years ago, and there remained too many of the twinkling lights that he couldn't identify. He liked to watch them nonetheless; they reminded him of the beauty of creation and how his own significance paled in contrast. He chuckled a little to himself. Not a bad thing for any man to come to the realization that he was so small.

He was brought back to earth by a noise across the street — a shout and a peal of laughter. The Donovans were hosting a party, no doubt one of many around the village. He hoped it wouldn't get too loud, and that Betsy could continue her peaceful slumber inside. He was about to set off toward the main road when he saw a crowd of men at the corner. He stepped back into the shadow of the doorway. There was something ominous about the way they moved, creeping silently along. As they drew closer, he recognized several of them. They had been present at the Orange Lodge meeting held at the hotel, and the fact that they were travelling in a group spoke of ill-intention. As the Donovans were the only Catholic family living on this short street, Lewis suspected that the Donovan house was about to be the target of whatever the Orangemen had planned. He stepped out of the shadows.

"Good evening, gentlemen," he called out in a loud voice. "Best of the season to you."

They stopped. Lewis could see that some of the men had rocks in their hands, and two or three of them carried guns.

"It's a fine night to be out walking, isn't it? I myself ate far too much dinner and now I need a little fresh air to clear my head."

"Out of the way, preacher," one of the men growled. "We have no quarrel with you." The man's hat was pulled far down over his face, but Lewis recognized his voice. It was the lodge master. This was no impromptu foray, then. It was not born of high-flown words uttered over too many glasses of whisky. It was a planned attack. Lewis felt a shiver of fear, not for himself, but for his wife and grandchild sleeping peacefully in the kitchen. This could easily get out of control.

"I have no quarrel with any man," he replied. "And even if I did, I could scarcely indulge in quarrelling at Christmas now, could I? After all, it's the season of peace and goodwill."

He said this as loudly as he dared without alerting

the Orangemen to the fact that he was attempting to warn the Donovans.

"Peace and goodwill to Protestants," someone at the back of the crowd shouted. "The rest of them can rot in hell!"

To Lewis's relief this shout brought the desired result. The Donovans' front door was thrown open and Mr. Donovan appeared, backed by several of his burly houseguests.

"What's going on? What's the meaning of this?"

The Orangemen muttered and shuffled their feet. They had been hoping for a sneak attack and seemed unprepared for a direct confrontation.

Lewis held his breath as they wavered. They might back down yet.

And then someone lifted his arm and threw. The stone hit squarely in the middle of Donovan's chest, and that was the signal for the rest of them to attack. More rocks pelted the house, breaking a window, and one man fired his gun into the night. Donovan's guests piled out of the house, their fists swinging.

Lewis realized that he could do no good by joining the fray. He ran down the street toward the centre of the village. He needed to rouse the constable. As he ran, he hoped that Betsy would have the good sense to bolt the door and stay inside. He had almost reached the house he was looking for when a horse galloped up to him. It was Archibald McFaul. Lewis quickly explained the situation.

"Are you fetching the constable?" he asked.

Lewis nodded.

"Good man. I'll go on and see if I can put a stop to this." And he galloped off.

Lewis hurriedly gave his information to the sleepy-eyed woman who answered the door, and urged her to tell her husband to hurry. Then he ran after McFaul. He arrived back at the scene just in time to see him bull his way into the middle of the fight, using the horse's bulk to force the combatants apart. Lewis waded in, as well. He grabbed a man who was flailing at another man's head and pinioned his arms behind him. So far it was only a fistfight, but he knew that it was only a matter of time until it occurred to one of the Orangemen to aim his gun. He could only hope that the constable arrived before then.

Suddenly, Francis was there beside him and Lewis watched as he threw himself at a man who was putting the boots to someone lying on the ground. The kicker was knocked off balance and Renwell assisted his fall to the ground with a deft trip that took the feet out from under the assailant. Neighbours began arriving and one by one the belligerents were separated and subdued.

It was then that McFaul showed the true measure of his character.

"This is a peaceful village," he called out from his vantage point atop the horse. "We are in a peaceful season of the year. A season when we all, no matter our beliefs, gather to celebrate the good fortune providence has seen fit to grace us with. There are many creeds in this village — Anglican, Quaker, Presbyterian, Methodist," this with a nod toward Lewis, "and

Catholic."

"It's the Catholic we don't hold with." This was shouted by the man Renwell had thrown himself on top of. Renwell grabbed him by the back of his head and forced his face into the ground, effectively muzzling anything further he might have to say.

"And Catholic," McFaul continued. "We have always respected the differences among us and celebrated the things that bind us together. This is a season for reflection, not action. I urge you all to desist this night. Go home to your families. Go peacefully, and there will be no consequences — am I right, Billy?"

Constable Williams had arrived belatedly, red-faced and puffing, with one bootlace still undone. As Lewis turned to watch his approach, he caught a glimpse of a small pale figure as it slid from the shadow of the hotel and continued along the main street. *Horatio, come to watch the melee?* But the boy didn't come down the side street and Lewis lost sight of him in the dark.

McFaul greeted the constable as he finally reached the crowd. "There will be no arrests this night, will there Bill? Not if they all go home now?"

The constable looked around in confusion, then wisely decided to follow McFaul's lead.

"No, I won't haul anybody in if you all go peaceable now. We'll lay this to rest here and now. Off you go now, but I want your guns."

There was a grumble at this. "Don't you worry — you can come and get them in the morning. You just can't have them tonight."

Lewis thought this an uncharacteristically brilliant move on the part of the constable. Not only would it help eliminate further violence tonight, but whoever wanted to reclaim a weapon would be forced to ask for it back. The constable would have the names of at least some of the attackers.

One by one, the brawlers were released from their holds and one by one the Orangemen slunk off. Donovan's guests were about to return to the house, but the constable stopped them.

"I think the party's over," he said. "You can all go home, too."

As soon as Lewis's services as peacekeeper were no longer needed, he went to check on his family. It was no surprise to him that his door was firmly locked.

He knocked. "It's me. I think you're safe now."

The door opened a crack. "What was that all about?" Betsy asked.

"It was just nonsense," he replied. "But it's done with now. Are you all right?"

Betsy opened the door further. "Oh, yes," she said. "I got the poker. If any of them had come in here they'd have left with a sore head."

He smiled. "I knew I could count on you. I'm just going to walk up the street and make sure the trouble is over with — for now, anyway." He had no real hope that this would be the last incident of the sort. Scenes like this were no doubt being repeated across the province.

As Lewis walked up toward the main street, there were still a few people slowly making their way home along the road. But Lewis spotted someone else there, as well, someone who tiptoed from shadow to shadow, someone who was trying not to be seen. *A brawler returning to finish what had been started?*

Lewis moved into the canopy of shadows and began to follow the slinking figure.

Chapter Twenty-Eight

Clementine had been on the edge of going mad all day, her nerves stretched and jangled as she looked for a way out. After Reuben left, she had begun to pack, weighing her choices carefully as she stuffed items into her valise. They would be able to take only what they could carry. Everything else — the trunk, the camera, all of the items she used in the pursuit of dead spirits, would have to be left behind. She and Horatio had gone down to the dining room to take their meal as usual; it would have excited far too much comment if they had stayed in their rooms. But she had been too nauseated to eat much, and she was unable to keep her attention focused on the conversation around her.

After dinner, they had returned to their rooms and waited. She rechecked her packing a dozen times and wept a little over the articles she would have to leave behind. The only other thing she could do was pace up and down the room. She had told her son what she wanted him to do as soon as he had a chance, and he waited with her. She knew he was bored, but she wanted him close in case an opportunity presented itself. He played incessantly with the jig doll he had been given, the jointed wooden feet making a constant clatter that grated on her already taut nerves.

Finally, it was suppertime, and again she forced herself to go to the dining room; this time she could eat nothing at all, but she did take a glass of wine, which helped soothe her nerves a bit. The preacher and his family were noticeably absent.

"They all went for a nap." The innkeeper chuckled. "My guess is that they're out for the count. They'll wake up tomorrow morning and wonder what happened to the day."

This was welcome news. *Fewer people to dodge.* She knew that the cook went home after the supper dishes were cleared up. The innkeeper's wife was still in bed. That left only the innkeeper himself and the son-in-law. She would wait a while more, until the hotel was locked and shuttered for the night; then with any luck, she and the boy could slip out the front door unnoticed.

Luck did not favour her, however. The cook did not go home. She, too, waited until the innkeeper had gone to sit with his invalid wife and then she and the son-in-law tiptoed into the front parlour.

Clementine had been mildly amused by the budding romance, but now she cursed it. There was no way they could slide past without being seen — as befitted a gentleman with honourable intentions, Renwell had not closed the door to the small room.

The couple remained there for an hour or more. She could hear the low murmur of their voices if she went to the top of the stairs, and she did this every five minutes or so. *Would they never leave?* Finally, she heard footsteps. The cook had moved into the hall.

"Goodnight then. I'll see you tomorrow," she said.

Whatever her suitor replied was indistinct, but she heard the front door open and close again, and then more footsteps as Renwell walked to his small room at the back of the hotel. She was about to set her plan in motion when she heard what sounded like a gunshot. She ran down the stairs, reaching the bottom just as the innkeeper entered the hall.

"There's a bit of a disturbance on the back street," he told her. I don't know what it's all about, but Mr. Renwell has gone to find out. I can't imagine there's any real danger."

"My goodness," she said. "Is someone being robbed?"

"No, nothing like that. Likely just a few people who've had a little too much drink. Nothing to worry about. If it would make you feel safer, you and the boy could come and sit with us in our room. My wife, of course, is rather anchored there, and anxious for company."

Perfect.

"I think we'll be all right on our own," she said, "but thank you for asking. I'll make sure my door is securely locked. You go and be with your wife. She needs you more than we do, I'm sure."

He nodded and went back down the hall. She waited until she heard his door close and then ran up the stairs.

"Now," she hissed. "I'll be there in a few minutes."

Far less likely that they would be seen if they went separately. Clementine stepped out onto the second floor verandah and watched as the boy slipped down the street. She would give him time to reach the stable and then she would follow.

She had to wait longer than she had intended, for people were pouring out of the nearby houses to see — or join in — the fight, she couldn't really tell which. Finally, it appeared that the excitement was over as groups of men emerged from the side street. She waited until she saw the constable go by with an armload of guns, then crept down the stairs. Horatio had left the door unlocked for her. She silenced the bell with her hand and slid out into the night.

Clementine hoped that everyone would now be back in their houses, recounting the details of what had happened. Wives and children would all be sitting in their kitchens, no doubt, while tales of derring-do were spun.

She decided to keep to the shadows as much as she could and hoped that the boy had managed to harness a horse without alerting the stable-keeper. She had concocted a story about being called away suddenly, just in case, but it would be far better if they were neither seen nor heard.

"Out for a stroll? It's a dangerous night for a midnight walk."

Clementine jumped when she heard the voice.

The damned preacher! She considered bolting, but thought better of it. She could never outrun him, not even if she dropped the bag she was carrying. *Better to stick to the story and hope it would hold water.*

"Oh, Mr. Lewis," she said. She didn't bother affecting the southern drawl. "I'm so happy to see you. I wanted to say goodbye but I couldn't find you. I've been called away rather suddenly, I'm afraid."

"So suddenly that you couldn't pay your bill? My, my, that's an emergency indeed."

She hesitated. *Did he know for sure that she was skipping out, or was he just guessing?* The one thing she had learned in all the years in the game, though, was to keep the story going until you were sure it was lost.

"My mother has been taken ill suddenly," she said. "I didn't want to disturb the innkeeper. Please let him know that I'll settle up with him when I return."

"I expected a better story from one so accomplished in the fraudulent arts," Lewis said. "You seem to be losing your touch. What happened today when Reuben came visiting? You seemed pretty rattled."

She regarded him warily. *How much did he know? Too much, it seemed.*

"I had all the moaning and groaning and ghosts up on the second floor pegged as nonsense right from the start," he went on. "I've known for some time that you went by the name of LeClair while you were in New York and that Mr. Gilmour was following you in the hopes that he might collect the reward that

was offered. Just a little while ago I figured out that
Nate's return was a scheme hatched so that he could
get away cleanly and Reuben could inherit the farm.
Do you want to fill me in on the rest of it? Something
else has gone sadly amiss, I would guess, otherwise you
wouldn't be scuttling away in the dead of night. I take
it Horatio, or should I say Joe — that's his real name
isn't it? — is waiting with the horse and cart a little
farther up the road?"

Did any of it even matter now? She decided it
didn't. "Nathan Elliott just came home."

It was the last thing Lewis had expected to hear
and he struggled to make sense of this statement. "But
Nate is dead."

*So he hadn't put all the pieces together yet. Too
late to backtrack now. Carry on and hope he can be
diverted somehow.*

"No," she hissed. "My husband is dead. And now
Nate is back."

She looked around, but there was no one else
on the street. There was little likelihood that anyone
could hear.

"We were trying to cover our tracks, so we booked
a squalid little room in a poor neighbourhood in New
York. The previous occupant had been unable to pay
his rent and had disappeared abruptly. He left some
things behind — a few pieces of clothing. They were
little more than rags, but there were some letters in a
jacket pocket. They belonged to a Nathan Elliott. We
didn't think anything of them until Reuben showed up,
looking for his brother."

Lewis nodded. Reuben must have been desperate. He thought he had located the long-lost Nate, only to find that he had once again disappeared like a wisp of smoke.

"We knew that Van Sylen had offered a reward and that sooner or later someone would catch up with us. Jack offered Reuben a deal that was supposed to have taken care of both problems. Jack would pretend to be Nate, and Reuben would help Jack disappear."

"Jack?"

"My husband." Her voice broke a little as she said this.

"So it was Jack we buried?"

She nodded. "He was supposed to have met me in Niagara Falls. He would sign the agreement, and I was to bring it here to collect the money. When he didn't show up, I came here anyway. I didn't know what else to do. I wondered for a time if I'd been double-crossed, if Jack had taken the money and run. Then I discovered that he truly had disappeared. Reuben claimed that everything had been going as planned and that he had no idea what had really happened. When you found all those bodies, I finally realized what was going on. It wasn't Jack who was doing the double-crossing."

"And Reuben wouldn't give you the money he'd promised in the original agreement?"

"No. And I couldn't expose him without exposing myself. I thought I could rattle him if I threatened to go to the courts. That was also my insurance policy. I made sure everyone knew about it. That way it would be far too suspicious if a second Elliott disappeared mysteriously."

"And now the real Nate Elliott has returned, and the game is up."

She sighed. "It's all been for nothing. I wish we'd never heard of Nate Elliott."

"So the question is," Lewis said. "What do you think really happened to Jack?"

She looked at him squarely, trying to judge what he would do. "I think Reuben murdered him and left his body in the marsh. I think Reuben would murder me if he thought he could get away with it. I don't have any proof of this. All I know for sure is that it's time for me to be on my way."

"Where is Nate Elliott now?"

"At the farm, as far as I know. At least that's what Reuben told me this morning."

They could hear the sound of an approaching horse. Lewis turned and Clementine slipped back into the shadows. *It was now or never. Go to the farm; please decide to go to the farm. Go save the brother. Let me leave.*

"Just tell me one more thing," she heard Lewis call out softly. "What's your real name?"

It was the last thing she expected him to ask, and she took a moment to answer. "It doesn't matter. Just remember me as Clementine." And then she ran.

The man on horseback was McFaul, patrolling the street to be sure that everyone had returned to their homes and that there would be no further trouble.

Lewis thought furiously in the few seconds he had before McFaul greeted him. *Just how desperate would Reuben be?* If he had committed one murder, would he see a second as an equally convenient solution to his problem? No one besides himself, Clementine, and Reuben knew that the real Nate Elliott had returned, and Reuben would be unaware that Lewis knew. Reuben would assume that if Nate went missing now, no one would ever go looking for him.

"Ah, Preacher." McFaul had reached him. "All seems quiet now."

"I don't think you'll hear any more from the Orangemen tonight," Lewis replied. "But there may be trouble brewing somewhere else. Do you suppose I could borrow your horse?"

There must have been an urgency in his voice, because McFaul looked at him coolly and said, "Hop up behind me and I'll take you to wherever you're going. You can tell me about it on the way."

It was not far to the Elliott farm. Despite the fact that the horse was carrying two men, it took only a few minutes to reach the house. Lewis gave a barebones account of what he had discovered as they rode. He knew that McFaul had many questions, but the man seemed to realize that these could be answered later. They leapt from the horse and ran into the Elliott kitchen. There was no one there, although the stove was hot and the remains of a meal were on the table. Whatever Reuben had planned to do, he had waited until he had the cover of darkness to do it.

"I don't think they've been gone long," McFaul said, looking around the kitchen. "And they had quite a feast before they left." He laid his hand against a pot at one end of the table. "This is still warm."

Lewis stood in the doorway, surveying the scene. *The necessary knowledge is that of what to observe*, and like C. Auguste Dupin, observation had become of late a species of necessity with him. A man's life might well depend on what he could observe in this untidy kitchen.

It had occurred to him that Clementine's claim that the real Nathan Elliott had returned might be a feint designed to distract him while she fled, but he could see that the table had been set for two, and two glasses had been used, although only one had been drained. Reuben's guest could have been anyone, however — a neighbour, a relative, a friend.

He went to the sideboard and inspected the many bottles that were there — whisky and rum, mostly, along with several decanters and a number of unwashed glasses. But tucked away, just behind a jug of cider, was a small brown bottle.

It was a container of the sort used for tonics and elixirs. It was uncorked. Lewis sniffed at the open neck. There was a distinctive smell that he recognized immediately: the tang of herbs in a laudanum mixture. Betsy took something similar at times, when the pain was bad and they could afford it. When he tipped the bottle upside-down, not a drop came out.

Lewis strode to the table and picked up one of the dirty glasses. Nothing but the odour of rum from it.

But when he sniffed at the second glass, he thought he could detect the same flowery smell of the laudanum.

As he put the glass back on the table he realized that there were a series of clothes pegs beside the door, but that only one coat was hung there. It could easily have been Reuben's, he supposed, but when he thrust his hands into the pockets he discovered a small purse. Inside were two notes and a handful of coins. All of them were American. It appeared that Reuben's Boxing Day guest might indeed be his long-lost brother, Nathan.

Had Reuben rendered the first Nate — *Jack* — helpless with the laudanum? Had he taken his victim to the marsh, where the Holey Man had found him? And had he been dead already or still alive and too insensible to save himself? Having had such success with his first crime, had Reuben decided to use the same method for his second?

But the Holey Man is gone. No one can lay the blame there if another body is found in the marsh.

Suddenly, Lewis knew where they had gone. "The woods. He's taken him to the woodlot."

What better place? Reuben had maintained that his brother had disappeared there in the first place, and the coroner's jury had expressed doubts about the identity of the bones found at the Holey Man's shack. If something went wrong, and this body was found, Reuben could always claim that it was the missing Nate, and that he had been there all the time.

McFaul had been watching in silence as Lewis examined the kitchen, but now he sprang into action. "Let's go." He rushed to the door.

They went on foot. The trees grew thick in places, and a horse would make too much noise. They crossed the cleared fields and pastures close to the barn and soon reached the wooded area. Lewis led them to the clearing where Reuben claimed Nate's accident had occurred. He motioned McFaul to be as silent as possible. There was no one in the clearing, although there was evidence of continued logging. Several felled trees lay on the ground waiting to be chopped into smaller lengths. Lewis tripped on one of these, but managed to stifle a groan as his weight shifted to his bad knee.

McFaul grabbed his arm to prevent him falling. "Listen," he whispered.

Lewis could hear something off to their right. He and McFaul crept through the clearing as silently as they could. It was harder to see here, tree branches forming a dark web over their heads. Here and there widow-makers dangled in the arms of their neighbours, ready to come crashing down when least expected.

There, in the part of the woodlot where the trees grew thickest, Reuben Elliott was cutting brush. As they watched, he slashed at the branches of trees, both fallen and standing, and threw them onto an enormous pile. Had it been daytime, he could have been merely chopping, throwing the unusable brush into a mound to be burned later — a commonplace chore on a farm. Except that a shaft of moonlight broke through a gap in the overhanging branches and Lewis could see the toe of a brown boot at one edge of the brush pile. Reuben muttered and cursed as he worked.

There was a shovel leaning on a tree nearby, with a small pile of disturbed earth at the foot of it. He had intended to dig a grave, Lewis thought, but no one could dig far in the frozen earth. So he had settled for a less effective concealment perhaps.

Lewis signalled McFaul and they crept up around the back of the mound of brush.

As Reuben reached up to chop another branch, his back to them, he must have heard them as they rushed forward, for he turned, and in one smooth overhand motion, threw his axe. Lewis shouted and rolled sideways, knocking McFaul out of the way. The axe flew over his head and bounced off the ground, landing against the piled branches.

When Lewis looked up, Reuben was disappearing into the trees. McFaul signalled that he was going to the left and that Lewis should swing around to the right. Lewis could hear the man crashing through the undergrowth ahead of him and he tried to follow the noise. Suddenly, there was silence. Lewis stopped, hesitating. The trees had closed in around him again and he could see nothing but shadows. He caught a slight movement just at the periphery of his vision, but turned too late. The branch slammed into the side of his head and he went down heavily.

He had just time to shout "Here!" before he was struck a second time. He could hear McFaul shouting, but he sounded so far away — he would never arrive in time to prevent Reuben from delivering a rain of blows.

Lewis instinctively put his hands up over his head. He felt intense pain shoot through his left arm as the heavy oak branch crashed down again. In spite of the pain, he rolled to the right and kicked his feet out as he rolled. One of his boots slammed into Reuben's leg and the blow sent the man sprawling sideways. Then, unexpectedly, something arrested this motion and Reuben tumbled forward in a heap. As Lewis scrambled to get out of the way, he was astonished to see an axe embedded in Reuben Elliott's back. And there behind him, swaying, stood a man who could be none other than Nathan Elliott.

McFaul reached them just as Nate's knees buckled and he slumped to the ground beside the convulsing body of his brother.

"Holy Mary Mother of God!" McFaul said as he took in the scene. "Are you all right, Lewis?"

"I think my arm's broken, but I'm fine for the moment. What about Reuben?"

"He's still breathing, but I fear it won't be for long."

"Then go and get help. Maybe we can save him yet."

McFaul didn't argue. He nodded and ran back the way he had come.

Lewis pulled his scarf from around his neck and made a makeshift sling for his injured arm. His head was throbbing from the blows he had taken, but he hauled himself to his knees and managed to crawl away from Reuben and toward the other man. Nate was breathing, deep irregular breaths that sounded as though they might cease at any moment. Lewis leaned over him, flinching as he did so. The smell of rum was strong, but underneath this odour was the flowery stink of laudanum. Nate's eyes were open, the pupils nothing more than pinpoints. Reuben must have slipped the drug into his drink, drop by drop, until he became insensible. How had he ever managed to haul himself out from under the pile of branches, never mind locate the axe and find his brother in the dark? It was nothing short of a miracle. *I would be dead but for this man*, Lewis thought, for there was no doubt in his mind that Reuben had intended to kill him. *Please Lord, don't let him die now*.

He tried to shake the stuporous form, an action that caused a jolting pain in his arm. No response. He tried again, and Nate stirred a little. Lewis took a firm hold on him and with an effort that caused him to cry out with the pain, managed to haul the limp form to a sitting position and drag him far enough to lean his back against a tree. He slumped down beside the drugged man, closed his eyes, and waited for help to arrive.

Chapter Twenty-Nine

"Reuben Elliott was probably as good as dead as soon as the axe went into him," Dr. Keough said the next day when he came around to the Temperance House to check on Lewis's head, which he seemed far more concerned about than the broken arm.

Lewis was aware that he must have blacked out several times the night before — at least once before McFaul had returned with the doctor, the grumbling constable, and five strong men, Francis among them, and at least twice while he was being carried home. He had been fully conscious, however, of Betsy scolding him after he had been deposited in bed and she had been assured that his injuries were not life-threatening.

"Thaddeus Lewis, every time I let you out the door you fall through the ice or get hit in the head or break an arm. My word, Martha takes better care of herself than you do."

She had continued muttering while she applied a poultice to his head and Francis rushed to the hotel for some extra pillows to cushion his arm until the doctor could see to it.

Nate Elliott — for he had recovered sufficiently to confirm his identity — had been in far worse shape and had taken priority as far as the doctor was concerned. No one had been quite sure what to do with him when they had taken him out of the woods. They could scarcely dump him back at the Elliott house and leave him to recover by himself. Then Martin Carr had stepped forward.

"Take him to our house," he said. "Ma will look after him. She's an old friend."

According to Sophie, her mother sat by Nate's bedside while he recovered from his near-overdose of laudanum, soothing him when he tossed and turned, sponging his face when his eyes and nose ran, helping him sip the soothing posset she had brewed to alleviate the cramping abdominal pain.

"It was a very close thing indeed," the doctor said. "One or two more drops and I'm not sure he'd have come back from it.

"There was nothing more left in the bottle to give him," Lewis said. "It was completely empty. Of course, I don't know how much of it Hiram used, so there's no way of telling how much there was to begin with."

The doctor looked at him with astonishment. "Hiram Elliott didn't use laudanum. He was in no pain; in fact, he was largely insensible for the last months of his life. I would never have recommended laudanum in those circumstances. Reuben must have bought it."

Clementine had no proof that Reuben had killed her husband, but it was clear, to Lewis at any rate, that he had had murder in mind. He must have drugged the first Nate in the same way he had drugged the second. Had he thrown him in the marsh, hoping to dispose of the body later? Or had the first Nate realized what was happening and managed to temporarily shrug off the effects of the laudanum in the same way that the second one had? Could he have escaped the Elliott farmhouse and made it as far as the marsh, only to have the drug render him helpless once he was there? It was mere coincidence that the Holey Man had discovered him, whether dead or alive there was no way of knowing, but "coincidences ten times as remarkable happen to all of us every hour of our lives without attracting even momentary notice." M. Dupin was quite correct about that, Lewis realized.

He didn't bother to inform the doctor that the drug had been used in an evil way not once, but twice. He knew there had to be an inquiry into Reuben's death and the events leading to it, and that he would be called to testify. But he had decided he would stick strictly to the facts of what he knew and leave conjecture to the gossips.

Francis reported that there was little practical business being accomplished in the town of Wellington over the Christmas week. There was too much to talk about. The Boxing Day brawl, which everyone — even some of those who had instigated it — agreed was shameful, and the astounding news that Nate Elliott wasn't Nate Elliott at all, nor was his wife who she said she was, and that Reuben Elliott had died in a grisly fashion out in the woods.

Several of the handful of people who had met the first Nate Elliott now claimed to have known all along that he was an imposter.

"I didn't think he looked right," the postmaster said. "Nate was always a lot taller."

"Weren't Nate's eyes blue?" the cooper said. "The first one was too dark to be Nate."

"Now why wouldn't his wife have known who he was?" Bella MacDonald asked, until it was pointed out to her that she wasn't the real Nate Elliott's wife at all, and even if she had been, the first Nate Elliott had been chopped up and stuffed into barrels, making identification difficult, to say the least. Not to mention the fact that she could hardly be questioned about her knowledge now, given the fact that she was nowhere to be found.

Daniel had been beside himself when he realized that yet another guest had neglected to pay.

"Two rooms it was, two rooms, and at top rate! First Gilmour, now Mrs. Elliott. I swear, never again do I rent my rooms without asking for the money ahead of time. This hotel business just isn't what it's cracked up to be, is it?" He sighed. "I don't suppose you know where she's gone, do you Thaddeus? Is there any way we could track her down?"

Everybody seemed to think that Lewis would have answers to all of their questions, and over the next few days Betsy shooed away numerous visitors who appeared to be nothing more than curious about the details of the strange incident.

There were few people other than family that she allowed into their little house, but one who was granted entrance was Clara Sprung, who came only once, and stayed for only five minutes.

"I just want to hear from your own lips that it was all a contrivance," she said. "I think if I hear you say it, I'll believe that Amelia is really gone and that I won't see her again."

Lewis reached out with his uninjured hand to pat her shoulder. "I'm sorry. What you saw in that room wasn't real, but rest assured you will see your daughter again. I'm sure she's in heaven and will be there at the gates to meet you when your time comes."

She nodded. "I knew that. I knew it all along, but I guess I just wanted to believe otherwise. Thank you."

Archibald McFaul was allowed in the door, as well.

"As the only person in the woods that night to come out unscathed, I thought I'd better drop around to gloat," he said. "Seriously, though, I thought you were done for. One more blow to the head and you'd have been in real trouble. I tried, but couldn't get there fast enough."

"A hard-headed Methodist like me?" Lewis said. "I might have survived one more." And McFaul chuckled. Lewis liked this man immensely, and he had certainly solidified his reputation as a village leader, both in disrupting the riot and in helping to chase down Reuben Elliott.

"I was going to ask you this anyway," McFaul said, growing more serious, "but now I'm convinced that it's the right course. You told me once that you're an educated man."

Lewis nodded.

"If you've listened to the village grapevine at all, you're probably aware that I have diverse business interests. I'm finding that the routine administration of many of these is taking up far too much of my time. I need someone to see to some of it for me. Someone I can trust."

"Do you mean like a clerk?" Lewis said, but his spirits fell as he said it. He would take whatever McFaul offered. He was in desperate need of income, but the thought of being shut up in a poky little office every day was depressing.

"No, not as a clerk. Men who can add up a column of figures or check off a shipping list are easy enough to find. I need someone who can handle a certain amount of my correspondence for me, and who can be trusted to correctly file legal documents of various sorts. It wouldn't be full time, mind you, and it would require you to travel to the courthouse in Picton on a fairly regular basis, but if you're interested, you seem like the ideal candidate."

Lewis needed no time to consider this offer. "Agreed!" he said immediately. "But I can't start until I have a little more use of my left arm."

It was perfect, he pointed out to Betsy after McFaul had left. It would give them some money, yet leave him free to tend to her on her bad days. He would be settled in one place, but asked to travel a bit. He would once more have an open road unwinding before him. He would travel no farther than Picton, it was true, but he had missed the steady drumming of a horse's hooves and the feel of a hot sun or a winter wind striking his face. He would be able to breathe again.

"Best of all, it will give us time to collect up a little nest egg, in case we have to trail after Martha some day."

On the fifth day of his convalescence, just when Lewis had had enough of lying around the kitchen and was about to ignore Betsy's protests and go out, he had another visitor. It was Nate Elliott, recovered from the more unpleasant effects of his overdose, but still pale and a little shaky.

"I thought I should come and talk to you," he said. "There's still so much I don't understand. Apparently, I had a wife and son at one point?"

"That's what they claimed, anyway."

Lewis had questions for Nate, as well. "What made you come back?"

"I finally found a few weeks' work and could pay my back rent. It bothered me that I'd skipped out in such a hurry, and I wanted my letters back — more than anything to remind myself why I'd left. I had no sentimentality about the old homestead or my family either, I assure you. When I went back to the room, the landlady told me that my brother had been there and had taken the letters. I knew there was only one reason Reuben would have come looking for me — the old man was dead or dying and had somehow tied everything up in knots."

"Did you know that Reuben had found a substitute for you?"

Nate shook his head. "No. The landlady said nothing about it, and I'm not sure it would have made any difference to me anyway. I truly debated just going on my way. I didn't really care what happened to the farm."

"What changed your mind?"

"I know you're a preacher and probably won't approve, but I'll be honest with you — I wanted to see that miserable old bastard dead in his grave."

It was a stark admission. Lewis had heard Hiram Elliott described in various unflattering ways, but he had wondered how a father could engender so much hate from a son. And then he realized that he had come perilously close to doing the same to his own son, not in degree, perhaps, but in spirit. At least he had realized it in time, and had repaired much of the rift that had developed between him and his eldest boy.

"I didn't count on seeing Reuben dead, as well," Nate went on. "We never got along, but I realize now that it was the old man who was responsible for that. I would have liked to know him better, to see if we could have been friends without my father there to sow poison between us."

"Reuben made his choices," Lewis said. "One might argue that it was all your father's doing, but Reuben was chained by nothing but his own greed. He could have left at any time, just as you did."

"I suppose that's true," Nate said. "But I certainly didn't expect him to try to kill me."

"He'd set himself on a path that was full of pitfalls. When you arrived, he must have convinced himself that there was no other way out. He'd have murdered me, as well, if it hadn't been for you. I'm still trying to figure out how you got yourself out from under that pile of branches to stop him."

"I have no idea," Nate said. "I have absolutely no recollection of any of it. One minute I was sitting in the kitchen drinking with Reuben and the next thing I knew Eliza Carr was dabbing at my forehead with a cold rag, bless her heart. The constable came around and wanted all the details, but I could tell him nothing."

"That will stand you in good stead at the inquest, I expect."

Nate nodded. "According to the constable, it will almost certainly be ruled self-defence. I just wish I could remember that it was so."

"Oh, don't worry," Lewis replied. "That's exactly what it was."

The verdict at the inquest was exactly as the constable predicted, and Nate Elliott was exonerated from any guilt in the death of his brother. The hearing was very short, the coroner seeing no need to belabour the details of a train of events that seemed so straightforward. The jury consisted of some of the same men who had ruled in the previous inquest, and afterward they couldn't help but point out how prescient they had been.

"Everybody gave us a hard time over our findings," one of them said, "but now you know we were right — it wasn't Nate Elliott after all. Was it?"

"What are you going to do about the farm?" Lewis asked Nate as they stood outside the courthouse.

"I don't want it. It's got nothing but bad memories for me. I'll just sell it, I think. But I don't really want the money either. As far as I'm concerned, it's tainted. In any event, some of it will be needed to clear up a few of the messes Reuben made. I'd like to put up some sort of gravestone for my imposter, although I don't have a name to go on it, other than 'Jack.' That will do, I suppose."

"There were a number of other names he used," Lewis said, "but I don't think any of them were the name he was born with."

"I don't suppose you've heard from my erstwhile wife?"

Lewis shook his head. "Not a word. I didn't really expect to though."

"If you ever do," Nate said, "please let me know. I'd like to pay her what Reuben promised."

"And the rest?"

"Oh, I'll take enough to give me a stake somewhere else, but I can't think of anything better to do with the rest of it than give it to Eliza Carr. She's always been a real friend to me."

"And it will make a great deal of difference to her," Lewis said, although he privately hoped that it wouldn't mean the departure of Sophie from the Temperance House kitchen.

Two weeks later, Lewis was surprised when a package arrived at the post office for Martha. He had been collecting the mail for Archibald McFaul, both of them agreeing that Lewis would work into his new position slowly. Collecting the post was, in fact, his only duty at the moment. Postage for Martha's package had been pre-paid, and although he looked it over carefully, there was no indication of who had sent it, or from where it had been mailed.

He dropped a handful of letters off at McFaul's store and made his way back to the hotel. There were not nearly as many guests as there had been in the heyday of Clementine Elliott's fame, but word had spread about the superior accommodations at Temperance House, and there were currently three rooms rented, for one night only, by customers who were making connections between the stage and the steamboat. As well, there was a farm family who had come into the village for provisions and who were treating themselves to some of Sophie's famous cookery. Not bustling, exactly, but good enough.

He waited until the dining room was cleared and his family had gathered in the kitchen for their own supper to hand the package to Martha.

"This came for you," he said.

"For me?" Her eyes lit up, for she had never before received a package in the mail. "What is it?"

"I don't know. You'll have to open it, won't you?"

She tore all the wrapping off the small parcel. Inside was a twist of paper, wound around a handful of lemon rock and molasses candies. All of the adults at the table looked at it with puzzlement, but Martha had a wide smile on her face.

"It's from Horatio Joe!" she squealed. She peeled the paper away, spilling some of the candy onto the table. "Look there's a note inside!" And then her face wrinkled in puzzlement as she showed it to Lewis.

There were four words in the message, but only two of them were legible at first glance. It said *Thank you* twice, but the words on the left hand side were entirely backward, a mirror image of those on the right.

Apparently, Clementine had landed on her feet.

Chapter Thirty

On a clear, cold Saturday afternoon toward the end of February, Lewis decided that he was finally strong enough to walk down to the harbour and along the sandbar to the dunes.

"You really want to go across the ice again? You're getting quite bold, aren't you?" Francis teased, but he agreed readily enough to go along.

The ice was solidly frozen and the wind bit at them as they crossed the channel, making their eyes water. They followed the trail along until they reached the clearing in the woods. The stench from the root cellar had dissipated, and anything that had been left behind had frozen, the slow putrefaction halted by the cold. The wreckage of the burnt-out cabin had been scattered by the crew of men who had gathered the bones, the crude stone hearth had been thrown down, the iron pot removed.

"What are we looking for this time, Thaddeus? You do have a habit of making the most amazing discoveries. I'm never sure what I'll see when I'm with you."

Lewis didn't answer, because he wasn't sure himself why he had come, except that he felt that he owed something to the wild creature who had lived here. One of many innocents caught up by the actions of others.

Francis stood by the shore and watched as Lewis picked through the fallen hearth stones. He made no comment when his father-in-law finally selected a flat piece of limestone, but he held the rock steady while Lewis scratched the letters on it with a nail. He helped scoop out a hole in the sandy earth under the cedar trees and together the two men lowered the stone into it, shoring it up with sand and more stones. When they were done, they stood before it in silence, their heads bowed. It was a plain enough remembrance, and would probably last only a winter or two before the stone heaved and the words were lost, but at least the intent was sincere.

The inscription was short. Lewis had been able to think of nothing more fitting than to simply mark it "Boy."

Also by Janet Kellough

On the Head of a Pin
978-1554884346
$11.99

Thaddeus Lewis, an itinerant "saddlebag" preacher, still mourns the mysterious death of his daughter Sarah as he rides to his new posting in Prince Edward County. When a girl in Demorestville dies in a similar way, he realizes that the circumstances point to murder. But in the turmoil following the 1837 Mackenzie Rebellion he can get no one to listen. Convinced there is a serial killer loose in Upper Canada, Lewis alone must track the culprit across a colony convulsed by dissension, invasion, and fear. His only clues are a Book of Proverbs and a small painted pin left with the victims. And the list of suspects is growing.

Of Related Interest

Lake on the Mountain
A Dan Sharp Mystery
by Jeffrey Round
978-1459700017
$11.99

Dan Sharp, a gay missing persons investigator, accepts an invitation to a wedding on a yacht in Ontario's Prince Edward County. But the event doesn't go as planned. A member of the wedding party is swept overboard and Dan finds himself deep in troubled waters as he searches for possible killers, not only in the present, but also twenty years earlier.

Daggers and Men's Smiles
A Moretti and Falla Mystery
by Jill Downie
978-1554888689
$11.99

Lights! Camera! Action! On the English Channel Island of Guernsey, Detective Inspector Ed Moretti and his new partner, Liz Falla, investigate vicious attacks on Epicure Films. The international production company is shooting a movie based on a British bad-boy author's bestselling novel about an Italian aristocratic family at the end of the Second World War. When vandalism escalates into murder, Moretti must resist the attractions of the author's glamorous American wife, consolidate his working relationship with Falla, and establish whether the murders on Guernsey go beyond the island.

Available at your favourite bookseller.

What did you think of this book?
Visit *www.dundurn.com*
for reviews, videos, updates, and more!